COLOGNE NO. 10 FOR MEN

To Barry,
Welcome Home
Enjoy!
Richard Ulrich
5/25/2015

COLOGNE NO. 10 FOR MEN

A Novel

Richard Morris

iUniverse, Inc.

New York Bloomington Shanghai

Cologne No. 10 For Men

iUniverse books may be ordered through booksellers or by contacting:

iUniverse
1663 Liberty Drive
Bloomington, IN 47403
www.iuniverse.com
1-800-Authors (1-800-288-4677)

Because of the dynamic nature of the Internet, any Web addresses or links contained in this book may have changed since publication and may no longer be valid.

Certain places described in this work are real, and certain events did take place. However, this is a work of fiction. All characters, names, and other events, places, incidents, organizations, and dialogue in this novel are either the products of the author's imagination or are used fictitiously.

Cover design by Audrey & Rick Engdahl

ISBN: 978-0-5954-2431-3 (sc)
ISBN: 978-0-5956-7997-3 (hc)
ISBN: 978-0-5958-6766-0 (ebk)

Printed in the United States of America

For my family

PROLOGUE

▼

Wilfred skipped through the next few days like a flat rock on still water. He had all the weapons he needed. Now all he needed was bodies. They will come, he thought. They will come.

He used Trinh day after day, offering him to Colonel Clary sunny side up and over easy. He began by dressing him in a fresh NVA uniform and then he caked it with mud and used it again. At night he retired to his hooch and patiently sewed rank insignias on it, changing them daily.

When he'd exhausted all permutations, he resorted to new civilian garb, once even borrowing a girl's pajamas and padding them appropriately. The face he altered, too, though Wilfred was fairly certain the colonel wouldn't risk being called a racial bigot again. He had Trinh make faces, selected an expression and told him to freeze. Borrowed glasses of varying styles and made Trinh wear them. Stuffed cotton in his mouth and under his lips. Drew scars and wrinkles on his face with charcoal.

Then he arranged Trinh's limbs in a myriad of configurations, discovering ways of bending and twisting his arms and legs that he didn't know were possible—grotesque ways that looked as though the members were horribly broken. Sometimes he had to use rope to hold them in position and hid the stay with clothing or gore. "My favorite mannequin," he said to Trinh one day.

The wounds were no problem. He dribbled ketchup from Trinh's mouth and ears, poured it liberally on portions of his body, and used animal innards for extra realism. Once he put a dog's eyeball on top of Trinh's own to simulate a hideous eye injury.

As word of Wilfred's fetish for disemboweling animals spread through the countryside, he found the critters harder to find. In one village he saw a dog, an ox and a water buffalo fleeing into the paddies at his approach. At another, he penetrated a booby-trapped tunnel complex only to find it full of ducks and pigs hiding in the darkness. At yet another he found a flock of chickens cowering in a barnyard and was certain he detected fear in their eyes.

Wilfred felt that his work was highly creative—artistic, even. Trinh had other opinions. But the interpreter impassively persevered, his fear of the madman growing with each new obscenity Wilfred perpetrated upon him.

Colonel Clary had his suspicions. "Why are there always two?" he asked Wilfred.

"Sir. Even VC were meant to go through life two by two. It's part of God's plan."

"Oh, yeah," Clary said, not completely convinced. Something was wrong, but he couldn't put his finger on it.

"Well, tell me this," he said. "Why are their rifles always so clean? They look like they've never been fired."

They never have, Wilfred thought, but he reported gravely, "Discipline, sir. Discipline."

Clary grumbled a grudging acceptance and not to be out-soldiered by primitive, heathen, commie natives, went back to LZ German and instituted daily rifle inspections throughout the battalion.

Eventually Wilfred's ideas on how to use Trinh began to wear thin and he enlisted the aid of an Italian and a Latino from the company, but soon discovered that although the hair and complexion weren't too bad, he just couldn't get the eyes right.

"That one doesn't look Oriental," Clary said.

"Probably a French father," Wilfred explained.

"Mother too, if you ask me."

That was it. He couldn't risk using the G.I.'s anymore and neither could he use Trinh. The skipping rock was sinking fast, and after three days with no kills, Wilfred grew desperate. "We've got to find some bodies," he told Reckert.

Then came the break he'd awaited. The company was moving through a mountain forest near the edge of the plain when the word came down the line: "Fresh graves." "Fresh graves." "Fresh graves."

"Fresh graves!" Wilfred screamed, and he galloped up to take a look. "Oooh! There must be fifty or sixty of them. Must be from that battle D Company had yesterday." He was so happy he nearly cried. All his hard work was beginning to pay off. "O.K., lads. Unearth them."

He sent Henry and Rodriguez on a special mission. "We need blood, boys. Lots and lots. Hurry back before it clots."

Everyone else in the company took part in the dig, and bodies began appearing everywhere. It was quite an undertaking. The corpses were coated with dirt but otherwise perfect—horribly mangled and wearing the most repulsive expressions.

Wilfred was only sorry that Louis King was not there to share in the fun. He would have gone crazy out here, Wilfred thought.

He found Reckert. "It's a breakthrough, Robbie. A giant leap forward in the art of non-war."

"What?" Reckert asked.

"The recycling of bodies. Do you know what this means? Do you understand the implications?"

"I-I'm not sure."

"Man won't ever need to kill again. All he has to do is use the same bodies over and over. Go ahead. Fill their veins with chemicals. Coat their skins. Freeze them. Can them. Freeze-dry them, for Christ's sake. And use them till the end of time. Kill them and count them again and again and again and again."

Wilfred had the bodies moved away from the graves to the edge of the plain and arranged them in a nifty battle formation. As the men were finishing, Henry and Rodriguez arrived driving a team of oxen.

"We thought we better bring it on the hoof," Henry said to Wilfred. "You said 'fresh,' and 'fresh' is what you gets."

"Great. Now how do we get to all that blood? Wait. That new man in Lorde's platoon. What's his name—Reinholtz? He's a butcher, isn't he?"

"I think so," Rodriguez said.

"Get him," Wilfred said.

Reinholtz, the butcher, was the perfect choice, once he got started. "Y-you want me to butcher him? An-and drain his blood?"

"That's right," Henry said.

"B-but I don't have any blanks. How will I stun it? I don't want it jumping all around on me."

"Use a real bullet, shithead," Henry said.

The butcher led the animal to a tall tree, put the pistol to the side of its head, and shot him, and then tied its rear legs with a rope, and threw it over a stout

With the help of four stout troopers, the butcher hung it up to drain and slit its throat. "Ain't grain-fed, that's for sure," he mumbled.

They collected the blood in ponchos and canteens and poured it over the bodies and Wilfred inspected each for authenticity. Then he placed the G.I.'s in an opposing fighting formation. They didn't mind at all: it was easier to fight dead gooks than live ones. He told them to expend as much ammunition as they could and had Captain Simms call Clary.

"Must be the 105th NVA Battalion," Clary said to Wilfred and Simms when he arrived. "D Company got into it with 'em yesterday. They were pinned down for a long time. Took a lot of casualties, but didn't zap too many NVA...." Charlie must have pulled out most of his dead while D Company was pinned down, Wilfred thought. "...Funny. You didn't seem to have much trouble with 'em. Not one friendly casualty. That's astounding!"

"Dumb blind luck, I guess," Wilfred said.

The colonel walked through the field of battle surveying the carnage. "Filthiest soldiers I've ever seen. Looks like they've been wallowing in mud. They take no pride in cleanliness, that's for sure."

"They've never heard that cleanliness is next to godliness," Wilfred said. "That's why we're here—to teach 'em things like that."

"Strange how they can be so poor at personal hygiene but still keep their weapons so clean."

"I guess they believe in first things first."

"What are the counts, Simms?" Clary asked.

"Fifty-five KIA—NVA, sir. No friendlies."

"And how many weapons?"

"Six rifles, sir," Wilfred said. He was trying to conserve.

"Six! Is that all?"

"A good many Charlies got away, sir. They must have taken the other rifles with them."

"Humph," Clary said.

When the colonel left, Wilfred told Simms to post guards on the bodies. "We don't want any Charlies sneaking in and filching the stiffs and burying them again."

"Why not?" Simms asked.

"Too much work digging them up again."

"Digging them up again?"

"We gotta use them again tomorrow—before they rot up too bad."

That night at chow Wilfred was feeling proud of himself. Under his brief command, A Company had earned an infinite kill ratio of 73 to zip. He couldn't resist pointing this out to Reckert. "We've shut them out," he chirped. "Decisively."

"What are you going to do for an encore? That's what I want to know."

"Well, I've been thinking of going public."

"What does that mean?"

"Robbie, I think one of the important services that contemporary wars perform is to entertain the public. Every night at six and eleven, and again on the morning news."

"Kind of like a daily horror show?"

"Yeah. And I somehow think we're letting those people down if we don't contribute to their enjoyment. After all, they're paying for the show by buying the products and paying their taxes."

"We're being downright unpatriotic," Reckert said, "keeping all this gore to ourselves."

"I think so, too."

"So what's your plan?"

Wilfred dug out his wallet and pulled out a business card.

"I think it's time to call on Frank Storp. He wanted bodies, and bodies we have."

After supper Wilfred sent himself on a secret mission to LZ German. Leaving Reckert in command of the company, he boarded the chow chopper and found Storp at the Brigade Information Office. "Frank, I need you in the field by ten hundred hours tomorrow. I have lots of bodies."

That night in a bunker at German, in sleepless excitement, he laid plans for the next day and then relived the experiences that brought him here....

PART I

▼

THE WAR

"'Gentlemen. What's the mission of the Infantry?'
and we all shouted, 'To kill, sir,'
and the colonel said, 'I can't hear you,'
and we roared, 'To kiiii—ll, sir!'
and he said, 'Never forget it.'"

CHAPTER 1

▼

RECKERT AND CAN

"FUCK COMMUNISM," blared the large, professionally lettered sign hung on stout square legs mired in foreign clay. Behind it another announced: "1st Battalion, 13th Cavalry, Airmobile Division." A smaller sign greeted, "Welcome To The War."

Wilfred bounded through the door into the battalion orderly room where a young buck sergeant sat alone behind a desk, thumbing through a girly magazine.

"Lieutenant Carmenghetti, reporting for duty." He handed the sergeant his orders. "What's your name?"

"Sonny Williams, Lieutenant."

"Nice to meet you. What do you do here?"

"Tell guys where to go when they come in, and where the shitter is. Help 'em get their uniforms and gear and find their classes. Stuff like that."

"Have you been here long?"

"In Nam?" Wilfred nodded. "Eleven months. Got six to go. Then it's back to the states and kiss this uniform good-bye."

"Seventeen months? What did you do, extend your tour?"

"Damn straight. A lot of guys do. Beats stateside duty all to hell. Hardly any work to do, nobody gives you any shit, and the Army takes care of your every need. You get combat pay, and then everything's free: chow, rags, public housing, socialized medicine, two or three paid vacations a year, to Bankok, Hong Kong,

Singapore. Even free entertainment. Why, if the commies knew they were fightin' the socialists, they'd switch sides and the war would be over tomorrow."

"Socialists?"

"You bet. Outside of Russia and China, the U.S. armed forces is the biggest socialist dictatorship in the world. We can even supplement our income and combat pay by buying stuff wholesale and duty-free at the PX and selling it off base at a dandy profit. Best thing we got, though, is socialized sex."

"What?"

"No shit. We bring in mamasans, you know, to clean the quarters. It's one of the best public welfare programs we have for the de-prived majority: a good boom-boom gal can support her mama, papa, and ten or fifteen brothers and sisters. Hey, you want your quarters cleaned tonight?"

"You're kidding."

"Put her on your doorstep at—let's see—" He picked up a small notebook from the desk. "Oh, about eleven o'clock. You can have her for forty-five minutes."

Then it hit him. You're a pimp. "What would it cost me?"

"Thirty bucks. You gimme thirty bucks and I'll fix you up with the cutest little gook gal you ever saw. Course, I gotta have the cash up front, sir. You might not show, and then I lose the time slot. What do you say?"

Wilfred bounced around the screen door marked "Alpha Assassins" and into the wood barracks. Double steel bunks lined the sides. Two were draped with mosquito nets, and one contained a recumbent form curled beneath a mottled poncho liner.

"Hi. I'm Robert Reckert," another second lieutenant greeted. He was more than a foot taller than Wilfred.

"Wilfred Carmenghetti. Who's that guy?"

"I don't know. Whenever I come in, he's sleeping."

"The sleeper. Hmm. Say, did you run into that desk sergeant at battalion, what was his name, Williams?"

"The solicitor general?"

"He tried to fix you up too?"

"Yeah, but he's got competition. If ladies are your pleasure, tomorrow I'll take you to Sin City."

Explosions rocked the barracks. "Get up!" Wilfred said as he fumbled for his shoes. "We're under attack. Where's the arms room? We gotta get guns." With each blast a red-orange glow flashed through the windows, making beds and bodies appear magically for an instant in the darkness.

Reckert sat straight up, threw off the covers, and said, "What?" The other body snorted twice, rolled onto its back, and began snoring loudly and mutinously.

The assault continued. "We're under attack," Wilfred said, stumbling to his feet. "We have to find the arms room and get rifles."

The stiff, half-awake Reckert relaxed and bitterly snapped, "Jesus Christ, Wilfred. Go back to sleep. Those are our guns."

"Who are they shooting at?"

"They aren't shooting at anybody."

Wilfred was stupefied. "Why not?"

"They're H & I fires—Harassment and Interdiction. They do it every night at a different time—fire off in all directions. They aim at where Charlie might be—likely avenues of approach and trail crossings and suspected assembly areas."

"Oh, I get it. The old hit-him-where-he-ain't trick."

Reckert borrowed a jeep, and they set out for Sin City. "So what are you doing in Nam?" Reckert asked.

"Why are men drawn to war, like sharks to blood? I don't know. I came to help save the world from godless communism."

"Did you enlist?"

"Yep. What about you?"

"Yeah. I was graduating from college, and my number was coming up, so I enlisted to go to OCS. But I was hoping for a tour in Germany."

"Fat chance." They both laughed.

"Are you going to make the army a career?" Reckert asked.

"Hell, no."

"Do you support the war?"

"It's the only one we've got. I didn't want to miss the fun."

"At least you've got a good reason."

"What do you think about it?"

"I think we ought to leave, and I'm really not interested in killing anybody."

"Hmm. Where are you from?" Wilfred asked.

"Iowa. I grew up on a farm. How about you?"

"We moved around a little. Cleveland, Pittsburgh, Philadelphia. What's that smell?"

"Burned shit. They burn it with diesel oil in those fifty-five gallon drum halves we shit in, to keep down the flies."

On the way to Sin City, Wilfred made him stop at the PX. He needed some cologne. Behind the trappings and duty-free gifts for R&R—clothing, sporting goods, electronics, all duty-free—he found the wall full of perfumes, deodorants, and aftershaves and picked out a bottle labeled "Cologne No. 10 For Men." He gave it a whiff, bought it, took it outside, and put some on.

"What'd you get that for?"

"Don't you like to smell good? And, man, this stuff makes BO and exhaust fumes and burning shit smell like an Asian garden."

"You won't need that where we're going. Those girls don't care what you smell like. They just turn their head to the side when they do it."

They passed the officer and NCO clubs with their Olympic-size outdoor pools, headed past the chapel and library, parked at the gate, and walked into an off-base peninsula surrounded by barbed wire.

"This is it, Carmen. Pearl of the Orient—Sin City, Vietnam." Stucco garages painted pastel colors had signs like "Hawaii," "California," and "Heaven." Vietnamese girls stood out front in tight cocktail dresses, snug white slacks and gaudy western blouses, or loose white slacks and flowered tops. A dozen G.I.'s meandered down the fairway.

"Anything your heart desires," Reckert told Wilfred. "Barbers, food, booze, massage parlors, steam rooms. And girls, girls, girls. Take your pick."

"So how much are the girls?"

"Two-fifty."

"Two-fifty! Why that sonofabitch."

They passed two white-helmeted M.P.'s, and Wilfred whispered, "Do they run this place?"

"They and the docs. The girls here get checked and shot once a week, whether they need it or not."

"Socialized sex."

Reckert suggested they get a steam bath, so they wandered through the doorway into an establishment called Far West.

"Come in," said the smiling man behind the wooden barber chair. He looked sixty, but Wilfred suspected he was forty. Across from him a boy sat by an engraving machine behind a glass counter containing lighters and trinkets. The boy looked nine; Wilfred placed him at thirteen. Behind him were travel bags, jackets emblazoned with "Vietnam," and conical straw hats.

"You want hair cut? Steam bath? Massage? Girl?"

"Steam bath and massage," Reckert said.

"Numbah one, numbah one. You like. Ly! *Lai day!*"

A girl in black pajamas appeared through a curtain, led them back a foggy hallway, gave them each a towel, showed them where to undress, and led the towel-skirted gentlemen to the steam room. There they sat on wooden benches, as hot mist slowly cooked out tiny beads of sweat all over their bodies and boiled away Wilfred's cologne. A year later, a black shape appeared and led Reckert away. Then another came, and Wilfred followed submissively, passing through another curtain into a tiny room with a body-sized wood table. The girl motioned him to sit, and as he did he looked into her face.

This was a different girl, not five feet tall, and he was struck by her beauty. She wore white cotton slacks and a thin hip-length long-sleeve white shirt. Shiny black hair held by a red elastic band fell to her waist. She appeared to be in her late teens, five or six years younger than Wilfred.

"I Can," she incanted with a British A.

"Cahn? I'm Wilfred," and it seemed to him strange but exciting that the impersonality had so quickly dissipated.

"Wilfed," she mimicked, her big eyes gazing into his.

"Not bad," he said with a chuckle.

"You nice." Wilfred felt himself turning liquid. "G.I. numbah one. And tee-tee." She raised her hand to the top of their heads to indicate that they both were short. Looking at his straight black hair, she said, "Same-same Vietnam." Then she shocked him with a smile of childish innocence, and Wilfred was enthralled. "Sit here," she said.

She massaged his hands between her tiny palms and pulled each finger with a crack. As she repeated the massage, he began to wonder if she was trying to communicate through their hands. She looked into his eyes and slowly released him. Then she kneaded his shoulders deeply and he was impressed with her strength. And when her hands stayed too long, ending in what might have been a caress, he wanted to touch in return.

She took his face in her hands. Looking into her deep brown eyes, he wondered if she intended to kiss him. Then she rolled his head back and forth gently and abruptly swung it to the side with a crack. He was amazed to find that he was not paralyzed from the neck down. She cracked the vertebrae the other way, and again he felt more relaxed than before.

Now she had him lie down on his stomach and proceeded to bend and fold and swing and crack his arms and legs, and chop his back with both hands. He closed his eyes and began to drift away under the vibration. Then the table shook and he felt the balls and toes of her tiny feet traversing his back, pressing and pinching, and "cracking" his spine. Down again, she said, "Turn ovah," and he did so, oblivious that the towel around his waist had not followed. She chopped and rubbed and kneaded his arms and chest and legs and feet, then stopped.

"Lutemma?" she said, and he opened his eyes to find her staring at and pointing to his slumbering soldier. He wasn't sure what she had in mind. In reply, he ordered the trooper to attention and then closed his eyes to increase the suspense.

Whatever it was, it was wet and warm and wiggly. Eyelids barely raised, he watched her try to swallow it whole, stop after consuming only half, attempt to eject it again, yet never give up her grip, and continue on in this ambivalent and fearful battle between gluttony and anorexia until Wilfred—eyes squeezed shut—was in a frenzy. At last, moderation conquered, and she spat it out, and in a moment, he heard an almost shy voice ask, "Lutemma? You want me?" and he threw open his eyes to the offering of soft rounded nakedness through a long veil of hair falling from her tilted head.

In a fury of lust, he assented, not even asking the price, and was instantly grateful when the warm and wet massage resumed, this time with the belly and breasts of the maid upon him, and her lips and tongue exploring his.

She moved down upon him, and he felt her rising and falling, slowly at first. As his hands traveled down over her hips, he rose to join her, then drew away, moving uncertainly, wanting not to hurt her, and to make love with her, not to her.

Wilfred was astonished. She wasn't giving him the mechanical trip he'd expected. He felt her body offering affection, and he accepted it and reciprocated, thrusting deeper and deeper—every stroke reaching up into her further and further to get closer and closer to some glorious depth. His hands roamed her silky hair and breasts and nipples and shoulders and back and hips and thighs—infant smooth—and cradled her as he rolled on top, and again found her mouth and eager tongue.

Their motions waved together like wind and wheat, and Wilfred felt himself drifting into ecstasy. He heard her moan, and felt her nails digging into his back, and felt himself near tears from wanting to give and end the excitement, yet wanting it never to end. At last he could withhold the explosion no longer, and again and again he pumped his seed into the slender young creature.

They collapsed together, and he didn't want to leave her, and he left it in until long after it was shriveled soft and helpless. Finally he eased off, rolled over onto his back, slid his arm gently around her shoulder, pulled her to him, and rested his hand on her tiny round breast, and they lay together for a quiet time in ethereal peace.

"Ooooh, Wilfed," she said, eyes still shut tightly as if she never wanted to come back.

He held her and fondled her and heard his own voice say softly, "Oh, Can. You're wonderful. I—"

She looked into his eyes with sadness and fear and courage, and whispered breathlessly, "Wilfed numbah one."

She refused to take his money, and they lay together in the afterglow, her hand resting possessively on his off-duty private. And when Reckert's impatient voice intruded from down the hall, he didn't want to go.

"What do you mean, you're in love," Reckert asked later. "You exchanged five words of Pidgin, screwed this girl just like hundreds of other guys have done before you, and suddenly you're in love. What's that called? 'Love at first fuck'?"

"I know it sounds crazy, but I love her—I really do."

"But she's a whore!"

"Not to me. She never charged me a penny."

"Big deal. She's out $2.50, and for that she buys your undying love."

"I love her, Reckert."

"Buddy, I think your love needs to be put to the test. I'm gonna pick out another girl for you to screw, and this time a really sexy whore, and if you feel the same about Can after that, maybe I'll believe you."

CHAPTER 2

▼

MÁ

The next day Reckert took him to "Heaven" where Tan worked him over. Wilfred emerged enthusiastic but unmoved. "She's good, but I don't want her. I want Can. And I think I always will."

"Impossible, man. People don't fall in love like that. You've got a crush on Can, but I bet if you go back to her tomorrow, it'll all be different. She won't live up to your memory of her, and that'll be the end of it. You'll see."

A day later Wilfred told the barber, "I want see Can."

The barber's smile fell. "Oh, you…Wilfed. She no here." He smiled again. "But have many girls. Numbah one. You like."

"She say you dinky dau," the boy put in, and the barber killed him dead with a flick of an eyelash. The boy twitched, slumped into his chair, and said no more.

Wilfred looked at Reckert quizzically. Reckert said, "Means crazy. She's a perceptive girl."

Wilfred was undeterred. "Listen," he told the old man. "I don't want another girl. I want Can."

"Solly, solly. Can no here."

"I wait," Wilfred said, moving over to the frightened boy and looking disinterestedly into the jewelry case.

"You want lightah?" the boy asked. "I do numbah one. Put patch here, years here, choppah here. Five dollah cheap, G.I."

They watched the boy guide the metal finger around the patterns while the wheel obediently ground copies into the steel. As they paid, Wilfred whispered, "Where Can?"

"She no here."

"We can at least get a steam bath and rub," Reckert said.

Wilfred found the bath relaxing, and the cracks and chops and pushes, delicious. Then the masseuse whispered, "I come back," and slipped out, leaving his languid body face down on the table. Soon he felt the hands again, rubbing his back in little circles. Then the chop-chop began anew, harder, until he started feeling pain. Tiny fists bludgeoned him and sharp pains stabbed his kidneys and liver. Just as he was about to complain, the masseuse leaped up and began dancing violently on his back, her feet leaving, and heels smashing down onto his shoulder blades, driving the air from his lungs. More pain. She jumped down and slipped her fingers under his shoulder to motion him over. He rolled without opening his eyes and felt the chop-chop on his chest growing to another crescendo—pounding and crashing and bruising him viciously. When the pain finally became more than he could bear, he opened his eyes, and there was Can, beating him like a double jackhammer. "Dinky dau, num ten, sombitch," she screamed. "Wilfed love Tan. No love Can!"

"Can!" he shouted, lunging and grabbing her wrists in a supreme effort at self-preservation.

"You…you…" she stammered senselessly as she pulled and tugged and struggled to get away.

Desperately he hung on until her strength ebbed and her eyes gushed. "Wilfed numbah ten," she sobbed and collapsed to her knees on the floor, nearly pulling him down on top of her.

"Oh, Can. I'm sorry. You're right. I number ten." He let go and stroked her smooth black hair. "Come here," he said.

"No come."

"Can. She means nothing to me. I love you."

"No love Can. You numbah ten."

"I do love you."

"Dinky dau."

He slipped off the table, sat beside her on the cold concrete, and tried to pull her close to him.

"No love Can!"

"Please, Can. Love Wilfred."

His heat was rising, and he felt like he was making some progress when she stiffened, turned to face him, and spat, "You want love Can, you gimme fifty bucks."

"Whew," he whistled as his arm dropped from her waist like a lead weight. She knows the test for true love, he thought grimly and took account of his assets and liabilities. It would hurt, but he could hack it, and it would certainly be worth it.

"I do love you," he whispered as he cleaned out his wallet.

It wasn't worth it. She lay on her back, knees bent, head to the side, eyes open, and calmly took his money, while he gained new insights into necrophilia. Shit. The bitch!

"Didi mau!" she hissed, pointing to the door.

Wilfred stalked past the proud and sullen man and boy without a word.

Reckert was waiting outside, eager for a report, but it was not until the two were bouncing back in the jeep that Wilfred had cooled down enough to explain what had happened.

"Got fucked, huh?"

"It's not funny."

After a steak dinner in the officers' mess, Wilfred was able to get Can off his mind for a while. "How come no one has a gun? How can they send us to war without a gun?"

"Guns are dangerous, man. They don't let us carry them until we go to the field. And we don't need them here anyway. Fortress Vassar is impregnable with all its rings of defenses."

"Looks like a stateside base to me. Looks like we're going to stay forever."

At the officers' club, Reckert said, "You know that bus driver on the way in said that second lieutenants last twenty minutes in combat, because we're the guy that always stands in front of the guy with the radio on his back—the RTO."

"That's total bullshit, totally bassackwards improbable."

"What do you mean?"

Wilfred pulled a coin from his pocket. "Look, Reckert. Let's flip this coin. Heads you live, tails you die. Now we flip. What are the odds that you die on the first day?"

"Fifty-fifty."

"O.K., but say you flip it a hundred and fifty times and it always comes up heads. What are the odds you die the next day?"

"Fifty-fifty."

"Bullshit. That's what the books tell you, but you know there's a much greater chance it'll come up tails the next day."

"What?"

"You know it's true. What if you flip it three hundred times and it always comes up heads? What then? The next day you're going to die, man. The VC love to zap you when you're stepping on the plane to go back to the world."

"You are dinky dau, man."

"That's why we gotta zap them first. Remember what they told us in OCS: 'Gentlemen. What's the mission of the Infantry?'"

"I don't remember," Reckert said.

"What? And then we all shouted, 'To kill, sir.'"

"Nope. Don't remember that."

"Bullshit. And then we shouted louder, 'To kill, sir,' and the colonel said, 'I can't hear you,' and we roared, 'To kiiii—ll, sir!' and he said, 'Never forget it.' You remember that."

"I try to forget."

"I am Infantry. Follow me," the short lieutenant said as they staggered home at two A.M., past the snoring soldier. Wilfred fell into a restless sleep and dreamed that a small, soft, body crept under the net with him, snuggled close, slipped her arms around him, and slept with him. The next morning as he made up his bunk, he never noticed the long strand of black hair that fell from his pillow to the floor.

"Hey, Fred. Did you get any last night? I could have sworn I heard sounds of the beast with two backs coming from your bunk—smacking and grunting and blowing. Was I dreaming?"

"Yes," he said, shocked by Reckert's invasion of his dream.

"She really has you hooked."

"Buzz off, prick."

"'Mom, I'd like you to meet my wife. Go on, honey, show Mom how you can talk.' 'Numbah one hooch here,' say Can. 'Oh, no!' says Mom. 'He's giving me slanty-eyed grandchildren.'"

"Stop!"

"'But Mom. She loves me. And she's very sensible. All I did was give her fifty bucks for a two-fifty fuck, and she's been after me ever since.'"

"I'll murder you."

"You know that when we go to LZ German, you'll have to leave her behind anyway. And you sure can't take her to the field. You'd get her killed."

"I can take her to German. Then she'll be close."

"Well, how are you going to do that?"

After a few more trysts, Wilfred decided it was time to meet Can's mother, and he set out for town. This time he went along the curving, palm-lined dirt street, following Can's directions. He passed one-room houses with mud walls and thatch roofs, and then stucco dwellings with tile roofs resembling ageless French farmhouses. At the market square, he smelled manure, wood smoke, and fish sauce, and heard voices haggling and chickens squawking in bamboo cages. He passed a Catholic school and a Buddhist temple, and a young man in a tan western business suit putted by on a new motorbike. On the other side of town mud walls and thatch roofs reappeared. Then he was among cardboard refugee shacks and began to wonder from what depth of poverty Can had bloomed.

A ten-year-old boy in shorts and a sport shirt appeared from between two hovels, followed him briefly, hesitated, and then ran to his side and said fearfully, "Mistah Wilfed?"

"Yes?"

"Can. *Lai day.*"

Wilfred trailed him behind a jumble of shacks and down a narrow dike through rice paddies so small they seemed hardly worth cultivating. Across one Wilfred saw an old man squatting on a dike, defecating into the still water.

Then, there she was, standing in the path in black trousers, a plain white top, and conical straw hat. He was surprised to see her in native garb, and the girl he thought he knew was suddenly a stranger. He sent her a smile, but her face, far from beaming the welcome he expected, looked afraid. She turned to accompany the boy, and Wilfred followed.

They stopped at a mud hut with dirt floor and grass roof where an old woman with deeply wrinkled brown skin and a smoking black cheroot jutting from the side of her mouth was squatting by an open fire outside. A stout spit crossing the flames carried three blackened pots. When Wilfred approached, the woman turned, and still clenching the cigar between her rotten teeth, gave him a wide, gappy grin. Wilfred concealed shock at her dental deficiencies and smiled back.

"Má," Can said. "Lutemma Cah…meh…geh…ee," she carefully pronounced his name for nearly the first time.

Má smiled at Wilfred from her squat, then frowned at Can and began speaking rapidly in Vietnamese. "Why do you bring me a hideous, pale, horrible-looking foreign dwarf when there are so many handsome men of your own country ready to slip you their stalks and give me beautiful grandchildren? The eyes. Skin. So ugly, these shit-burning pigs. Your father must be turning in the ground, clawing to get out and murder the pest and send away his ignorant daughter. I pray to the ancestors, let him come and do it. Hurry, my husband. Save us from this fornicating foreign devil. Oh, my daughter. You are so stupid. And the pig too, if he likes you. Oh, why must it be the foreigners who are rich? Why must they come and murder our sons and steal our daughters? Oh, Buddha, save us from foreigners!"

"Please be nice to him, mother," Can entreated.

"Get your brothers and sisters," she told Can's brother, "so they can see this animal that your sister has brought, and so that he can see how many mouths we have to feed and know what handsome, mannerly children look like."

"Eat now," Can said, and she walked around the fire and motioned for Wilfred to follow. She squatted and looked up at him, and for the first time he saw a glint of love in her eyes.

Something smells like rotten fish. He squatted awkwardly beside Can as her mother heaped their bowls with rice, nearly swooned when the other pot was uncovered and the rotten smell engulfed him, and then watched with nausea as the mixture of fungus, dried shrimps, and fish sauce was liberally spooned over the rice. Can handed him the bowl and some chopsticks, and her má, with a grinning nod, invited him to sup.

Deciding it would be unforgivable to insult the mother's cooking, he closed his eyes and nostrils and took a bite. Salty…fishy…like salted fish…anchovies or kippered herrings. Not too bad.

"You like, Wilfed?" Can asked.

"Number one," he replied and repeated it to her ma.

Eight children, aged two to ten, came up now, all dressed in new clothes. Can named each, and the sounds bounced off Wilfred's brain like Ping-Pong balls.

Now Má spoke sharply to the oldest boy, and he jumped up, uttered a command, and led the children away.

It's a matriarchy, Wilfred thought, and he asked Can, "Where is father—papa?"

"Ba dead."

"VC kill?"

She shook her head no.

"Ba VC?" He feared her answer, though he wasn't at all sure she would tell him the truth, especially in front of her mother.

She glanced at her mother, who nodded defiantly.

"VC," Can said with a worried look.

Wilfred was pleased that she'd answered honestly. "Love Can," he said softly, and he thought he saw her face flush.

The old woman puffed on the butt a few times and then, glaring at Can, lashed into a flurry of words with Can interjecting torrents herself in return:

"There will be no fornicating here in front of the children and with the neighbors nearby, young lady, so you can tell that pig it's time for him to get back to his sty, and you can tell him that if he should make the mistake of letting his snake sneak out in front of my children I shall whack it off with my cleaver, slice it up, and serve it to him over rice!"

"You always think the worst, my mother, and you never trust me. What do you think I am, a whore? I tell you, I only rub their backs. I have never made love to any of them, especially the lieutenant, though he wants to very badly. I—"

"You lie very badly. I know what you do. You—"

"You know nothing. But I will tell you one thing: the lieutenant is not leaving until I say so, mother, or else I will leave with him, and I will never come back, and you will never see me again nor get a single piaster from me ever again."

"Don't you talk like this to me—I who have borne you and raised you, you ungrateful child. I should have thrown you out long ago—sold you to a foreigner—for all the trouble you have given me. Go. Leave with him. Never come back. See if I care."

"We're not leaving. And you're going to be nice to him, or we're going to have a fight like we've never had before. You be nice to him and leave us alone, I'm warning you."

"I tell you," said Má, raising her cleaver, "if he makes one move toward you, I shall bury this in his back."

Whoa, Wilfred thought. A violent mother and a VC father!

"I talk Can?" He nodded at a door to the house.

Another burst from Má in her native tongue: "You are not going in there with him!"

Can told Wilfred, "Talk here."

"I go Sang Tran, four days. Can go Sang Tran, four days. I see Can in Sang Tran."

Now he thought the old woman would pick up the pot of fish sauce and scald him to death. Her eyes leaped and she threw the butt into the fire and swelled into a typhoon—megawatts leaping, gales roaring from between her teeth, torrents pouring from her eyes, her wind making a fearful moaning sound. Then she subsided and Can wrote the subtitles: "Bookoo baby. Ba dead. Tee-tee money.

Can give money Má. Má say Can go, baby die. Má say Can go, Wilfed give Má five hundred dollah month."

"Five hundred dollars! I can't afford five hundred dollars." Can had a brief exchange with Má.

"Can no go," she said, and water glistened in her eyes.

Wilfred was stonily silent.

Then the old woman spoke, and Can said hopefully, "Má say four hundred dollah!"

Wilfred couldn't believe it. The old witch was haggling over the rental fee of her own daughter. He crossed his arms and turned away in anger and disgust.

"Má, please. I love him!"

"All right, all right. But tell him this is my final offer. Tell him that. Tell him three hundred dollars a month."

With a touch of terror in her voice, Can told Wilfred, "Má no say again. Má say three hundred dol—"

"Stop," Wilfred said, spinning around. He stalked over to Can, pulled her to her feet, wrapped his arms around her, and said to her, "You tell Má, I give Má…no money. Not one dollar," and he felt Can sink a little in his arms. "I give money to Can. Two hundred dollars every month."

Can was ecstatic while Má thought, stupid dinky dau shit-burning American pig. Money is nothing to them.

Wilfred stayed till late into the afternoon, and though he and Can had the itch, they could not escape Má's arrogant eyes, nor the smaller ones peering around corners.

That night in the barracks, he whispered to her, "How you go Sang Tran?"

She shrugged and said, "Can go Wilfed. Can love Wilfed."

He caressed her hair with his hand and said, "Wilfred loves Can. I'll figure out how."

PART II

▼

THE GAME

The Army's my shepherd.
I shall not hope.
It maketh me to lie down in green paddies.
It leadeth me beside the still ambushes.
It restoreth my ammo.
It leadeth me in the path of booby traps
for its fame's sake.
Yea, when I walk through the valley of the
shadow of death,
I will fear the VC,
for the Army is with me.
My rod and Its staff discomfort me.
It preparest a combat assault for me
in the presence of mine enemies.
It annointest my head with blood.
My veins runneth over.
Surely buddies and medics will follow me
all the minutes of my life
but I will dwell in a plastic bag forever.

—written on a latrine wall at Camp Vassar

CHAPTER 3

▼

MR. MINH

They formed an inconspicuous huddle at the airport flight tower, shielding themselves with an offset in the building and keeping a low profile under the windows. Can's uniform, including his rakish Italian sunglasses, was identical to Wilfred's. A group of men waited on the tarmac for their ride to the front.

"Ah, the old shell game." Reckert said in his W.C. Fields accent. "A little sleight of hand. Watch closely, ladies and gentlemen. Then tell me who is under which shell."

Wilfred showed Can how to drop to one knee and rest her arms on the other. She did so, then came back to her squat, brushing off her knee and saying, "Numbah ten."

"You G.I. now, Can. G.I. no squat."

She sighed and returned to her knee. "Dinky dau."

The sky brightened, and sounds of night gave way to trucks humming and clanking and helicopters whopping. The lieutenants checked in and waited till they saw the two floppy rotor blades start up and the men rise before walking toward the big helicopter. Wilfred gauged from their number that the flight would be full, and when he saw the sergeant with a clipboard at the door to the plane, he felt a twinge of excitement.

"Can, stay with Reckert and don't speak. Robbie, try to get to the front of the line. I need to be near the rear. If anyone talks to Can, tell him she's got laryngitis." Can looked at Wilfred apprehensively and he responded with a smile.

Reckert and Can easily found their way to the front of the line since no one wanted to go, but Wilfred had to muscle his way aggressively into the back.

"O.K. Give me your names," said the sergeant. "Then get on board. And don't all come at once."

The line started moving, shouting out names, and walking up the rear ramp of the plane.

"Reckert."

"Gotcha. Next?"

"He's got laryngitis," Reckert said. "Name's Carmenghetti."

"Carmenghetti? Oh yeah. Here it is. O.K. Next?"

Thirty-five names later, Reckert and Can safely in the bowels of the plane, a soldier in sunglasses identical to Can's whispered to the sergeant, "Carmenghetti."

"Speak up, sir."

Wilfred pointed to his throat, pulled back the strap of his backpack, displaying his nametag, and waved the sergeant close. "I've already been through. I had to go back and get my rifle."

The sergeant vaguely recalled a short lieutenant with laryngitis, sunglasses, and no rifle earlier in the line. He shook his head in amazement, wondering how long this 90-day wonder would last in combat. "Gyood luck, fella," he said, glancing at God, and Wilfred walked onto the plane.

"Come every day at ten o'clock," he told Can under the huge flame tree with bright red blossoms in the schoolyard. "Some day I come." Pressing two hundred-dollar bills into her hand, he pulled her to him, and looked into the watery brown pools of her eyes. I go, Can. I don't know when I'll be back. I love you."

"Love Wilfed."

The lieutenants hitched a ride on a truck to where A Company was guarding a railroad bridge near LZ German. It was one lane wide and four hundred yards long. Its steel truss boxes spanned twenty concrete piers. The roadway passed through the bottom of the boxes twenty feet above the water. The rails had been torn up and the roadbed surfaced years before, when VC mines and raids had halted rail traffic throughout the country. High water marks on the piers showed that the river could reach ten feet higher. Now it was low, with half the sandy bottom exposed and the river shallow enough to walk across.

Wilfred saw bunkers guarding the bridge entrances, and coils of barbed wire stretched at water's edge far down the bank. Searchlights and generators sat near the water to illuminate the bottoms of the piers at night and VC underwater demolition squads. Above, G.I.'s with M-16s checked ID cards and searched baggage for weapons and explosives.

When their truck came to the guards, Wilfred asked for Captain Simms, A Company commander, and was directed to a bunker below the bridge. A stocky man emerged. He had wild eyebrows and a brown brush cut, and a pistol holstered under his left arm. He marched toward them, First Sergeant Biggs at his side. The two new lieutenants instinctively raised their hands in salute.

"Don't ever salute," Simms said. "When you salute, you tell Charlie who the officers are, and Charlie likes to shoot officers. Reckert, I'll make it short and sweet. Three weeks ago Lieutenant Harris, the platoon leader you're replacing, had the back half of his head removed by a sniper and went home in a bag. Carmenghetti, you're replacing Lieutenant Fox. Charlie fragged him in his hooch one night. They took off his legs at Vassar. I used to be a nice guy, fellas, but now I'm a bastard. We do everything by the book. And I'm telling you right now—if you or any of your men step out of line, I'll come down on you like a ton of bricks. Understand?"

"Yes sir," the pair said.

"Reckert, you got third platoon—up the bank and across the road and you're there. Your platoon sergeant's Sergeant Andrews. He's been running the platoon for three weeks and can fill you in. Carmenghetti, you got second platoon on the other end of the bridge. Sergeant O'Shaunnessey will get you started. Both sergeants are old soldiers. Learn from them and depend on them. Get to know all your men and be tough from the start because you better believe I'm gonna be tough on you. Any questions?" The lieutenants shook their heads. "All right. Go get settled in and be back here at 2000 hours for briefing. Don't be late."

Wilfred suppressed an involuntary twitch in his right arm. He dragged his pack up the bank, jerked it onto his back, and staggered under the weight. Halfway across the bridge his legs began to tire and his pace slowed. The straps were cutting into his shoulders, and he had to bend forward to relieve the strain. A round-faced girl in black pajamas and straw hat glided toward him with quick little steps, her heavy baskets drooping from each end of a pole across her shoulders. She deftly swung the pole parallel to the bridge as she passed him, one basket in front of her and one behind. Wilfred wondered if this method of loading the human beast was more efficient than his backpack.

At the end of the span, he saw more guards checking vehicles and I.D.'s and, beyond them, three lean-to coke and beer stands like he'd seen at Onkay, manned by a similar assortment of miniature salespeople and patronized by relaxing G.I.'s.

My god. Those soldiers. They're my men. Abruptly, he turned his mind to thoughts of command, straightened his body, quickened his step, and approached the guards.

"I'm your new commanding officer," he said to the biggest guard he could see, shedding his pack lightly and laying it down where someone might offer to pick it up for him.

"Can I help you with this, sir?"

"Thanks, soldier. What's your name?"

"Welbourne, sir. Alan Welbourne. It sure is good to have a lieutenant again, sir. The Lord sent Lieutenant Fox home, but now he's given us you. Praise the Lord, sir."

"I want to see Sergeant O'Shaunnessey right away."

"Right this way, sir," Welbourne answered in a twang. With one hand he slung Wilfred's pack over his shoulder, and they started down toward bunkers below.

First Sergeant O'Shaunnessey was a tall, gangling man with slightly stooped shoulders. He was in full uniform including steel pot, his sleeves neatly rolled above the elbows. His deeply lined face wore an aspect of careworn fatigue. "Lieutenant Carmenghetti?" his voice boomed.

"Sergeant O'Shaunnessey?"

"The one and only, sir. Good to have you with us," he said, extending a hand and a smile. The sergeant invited Wilfred to his hooch for some Irish stew, dark bread, and coffee he'd received from his wife in a care package the day before.

O'Shaunnessey's hooch had an attached porch roof made of two ponchos sheltering a table, ammo box chairs, and a metal cooler for his personal stash of beer and soft drinks.

Welbourne set down Wilfred's pack and turned to leave. "Go with God," Wilfred said. O'Shaunnessey stiffened. Wilfred gave him a sly grin.

"You had me going, sir," the sergeant said when Welbourne was gone. "I was afraid you might be just like him, and he's a little bit spooky, you know. Talks to God a lot."

"Really. He said his MOS was commo, but I didn't realize the extent of his expertise."

"He's been begging for a radio job ever since he got here and his radio skills are exemplary, but no one wants him because his preaching makes them nervous." Wilfred said he'd like to try him since it might be fun, and you could never tell when his skill in supernatural communications might come in handy.

While they ate, the sergeant said, "We're seven men under strength. Morale is low from casualties and lack of support at home. The men don't know what the hell we're doin' over here, and neither do I. Their friends back home are burnin' their draft cards and marchin' or hidin' out or runnin' to Canada or enjoyin' their college deferments.

"Yeah. My sister's been marching and sitting-in at Vassar."

"I don't blame them. All we're doing is killing people and wrecking the country. We can't win. We ought to pull out."

"How can you fight if you feel this way about the war?"

"I'm a professional soldier. I get paid to do what my country tells me to do and by God I'm gonna do it. I have to set aside my personal opinions. Besides, it gets real easy to fight when someone's shootin' at you....

"...The company usually goes to the field for three weeks and then comes back to a firebase for a week of stand-down and security duty. The men usually need a good rest after three weeks in the boonies."

The Duster on the bridge began pumping off 40mm rounds, exploding them on the hillside above them. "What's happening?" Wilfred asked, suddenly sober.

"Just H & I fire, sir. Once a night at a different time. Keeps 'em off the mountain."

H & I. Wasteful and idiotic, but comforting.

A tall, slender Vietnamese man emerged from a shop, walked toward a small Japanese truck with a canvas top and sides, and climbed in. He was neatly clad in slacks and sport shirt. His right cheek bore a long, wide scar from a shallow bullet wound. He limped slightly, for after another bullet had shattered his left leg, he'd spent five days moving through the mountain jungle on a litter with only a bandage around the oozing wound. When it had finally healed, the leg was an inch shorter than the other. He felt fortunate to even have it, however, for while it was mending, they were sawing off his left arm, piece by piece, as poison from a hole in his hand slowly moved into his forearm, elbow and upper arm. Now the folded and pinned short sleeve covered his shoulder like an empty bag and the bone fragments around his mended femur periodically seized him with pain that made every muscle in his body clench. Still, broken and scarred though he was, he attracted little attention in a country where so many people were disabled by war. And the right arm had compensated by doubling in strength and dexterity.

A boy approached him. "Mr. Minh. A Vietnamese girl wearing an American lieutenant's uniform went into Mr. Tuong's massage parlor a few minutes ago, and Mr. Tuong took her back into the rear."

Minh thanked him, parked near the massage parlor, slipped inside, and stood in a corner of the front room.

Soon Tuong came through the curtain alone, walked to the swinging doors, opened them inward slightly, carefully searched the street, started when he saw Minh's truck, closed the doors quickly, and turned toward the counter.

"Do you need anything today, Mr. Tuong?" Minh asked quietly with explosive effect.

"Oh, Mr. Minh. How very nice to see you again," Tuong said, breaking into a smile and ambling across to greet his guest with both hands outstretched. "I was just planning to send a boy for you. I need some jackets and lighters and beer."

"Good. I am glad I came by then. I have what you need right in my truck which I can sell you for very little."

"Very good. I am so happy you have come."

"Have you heard any news from your sons?"

"I hear very little, Mr. Minh. They are slaves in the army of the Americans, but help our army whenever they can."

"That is good, Mr. Tuong. Too long have the white imperialists murdered our countrymen and stolen our rice, rubber, oil, and sand, and used our young girls to satisfy their lusts. We must all work together to destroy them and bring freedom back to our land and make it one country again."

"Yes, Mr. Minh. And, as always, I am anxious to help you and the Liberation Front in any way that I can."

"You are a good man, Mr. Tuong, and I know you will help. Unfortunately, there are many among us who prefer to become rich from American dollars at the expense of their fellow countrymen. Some even are spies. We must find these snakes and cut off their heads with machetes. Don't you agree, Mr. Tuong?"

"Oh, yes, yes, and I may have a new way to help. A new girl came to me today wearing the uniform of an American lieutenant named Carmenghetti. She asked for a job as a masseuse, but says she will not be a whore. She is a good masseuse, and wants very little, so I hired her and made room for her with another girl."

"She must get money from the lieutenant if she is so little interested in money."

"Very wise, Mr. Minh."

"Perhaps we can use her to get information from the lieutenant."

"That is what I had in mind, Mr. Minh."

"Then that will be your task, Mr. Tuong, for the good of your country. Do not fail."

"It will not be easy, for I believe that she is infatuated with him."

"If that is true, can we use that emotion, perhaps, to turn the head of the lieutenant to our side?"

CHAPTER 4

▼

JOSHUA HENRY

"As you know, I'm Lieutenant Carmenghetti," he said to his squad leaders. "I'm replacing Lieutenant Fox who is on some paraplegic ward back home trying to figure out what he did wrong. I'm going to be different. They say Fox was a nice guy, and that's what got him killed, and by that they mean he was too lax. You'll find I'll be different."

"For me you'll do things by the book. I'll be checking everything. I want clean weapons and chest-deep foxholes, and everyone will wear steel pots. I'll check guards every night, some nights twice, and any man sleeping will get court-martialed. I'll ask for your advice on tactics, but I'll make the decisions, and everyone will do their job aggressively. It's the only way to win the war. I guess that's it."

Wilfred was shocked. It was another voice talking, not his own, but one he'd heard many times before in his training. Still, there was nothing else to say. This was a real situation with real sergeants in a real war.

He asked for questions, and after a long silence, Sergeant Roosevelt asked when they would be going back to the field. Wilfred told him they wouldn't know until the night before. Then Wilfred asked O'Shaunnessey to give them a time check, and he said, "When I say 'hack' the time will be 1432 exactly." They set their watches on 1432 and prepared to push the knob and start them ticking. "Five, four, three, two, one, *hack*, one, two."

Wilfred asked for the passwords for that night, and O'Shaunnessey said, "Sign: chocolate. Countersign: cookies. Chocolate cookies, sir." Words unfamiliar to the Vietnamese.

"You got anything?" he asked the platoon sergeant.

"A few things, sir. Mail call and beer call are at 1630. As usual, it's two beers per man. Supper's at 1700. We'll have the usual 25 percent alert tonight, if that's O.K. with you, sir, with four three-hour shifts: 1800, 2100, 2400, and 0300. Roll call at 0600 and breakfast at 0630. Squad leader meeting, 0730. Sick call, 0830. Each squad gets three passes to town for tomorrow, effective from 1000 to 1600. Give me your rosters for passes, mess, clean-up, daylight guard, and latrine details at the briefing tomorrow morning. That's all I got, sir."

Wilfred appreciated the schedule, which he was sure was mostly for his benefit. "Anything else?" he said, glancing around the group but receiving no response. "O.K. Dismissed."

Alone again with O'Shaunnessey, Wilfred asked, "How did I do?"

"Do you want the truth?"

"Yes."

"They're probably all mumbling 'ninety-day wonder' and wondering if you'll expect them to die for their country. You came on pretty strong, sir."

"You know, if they're sloppy with their jobs, it could get me killed, just like if I fuck up it might get them killed. I want them to stay on their toes and to know who's boss."

"Oh, I understand, sir, and I'm with you all the way."

"What is it with all the moustaches?"

"The Army thinks they make us look fiercer to the VC, who are a little short on facial hair. Just more bullshit, sir. Charlie ain't afraid of our hair. But the men like them. Makes 'em look more like their hippie friends back home."

Wilfred asked where he was supposed to sleep, and O'Shaunnessey pointed to an empty two-man bunker. "When you get an RTO, he'll stay there too so you're close to your radio."

"I didn't know I had to live with my RTO."

Wilfred dragged his pack to his bunker. Inside was a rectangular hole with sleeping ledges on the sides. The roof was a steel sheet with two layers of sandbags on top. He blew up his air mattress, laid it on a ledge, folded his camouflage poncho liner blanket in half, placed it on the mattress, and suspended his mosquito net by wedging the strings through holes in the steel and under the sandbags. Then he went outside, sat on top of the bunker, and looked around. While the sun bore down, some men slept while others lounged on bunkers reading paperbacks, listening to tape recorders, writing letters.

"You the new louie?" a deep voice startled him from behind. Wilfred lurched. "I want talk to you."

"Yes?" Wilfred said, his eyes leaping at the sight of a huge man—black, bare-chested, and muscular. He had a pump shotgun cradled across his arms and wore a floppy-brimmed camouflage jungle hat with graffiti on the sides: "I zap VC," "Bad Motherfucker," and "Black Power."

"He won't gimme my fuckin' pass." The words were slurred and hostile, insubordinate, and proud.

"Who won't?"

"That chickenshit spick."

"Who?"

"Rodriguez."

Wilfred began to grasp the situation. "Did Sergeant Rodriguez give you permission to see me?"

"I told him I was comin'."

"You don't tell your squad leader you're coming to see me. You ask for permission. What's your name?"

"Private E-1 Joshua Henry, and I tell anyone I want anything I want." Wilfred broke into an astounded smile. Henry's own face parted into a grin, exposing brilliant white teeth, and a right front tooth capped with gold and cut so a white enamel NVA star showed through the cap.

"And how," Wilfred asked, "do you get away with that?"

"I don't give a flying fuck, that's all. What you gonna do? Send me to Nam? Gimme a vacation at Long Binh jail? You can't do that, sir. You needs me too bad."

"And who made you indispensable, Private?"

"I did. I'm the baddest motherfucker you got. Been on point for three straight months. Killed five Charlies." He languidly pushed the butt of his shotgun toward Wilfred to show him five notches neatly carved into the wood. "You know, you and me, man, we's gonna do some time together up there, and if you wants me to, and if I wants me to, I's gonna save your little white ass from gettin zapped by the Charlie."

"After I save yours."

"You talk big for such a little man."

"Oooh, I act big too. You'll find out."

"We'll see. Wait'll the lead starts flying round your head. Then we see just how big and bad this white boy is."

"What about my pass?"

"Forget it. Next time go through channels."

"Hey, come on, Lieutenant. I wanna see my girl before we go out again."

"You heard me."

"Mother! I don't need no pass." He began to stalk away.

"Private Henry. I'm alerting the M.P.'s that you're on your way. See you soon." Wilfred headed for Sergeant O'Shaunnessey.

The platoon sergeant suggested they let someone in his squad keep an eye on Henry and let them know if he left. Wilfred agreed.

Then he told Rodriguez that Henry was getting ready to go "over the hill" again.

"That's why I no let him go, sir," Rodriguez explained. "I think if he go now, he not come back for a week maybe. And one more day we go to the field."

"You say we're going to the field in a day?"

"Yeah. Not tomorrow, but next day."

"Where did you hear that?"

"One my men heard in town today."

"Terrific. I didn't even know."

"We knew we go soon, anyway. Now we know what day."

"Did he say where we're going?"

"Near big lake, I think. Small village."

"Where did he hear this?"

"From girl in whorehouse."

"Think there's anything to it?" he asked O'Shaunnessey.

"Hard to say."

"Rodriguez. See if you can find out what girl in what whorehouse and what village we're supposed to be going to."

"I find out."

"Now, what do we do about Private Henry?"

"He's done it twice before," O'Shaunnessey said, "and we've busted him all the way down to buck private, sir."

"Maybe we should send him to jail if he does it again."

"I don't think that work, Lieutenant. He just don't care for nothing. And we need him on point."

"Good, huh?"

"Yes sir, good," O'Shaunnessey said. "Bronze star for valor, purple heart, and five KIA."

"Good with shotgun. No get lost. Find four boobytraps."

"Damned superman. So what the hell do we do? Keep him chained up back here? Post a guard?"

They thought a while, and finally Wilfred said, "I'll talk to him. Make him promise to come back."

"I try that. He promises, then doesn't come back."

"I don't know what else to do. Tell him I want to see him."

Rodriguez left and soon Henry was swaggering up.

"You wanna see me?"

"I want to make a deal," Wilfred said.

"A white man's deal or a colored man's deal?"

"Listen, Henry. I don't want to fight with you. They say you're a damned good soldier. And I know what it means to have a girl in town. I've got one myself."

"Ain't that sumpin?"

"But we have a war to fight and we need to know that you'll be with us when we take off outa here."

"So what's the deal?"

"The deal is that I give you a pass for tomorrow, and you be back tomorrow afternoon by 1600."

"That it?" Henry asked, a little surprised.

"Nope. You fail to return by 1600, and next time we're here, I'll confine you to a bunker the whole time with a twenty-four-hour guard."

"Ooooh. Big, bad lieutenant."

"Do we have a deal?"

"Yeees, sir," he said, but his eyes quivered with contempt.

At 1600 hours on this day before Henry would get his pass, the riverside camp was infused with the shouts and laughs and bawdy stories of soldiers returning from town, all appetites sated, blood type: alcoholic.

The chow truck pulled up and the dinner detail unloaded the dark green cooler-like mermite cans onto the ground and began setting up chow line for the platoon. A hefty green mailbag and two and a half cases of nearly cold beer were carried to O'Shaunnessey's bunker. He called out names and passed out the letters and care packages, and then gave two beers to each man in line. Following the initial distribution came the redistribution—the haggling and promising and repayment of debts whereby many men obtained six or eight beers.

All food was cooked twice, once in the mess tent at LZ German and again by its own heat on the way to the bridge. The rice was sticky, the vegetables soggy, the steaks overdone. Wilting blocks of paper-wrapped vanilla ice cream completed the meal. Wilfred, O'Shaunnessey, and the servers brought up the rear, and seconds were tendered on food that remained.

Wilfred checked on the intelligence report with Sergeant Rodriguez who gave him the name of the girl and the establishment. The soldier had been less certain of the name of the town they would search, however.

When Wilfred finished reading letters from his mother and sister and opening care packages from his mother, he rolled down his sleeves, grabbed his rifle, steel pot and flashlight, and left for the company briefing. The bridge was closed now, convoys gone, beer stands deserted, and the water under the bridge dark in the long shadows of evening.

Reckert was leaning against a bunker looking at the river when Wilfred told him about Henry. He laughed. "A few hours ago, you were a delinquent yourself. Now you're a hard ass cop."

The other three lieutenants came now and everyone traded introductions. Second Lieutenant Billy Jim Newcombe had first platoon. He was a tall and strong Texan with leading man good looks and was a graduate of a large southern university.

Weapons platoon was run by Second Lieutenant Byron Lorde from D.C., who had an embarrassingly thin brown moustache and a vacant look. He seemed afflicted with mental absenteeism—truancy even. "Hey, man, where you at?" he asked, his eyes looking past Wilfred to something on the other side of the river.

Last was a tall, slender man with shiny black hair, intense probing eyes, and a very bad complexion. First Lieutenant Eric Fierden was a psychology major who had been in country for six months and spoke with what he considered appropriate authority. He'd been a platoon leader for five months, but now was Executive Officer, second in command to Captain Simms. Administrative duties shuttled him back and forth from the field to Vassar with errands on payroll, leaves, and the like. He addressed the others as lieutenant as if he had already been promoted to captain and seemed to expect them to call him "sir."

"I trust you'll do something about that psychotic Negro Henry, Lieutenant," he fired at Wilfred.

"I'll do my very best."

"Well, if you can't handle it, Lieutenant, at least try to maintain some decent records of his deviant actions so I can have him committed before he kills somebody."

"He's already killed five, Lieutenant."

"I don't mean gooks, Lieutenant. You know what I mean. I'm talking about psychotic, anti-social, deviant behavior."

At the briefing Simms reported on the battalion briefing, describing the results of the day's actions: "eleven enemy KIA and five WIA, two rifles, and four inches of documents captured, no friendly casualties, forty-seven new cases of VD, three cases of malaria, and one case each of heat stroke and immersion foot. The Doc says to be sure the men wear rubbers, take their malaria pills and salt tablets, and take their boots and socks off at night and let their feet dry out. Any questions or problems?"

"The name of that girl who said we were leaving the day after tomorrow is Trang. She works at the Paradise body shop."

"There's probably nothing to it," Simms said, "but I'll pass it on to battalion S2."

"Is it true?" Wilfred pursued.

"I'll let you know when we're leaving the day before. I don't even know myself. As far as where we're going, I don't know that either, but I do know that sometimes these little seeds are planted by Charlie to discourage us from going into an area. They try to make us think they know where we're going so we'll figure they're laying for us or have already pulled out. Or they may be trying to make us think they're trying to discourage us so that we *will* go in there and so they're free to operate someplace else. It gets complicated. I find it's best not to worry about things like that. Leave 'em to the snoops."

"Robbie, are the rubbers for the VD or the immersion foot?" Wilfred asked later. "And I can't understand why the Army reports inches of documents captured. What the hell does that tell us? Four inches could be the Brooklyn phone book."

"They can't read Vietnamese and don't know what they have."

"Oh. The next thing you know they'll give up the body count and start reporting pounds of flesh. Or blood. Yeah. 'Today we had a positive balance, on the ground, of thirty pints of blood: fifty enemy minus twenty friendly.'"

"The blood balance."

"Yeah. It's better than the kill ratio. It takes into account friendly and enemy dead and wounded with one statistic."

CHAPTER 5

▼

TRANG

The sun was setting, and Wilfred noticed that Dusters, light tanks with machine guns and 40mm cannons, had blocked both ends of the bridge. One faced town and one the mountain on the other side of the bridge. As he started across the bridge a growling and rumbling erupted behind him on the left, then the right, then across the river on one side, then the other, like angry beasts calling and answering, guarding their domains. Suddenly the water under the bridge lit up like a monument, generators feeding powerful searchlights with energy that flooded the river.

A soldier out on the bridge pulled the pin on a grenade, yelled twice through the din, "Fire in the hole," and let the handle fly. Wilfred hit the deck. He heard the soldier count to three as the timing mechanism raced toward the moment when the jagged pieces of steel would rip and tear in all directions. Then the ball of steel was in the air, falling toward the water, and the soldier was crouching, waiting and listening for the proper sound. A "boom" would tell him he'd successfully exploded it just above the water, dispersing the killing fragments in a wide circle. A muffled "thud" meant that he had not held it long enough before dropping it and that the shock wave had only caused a few fish to float belly-up on top of the water and bloodied the eardrums of the hypothetical VC sapper towing explosive charges under water toward the concrete pier.

Throughout the night at random intervals Wilfred heard the sounds of the deadly game:

"Thud."

"Too soon, you gyrene. Hold it a little longer."

"Boom."

"Not that long, idiot. What're you tryin' to do? Get us all killed?"

"Must've been a short fuse."

He groped his way through darkness to his bunker, picked up snacks, and found O'Shaunnessey sipping a drink.

"What'll you have, sir? Irish or bourbon?"

"A little bourbon and water, thank you."

"That's a relief. Irish is hard to come by." He poured some whiskey from a steel flask into a canteen cup and handed it and a canteen to Wilfred, who was spreading out his vittles.

They talked about combat procedures, and Wilfred asked, "Did you ever burn down a village?"

"Yes sir. We got a rule: if we take casualties from sniper fire coming from a village, we burn it down, level it with bulldozers, and move the people to a strategic hamlet run by the government and surrounded by concertina wire. Teaches 'em a lesson. Pretty soon they learn not to shoot at you. But I can still hear the cryin' and moanin' when they pick up what they can carry and get into the choppers."

"Tough. So how much of our area of operations do you think we control?"

"Ten percent, maybe. The people fear us more than the VC when we're around, but we're not around that much. We move in, search an area, and move out. The AO's just too big. There are four hundred hamlets in the AO, and the Vietnamese government would have to have soldiers in every one of 'em and troops patrolling all the areas in between if they hoped to control it. So I'd say that most of the time the VC are in charge—especially at night."

As the evening wore on they moved to other topics: the possibility of beating the Russians to the moon; the flower people with their love-ins and communes and anti-war, anti-establishment, anti-materialism, and do-you-own-thing ethics, LSD, mini-skirts, wigs, topless waitresses, and body paint.

They inspected the guards with O'Shaunnessey leading the way.

"Halt. Who goes there," came a voice from a bunker.

"Lieutenant Carmenghetti and Sergeant O'Shaunnessey," Wilfred said.

"Chocolate," the guard whispered.

"Cookies."

"Advance and be recognized." The two stepped forward.

"Halt," the guard said, and they obeyed. Wilfred noticed that the soldier had his rifle pointed directly at them from the doorway of the bunker.

"O.K., sir, Sergeant. You're recognized. Proceed."

"Anything to report?" Wilfred asked.

"No sir. Situation negative."

"Good. Carry on."

On his way back to his hooch, Wilfred gazed at the moonlit river, and his eye caught a column of rats running single-file over one of his bunkers. He shuddered and they were gone. But they left him a vision of VC scurrying through the area. "Fire in the hole," called a distant voice. "Thud" came the result, and more fish floated to the surface. As he passed a bunker he thought he heard the squooshy, moaning sounds of copulation, and a deep voice said, "O.K., man. My turn."

Since it was Wilfred's duty to know what was happening in his platoon, he shined his flashlight around the corner through the window and observed eight G.I.'s in varying stages of undress and a naked Vietnamese girl. He quickly turned off the light and slipped away into the darkness, driven by a chorus of angry obscenities. *And now I know what the curve in the Army flashlight is for: looking around corners into bunkers.*

He thought about Can with growing unease. *Was she in danger? He had to find out. The report on this girl Trang had him unsettled.*

The next morning he washed amid the odor of burning shit and put on some cologne. *Is this to make me smell good to others or to make things smell good to me?*

He went to the flame tree, and on the way the thought of Can rushed him, knocked him down, rolled over him, and replaced loving concern with salty lust. His penis grew and stiffened, and once aware of it, he was embarrassed; he wished it were restrained by the soft pouch and elastic bands of civilian briefs instead of being free to gallop uncontrollably down the leg of his army shorts, there to jut out beside his thigh below the bottom of his fatigue jacket, advertising his excitement.

There she was, a block away, standing under the tree in black blouse and slacks, her straw hat flung back, eyes turned downward to discourage passing servicemen.

"Can," he said.

As she looked up with a smile, she couldn't help but notice his bulge, and as he attempted an embrace, she cut him short, "Oh, no, Wilfed. No here."

Half-walking, half-running, they raced to Paradise, past the grinning Mr. Tuong, down the hall where drapes concealed the body rooms, now alive with the rhythmic, liquid sounds of coitus, up narrow back stairs, and into her bedroom where woven straw mats covered two crude wooden platform beds. Between them was a bureau holding a personal praying Buddha and a collection of small, framed photos.

The pair were rolling together like ocean waves when a girl in white pajamas entered, sat facing them on the other bed, began pulling on her long black hair with a brush and looking at their naked bodies with amused indifference.

Wilfred noticed her first, pulled out, crossed his legs, and sat up. Then Can saw her and said, "What are you doing here? I'm using the room." He observed the comeliness of the intruder, and noticing his attention, she smiled and slowly puckered her full red lips. Can read the invitation, pushed Wilfred aside, leaped up, said, "Di di mau!" and ranted and raved and pointed to the door. The other girl hissed and fired a few epithets of her own, but finally capitulated. She rose and sauntered to the door, winking at Wilfred as she left.

Now Can's venom fell on him. She pushed him back onto the bed, leaped on him like a cat, knees astride his stomach, and began hammering his chest with her fists. Screaming and sobbing, she pointed to the other bed, the door, and her crotch.

At last he was able to grab the wrists, and when her wrath was spent, he pulled her down beside him. Then they were loving again, his hands stroking and fondling and giving her the feast she desired. And once more they lay together in peace.

"Chow-chow?" she asked, and they went to a restaurant for noonday rice. He had noticed that the place where Can lived was named "Paradise." It was time to find out who this girl was who had said the company would leave tomorrow. Perhaps he could unearth a spy ring and save some American lives. Can had rice bowl raised, chopsticks in mouth when he decapitated her with his first question: "You know Trang?"

She spat her rice back into the bowl, eyes glowing, and wailed in return, "You know Trang?"

He shook his head, shrugged, and said, "No."

Can was perplexed. She turned her head to one side, eyeing him suspiciously. "That girl Trang," pointing in the direction of Paradise. "She numbah ten!"

"That girl Trang? Live with Can?"

"Yes. Why you wanna know?"

"She say we go to the field tomorrow."

"When she say you?" She was certain the two had met before.

"She no say me. She say G.I. Yesterday."

"Oh, yes, I know. She say me you go tomollow."

"She VC?"

"Yes, VC. No, VC. I donno. I know she numbah ten."

Thus ended the double interrogation. He'd nearly stirred Can into another fit of jealousy just when he was going to the field, when they needed to be sure in their love.

"Oh, Can. I love you. You number one."

"No love Trang?"

"No. I love Can."

They wandered around town, shopping, returned to the parlor at three o'clock, felt each other's warmth, and shared a long kiss. Then the war intervened and as he drew back to leave, she clutched his arms. "No go, Wilfed," she said. "No go."

"I come back three weeks," he said, his voice snagging on the words. Then her eyes melted, and Wilfred remembered the eyes of Felicity and Mother Madge at the airport. "VC no shoot me. I too small—tee-tee." He touched her face with his hand, and left.

At the bridge he picked up the acetate-covered map at company headquarters and rode the stream of men returning from town. Their mood was strangely quiet: fear of combat was settling over the camp like an immense apparition.

"Any sign of Henry?" he asked O'Shaunnessey.

"Nope, and he's got five minutes."

"Shit. What do we do now?"

"Give him another thirty."

Wilfred received one letter from Madge at mail call and declined his beer ration. He himself was feeling the anxiety of leaving their womb of bridge security, and felt the weight of duties bearing down on him.

At 1645, he again approached the platoon sergeant. Henry was still absent—the only man. O'Shaunnessey called First Sergeant Biggs with a description and directions to his usual hangout in town; Biggs told the Captain and called the M.P.'s. After supper, they checked again with Biggs. The M.P.'s hadn't found him. Wilfred said he should've listened to Rodriguez and kept Henry under guard at the bridge. He asked O'Shaunnessey whether he thought they really might be going to the field the next day, and the sergeant said he had "a feelin'" they would.

Wilfred went to his bunker, put a hand on the sandbags over the door, and swung down into the gloom.

"Where you been?" came a throaty voice.

"Who the fuck's that? It's you, Henry, isn't it?"

"Reporting in, sir. A deal's a deal."

"Why, you sonofabitch. We've got M.P.'s looking for you all over town. How come you didn't report in when you came back?"

"I just did, sir."

"How come you didn't report to your squad leader?"

"My deal was with you, sir."

"Then how come you didn't try to find me?"

"I figured you might be comin' back late—you never knows about lieutenants—and maybe I'd a walked around for hours and never found you, and then I'd be in big trouble. But I knowed you'd come back here sooner or later."

"You did this just to make trouble. Well, let me tell you—next time we're back here you aren't going anywhere."

"Oh, no, Lieutenant. That's a white man's deal, and I ain't buyin'. I kept my part of the bargain, and you's going keep yours or you's in some deep shit, little man."

"Don't you call me 'little man.' Get over to Sergeant O'Shaunnessey right now and tell him you're here. We'll deal with you later."

"Oh," Henry said, rising to leave. "You got another deal for me? Cool, man. Bye."

He left, and Wilfred pulled out his pack and began rummaging furiously, trying to distract himself and dampen his anger. The sonofabitch was just tryin' to get my goat. And damned if he didn't. Had me just where he wanted me. Made me blow my cool. Lose control. Manipulated me. Duped me. Made an ass out of me. Got his sweet revenge. Dammit!

At evening briefing Captain Simms said it was official: they would leave tomorrow. As he described the operations plan to his group of lieutenants, they madly scribbled the orders into pocketsize spiral notebooks. "We'll chow down at 0630 and load up the trucks at 0800, right after our relief moves in. Then we move to German and lift off at 0900 and Charlie Alpha to the East. That's a combat assault for you new men. Mission? Cordon and Search Phuoc Binh 3, a suspected VC hamlet near Dam Thuong Lake. Artillery prep of the LZ starts at 0920 and lifts at 0925. At 0925 the gunships will strafe the LZ and then circle the objective to keep any Charlies from getting away. Touch-down of second platoon will be at 0930." Wilfred swallowed dry saliva. "That's you, Carmenghetti. Don't screw it up."

CHAPTER 6

▼

CARMENGHETTI AND SIMMS

Wilfred felt his feet hit the ground and go pounding away from the plane. Blurs beside him began sailing down, and as he dove to the ground, the breath was jarred from his lungs.

The sound of the choppers faded, and he listened for gunfire, but heard none. Rising to his elbows, he surveyed the perimeter and his circle of troops lying in the low grass and shouted to O'Shaunnessey across the way, "All clear, Sergeant?"

"All clear, Lieutenant."

He found his green smoke canister, pulled the pin, and tossed it. A green puff rose like a genie and began dissipating and drifting toward the lake. He turned to Wellbourne, who offered him the handset, a telephone-like receiver attached to the radio on his back by a tightly coiled black wire. He took it, jammed it to his mouth and ear, and pressed the bar on the side. "Six, this is Two-Six. Come in Six. Over."

With a faint wop-wopping of helicopter blades in the background Simms hissed, "Roger, Two-Six. This is Six. Over."

"LZ green. Repeat. LZ green. Do you roger that? Over."

"Roger, Two-Six. LZ green. We're comin' in. Out."

The other lifts descended, bodies scrambled off, ducking needlessly under the big propeller, forming up in seconds, and running off in their designated directions—Newcombe's past O'Shaunnessey and northeast toward the lake; Reckert's, past Wilfred, heading north with Lorde's on his tail. Captain Simms came in on Newcombe's lift, looked around casually, found Wilfred, and came to his position. "So far, so good."

Newcombe reported to Simms first: "Three to six secure to the lake. Negative contact." Wilfred's position was six o'clock, and the lake was from twelve to three.

Lorde's report came next. "Six to nine secure, but we've lost the third."

"Six, this is Three-Six," said Reckert. "Nine to twelve is secure to the lake. I can see the fourth. Hang on, Four-Six. We're a-comin'."

Despite the momentary lack of coordination, the company finished the cordon in minutes. The captain called in three Vietnamese National Policemen, one with a loudspeaker, and told Wilfred to "gaggle up" his troops and "get going."

Wilfred formed his column with Henry in the lead and himself and Welbourne three men back. Simms fell in with O'Shaunnessey and the policeman with the speaker turned up his volume and began ordering the people out of their homes and into the narrow, dusty street.

"Hey, Lieutenant" said Henry. "Maybe you'll get your big chance today."

"Move out," Wilfred said, sweeping his arm over his head and pointing to the front to signal the men in the rear.

They walked down the winding path, by hedgerows, under palm trees, and came to a black-clad middle-aged woman standing in the road with five small children clinging to her. Her nervous smile revealed black stains from chewing betel nuts and gaps where the nuts had done their worst. Wilfred shouted back to Washington to have some men take them to the interrogation area.

Henry and Rodriguez went to the woman's hooch and stood by the door. Henry leaped inside with a bellow, fell to one knee, and whirled his shotgun around. Rodriguez began the search, looking at the walls, ceiling, floor, under the table and beds, in the large crock of rice in the corner. He slipped his bayonet into the thatch of the walls, stomped on the floor, listening for hollow sounds, and poked the knife into one place in the dirt that had aroused his curiosity. Henry covered him, while two others stood guard outside, and Wilfred came in and assisted in the search. The process continued throughout the village, the men working slowly and methodically, and the lead rotating to other members of the first squad.

They had inspected the eleven shacks and collected the fifty-odd villagers—old men, women, and children. Then Wilfred asked Simms, "Anything else we need to do?"

"Negative, Lieutenant."

They were nearly out of the village when Wilfred stopped the column. "Hey, O'Shaunnessey. Did anyone check out that pig sty?" The sergeant consulted Washington and Kaslovski and reported back that no one had, so Wilfred sent in Rodriguez and Henry. Henry looked disgusted and a bit tired, but he spotted a long bamboo prod in the corner, broke it in half, and he and the squad leader began weaving systematically back and forth across the yard, thumping the ground with their sticks. The other men watched with amusement as Rodriguez thumped one of the pigs and sent him squealing to the other side of the yard. Wilfred told them to make sure they gave the shed a close look. They did so, and Henry made the hollow sound that no one wanted to hear.

"I found her, Lieutenant. Right here. Give us some cover."

Rodriguez' squad aimed their rifles at the spot as Rodriguez and Henry kicked away the manure and dirt. Rodriguez said, "Get ready to shoot. We open it up."

"Watch," Henry said. "It might be booby-trapped."

They laid on their bellies in the dung, Rodriquez on one side, Henry on the other, arms outstretched, fingers on the top.

Rodriguez said, "Everyone get down, but be ready to shoot." He raised two fingers for all to see and dropped them. Then he said, "One...Two!" and they put their faces on the ground and flipped off the top. All was quiet. "Now what we do, sir?"

What do you do now, Lieutenant? He'd heard the words a hundred times in OCS as his instructors posed thorny problems and asked the candidates what to do, preparing them to make real decisions. But he hadn't expected the moment to come so soon. What should he do? He had an opportunity to make a decision, to impress the men with courage or cowardice, to gain a victory and win a medal, to act rashly, to err, to die. The words swept over him like an avalanche. He began to sweat; his eyes blurred.

"Lieutenant?" Rodriguez called again.

He gritted his teeth. "Get me some extra grenades."

Captain Simms stared at him. "You...going down in there?"

"You bet, sir," he said almost angrily. "There ain't no other way. Rodriguez. Follow me in."

Flashlight in one hand, pistol in the other, extra grenades on his belt, he stood by the hole.

"You want me to go, sir?" Henry asked with a sneer.

"You're too big. It's a job for a little man. Grab my legs and lower me down." He snapped on his steel pot.

Henry grabbed his ankles, lifted him up, and lowered him down and in.

"Pull me out!" Wilfred said.

"What's the matter," sang Henry. "Change your mind?"

"Let's roll in a few grenades first. It levels out six feet down. If there's anyone in there, I want to scare him back so he doesn't shoot my head off when I reach that level spot."

"Fire in the hole," Henry shouted as he dropped in a grenade. The explosion shook the ground.

"Another," Wilfred said, and the next grenade boomed. "O.K., now. Let's wait three minutes and drop another. Then they won't know when to expect the next one."

After the third grenade burst, Henry lowered Wilfred back down the hole. He landed gently and began to crawl, Rodriguez right behind.

The flashlight was of little use in the smoke from the grenades. But as they moved along, low-crawling rapidly on their elbows and knees, the smoke began to clear. The earthen walls and ceiling were sculpted into an arch. The floor was wet and muddy and in several places there were small piles of rubble that had fallen from the walls and ceiling. Wilfred hoped the grenades hadn't weakened the structure.

He started making noises—grunting and growling, chattering to himself louder and louder until he was bellowing.

Wondering if Wilfred was deranged, Rodriguez said, "Lieutenant. Be quiet. They'll hear us."

"I want 'em to."

"Why?"

"To scare the fuck out of 'em."

"It works. You scare the fuck out of me."

"Hey, Charlie," Wilfred taunted demoniacally. "We're coming for you, Charlie. Get ready to meet your ancestors." Then he grew bolder, pointed the pistol and squeezed the trigger.

Deafness. Solitude. Suddenly it was as if he were in space, deep and quiet. There were no sounds because there was nothing he could hear. "Damn!" he shouted, hearing his voice as if someone had pillows crushed against his ears.

He looked back at Rodriguez whose eyes returned fear and surprise. "Can you hear me?" Wilfred asked. Rodriguez watched the lips move and shrugged. Wilfred held up his flashlight and turned it off and Rodriguez did the same. Then they waited.

After several minutes Wilfred said, "Rodriguez," in a normal volume to test their senses and was relieved to find that his voice was closer. "Can you hear me now?"

"Yeah. But not real good. Jesus, sir, don't shoot again."

They set off again, moving another thirty yards, around bends, down gentle slopes and up, with no room anywhere to turn around. Wilfred continued to loudly threaten the insubstantial enemy, but frequently paused to listen.

Coming around a bend he heard a voice. He stopped, turned to Rodriguez, and pointed to the sound, which the sergeant confirmed with a nod. In cold terror, he reached for a grenade, wanting to wound or kill the VC, if they were there, or to send them into panic and surrender. The explosion might destroy his hearing, but if he put his hands over his ears, maybe it wouldn't; worse, it might bury them all alive, but the other grenades had not caused the tunnel to collapse, and he judged that this one wouldn't either. What worried him most was that the VC might pick up the grenade and throw it back at him, so he decided to risk a short fuse and the chance it might detonate in his hand and hold it an extra second before throwing it.

He held up the grenade, looked back at Rodriguez to make sure he was ready, and pointed to his ear until the sergeant covered his. Then he pulled the pin, let the handle fly, counted to four, threw a quick chest shot around the corner, and clapped his hands over his ears.

Quick thunder. Dirt sifting from the ceiling. A whining, crying sound and gabbling in Vietnamese. They had chosen surrender over entombment by a madman.

"Chieu hoi," Wilfred said. "VC, chieu hoi!"

He kept crawling, around a bend and over the pile of newly fallen earth and shale, making as much noise as possible. They entered a long, narrow room with an arched ceiling piled high with wooden crates. Wilfred's light found two figures cowering in a corner. Again he shouted "Chieu hoi!" as savagely as he could, pointed his pistol at them, and watched their hands fly up as again they begged to surrender.

As Rodriguez frisked them, Wilfred glanced through some of the crates in the room and found ammunition and grenades. "My God," he said. "That grenade could have blown this whole place sky high. No wonder they surrendered."

They crawled into the tunnel, and with the VC in the lead, made the long trip back. They arrived to a band of shocked men. Captain Simms pulled out the scrawny captives and Wilfred and Rodriguez. The VC were taken to the interrogators, and Rodriguez and three other men went back down and brought out thirty-eight rifles, mortar, and ammunition.

Wilfred collapsed, shaking, and wasn't settled enough to eat C-rations until two hours later when the weapons were up.

"Lieutenant," Henry said. "Here's your gun. Bad job."

The point man walked away, and as Wilfred laid the rifle on the ground, he noticed two notches cut into the plastic stock.

"I-I suppose you think you deserve some kind of a medal for that stunt, huh, Lieutenant?" Ever since Wilfred had emerged from the tunnel Captain Simms had been snapping at everyone.

"No sir. I was just doing my job." He was lying. There was nothing he would have liked better than a medal. After all, it would be the only way to prove to anyone he was courageous since he intended never to do anything courageous again.

"Well, you're not going to get one because you don't deserve it. You haven't paid your dues. You don't even know how to be scared yet. And you're not career. You don't need a medal. I'm the one who needs one, and I've been out here humpin' for five months. I even turned down a job at Brigade, but did they give me one yet? No. I'll be goddamned if you're going to get one after one day in the field. I'm the one who deserves one."

"I'm sure you do, sir."

"You're goddamned right. Now listen up good. I'm the one who captured those gooks, not you. You and Rodriguez scared them and chased them through the tunnel, but when they started to get away out that hole, I grabbed their arms and stopped them, and they would've got away if I hadn't stopped them. You, Lieutenant, are my witness, and you are going to fill out the request for my Silver Star."

"Sir?"

"Yes, and you're going to do it because I am going to fill out the request for your Bronze Star For Valor. It'll be our own private little deal, Lieutenant. No one needs to know."

"What about Rodriguez?"

"Put him in for a Bronze Star For Meritorious Service."

"But that's not even for valor. Everyone gets those."

"Lieutenant. You know if we hand out too many awards for valor, it cheapens them. Anyway, he probably won't even know the difference. His English isn't too good, you know."

"Yeah. I know."

"Good, then, it's settled. I'll have Lieutenant Fierden bring us the forms tonight."

Wilfred searched the ground beside him and broke a twig between his fingers. "Sir, I can't put you in for a medal. I didn't see what happened. I was down in the hole. I came out after the gooks did."

"One of those gooks was right in front of you—"

"Yeah, but I didn't see him trying to get away."

"I'm telling you they tried to get away."

"Sir, can't you get someone who was on top of the ground to do it for you. Someone like Henry? They could see what was going on a lot better than I could."

"Lieutenant. I want you to fill out the form."

Wilfred sighted Simms's eyes down cold steel and pulled the trigger: "Sir. I'd like to, but I did not witness your actions."

"You're refusing me, Lieutenant?"

"I'm sorry, sir."

"I won't forget this, Carming…Carming—whatever the fuck your name is."

The National Police questioned all the villagers and took back with them the weapons and ammunition and three prisoners, one of whom was the woman who lived in the house by the pigsty.

Before leaving the village, Simms reported his version of the operation to Colonel Clary and received highest praise. "I would have gone in myself, sir, but the tunnel was just too small for me to fit. God, those gooks are small. Anyway, I had two of my midgets go in and scare 'em out. Didn't take long. But it was lucky I was there to grab 'em when they tried to get away. I knew I was taking a chance with two of 'em, like that, but I stopped 'em, by God. Grabbed their arms and stopped 'em."

"Outstanding. Keep up the good work."

When time came to leave, Wilfred thought his platoon would be relieved of the responsibility of leading the afternoon march because of their extra effort that morning. He and his men were surprised when the captain said, "Second Platoon. Move out."

CHAPTER 7

▼

MATFIELD AND RODRIGUEZ

The company sailed single-file through wide expanses of glimmering paddies, silently tacking this way and that down earthen dikes, gliding between islands of palm-sheltered huts, crossing a dusty highway, and putting in at the foothills to a dark green mountain. Henry had taken one careful look at the map, glanced around to identify some key landmarks, and led them unerringly to their destination without using a compass.

Wilfred had spent the hours in phantasmagorial contemplation of the morning's events. Conflicting emotions streaked through his mind in random directions like a meteor shower: He was out of his gourd to do such a thing. He could have been killed. A Chi-Com grenade tossed his way. His own, hurled back. A bullet between the eyes. Snakes. Spring-loaded knives and trip-wires. Poisoned punji stakes. Dirt and rock falls blotting out the light, crushing his body. Oblivion. Why did he do it? Was he trying to prove his courage to those sullen hunters, Rodriguez and Matfield, and especially to Henry?

Then he saw the VC soldiers, riddled with jagged steel fragments, lying in blood, inert. He could have killed them. He heard his own voice screaming for their death. Stalking. Growling. Hunting. He felt the anger surge again. The pounding heart. The hate. He wanted to kill them. He would have enjoyed it and been proud of it. And he wanted to be back there now, doing it again. He saw esteem in the eyes of his men, but another reaction as well—fear. He'd passed the bounds of normal behavior, had shown too much courage and cunning, had verged on rashness and insanity.

They reached the area designated by Battalion for the FOB, their Forward Operational Base—a campsite with a defensive perimeter. He surveyed the terrain, a dried-up rice paddy—its dikes broken by track vehicles—with a stream running through it. He motioned for the line of men behind him to move ahead, and as each platoon leader approached, directed him to a section of the perimeter. Lorde's weapons platoon was kept within the perimeter to serve as a reaction force and to man the mortar.

Wilfred and O'Shaunnessey consulted on the platoon defense: six foxholes, two per squad, twenty feet apart; two three-man LPs—listening posts—in the woods on the hillside; machine guns on both ends of the line where their crossing fires could cover all of the field; two claymore mines just outside the perimeter and wires from them to the foxholes so that when detonated, their steel balls would saturate the entire field; a third aimed up a small ravine where the stream entered the forest.

Simms came to check Wilfred's plan and said, "Make damned sure those foxholes are chest-deep."

The supply chopper came in and the troops took turns leaving the perimeter to get their packs, mail, and beer, and then they went to work industriously even though the temperature was in the upper nineties. The beer helped, and they were strong and calloused and used to the labor. They also knew from experience the importance of good defenses.

While everyone else was digging, the two three-man teams that would man the listening posts disappeared into the woods to recon their posts. They had to find hiding places and become familiar enough with them to move to and from them in the dark.

Wilfred dug a six-inch deep six-foot square sleeping hole with his entrenching tool to get below flying shrapnel from enemy mortars or rockets while Welbourne foraged for bamboo poles for their hooch. Wilfred blew up their air mattresses and the RTO pushed two poles into the ground for vertical supports, lashed a third to the first two for a horizontal ridge, snapped their ponchos together, draped them over the ridge, and staked the corners to the ground. Welbourne climbed inside and tied the mosquito net to the ridge and down to the stakes. Air mattresses, poncho liners, and packs went inside. Not a bad system. Amazingly primitive for twentieth century mechanized warfare, but still functional.

He went out to inspect the foxholes and dispelled a vision that the men were digging graves.

"Is that hole chest deep?" he asked a private named Louis King.

"As deep as mine, or as deep as yours, sir?"

"Yours, soldier."

"Yes sir. But can I dig it head deep so I won't get shot in the head?"

"These holes are to fight from, not hide in."

"But sir, why do we have to dig holes in the afternoon, fill 'em up in the morning, and then dig new ones somewhere else the next afternoon, day after day. It makes me feel like that guy Sisyphus."

"The VC'll turn 'em into punji pits full of poison stakes if we don't fill 'em in, you know that. So what do you do in the world, King?"

"Dig graves. I get lots of practice over here."

"I guess you do."

"Say, Lieutenant, how do you tell if a man's dead?"

"I'll bite. How?"

"Dead men don't talk, sir. They's stubborn and damn good at keepin' secrets. Why you can ask 'em any question you wants to and they'll just sit there real quiet and superior-like and not even bother to answer. Course, they acts superior 'cause they is superior. They knows all the answers we don't, 'cause they sees the other side. But one thing worries me."

"What's that?"

"You almost never sees one smilin'. And the ones that is smilin' looks funny— like they found out they's been tricked."

At chow Reckert asked Wilfred, "What the hell were you doin' this morning? You could've been killed."

"Just doin' my job, Robbie."

"But no one expects you to risk your life over here. Heroism's out, man. You need to utilize all available war machines before risking a life. 'We waste bullets, dammit, not lives.' Haven't you heard that?"

"What would you have done?"

"I would've thrown in a bunch of grenades or dug 'em out with a loader. But don't risk your life. That's why we blow thousands of dollars on each combat assault by pounding the LZs with artillery and strafing them with gunships. Tactically, it's ridiculous because it alerts the enemy, but it's supposed to reduce the risk of friendly casualties. So what if it warns Charlie that we're comin'. If he hides, maybe we won't find him, and then we don't run any risk at all. But if he's got a strong force, it'll also tell him where to ambush us."

"So how would you run a Cordon and Search, smart guy?"

"I don't know. Skip the arty, skip the strafing, land the birds all around and charge in fast. It would be cheaper and more effective because we'd keep the element of surprise. But that's not the point. The point is that I'd like to have you around a while. You scared the hell out of me. You've got to start thinking about alternatives to personal heroism."

"But you know it's damned near impossible to get killed on your first day in combat. Flip a coin. I didn't even need to carry a gun this morning."

After dinner the officers planned the next day's foray into the mountains. "They're a sanctuary for NVA regulars who move through the area along the seacoast," Simms said. "The trees give 'em plenty of cover, and the mountains are close enough together that a group can cross the paddies from one to another in one night with the help of VC guides and porters. And the hamlets are close enough for them to get food and supplies." He looked up at the mass of green. "We can be pretty sure they're up there somewhere right now, 'cause we've taken so much shit up there before. It's your turn to lead out tomorrow, Lieutenant Newcombe, followed by Lieutenant Reckert, Lieutenant Lorde, and you, Carmenghetti."

After the briefing Newcombe said, "Wilfred Carmenghetti. The little man with the big balls. Nice work."

At the squad leader meeting, Wilfred gave an inspired pep talk on how the United States would win the war only if "we show aggressiveness and guts." He commended Rodriguez and told him he would put him in for a Silver Star.

Later, when Wilfred was sitting alone by his hooch writing the news to his father, Matfield and Rodriguez approached him.

"We like to speak to you, sir," Rodriguez said, dropping down on one knee while Matfield towered over them in silence.

"Shoot," Wilfred said.

"We don't like this blood and guts bullshit."

"What?"

"We want go home alive, and we don't want you taking chances with our lives."

Wilfred was stunned and incensed. "What do you think this is over here, some kind of a game? We have a job to do."

"No sir. Our job is to go home alive."

"Well, Sergeant. I think you'll do what I tell you to do."

"No sir. Not if you tell us to walk off a cliff, even if you go first. No, we watch you fall and say, 'Bye.'"

"I never took you for a coward, Sergeant."

"I'm not a coward, sir, but I'm not crazy either."

"Are you tellin' me you think I'm crazy?"

"If you don't care to live, you crazy."

"Damn it, I do care, but I care about winning this war too." It was the other voice again, coming from who knows where.

"That's fine, sir. You win the war. We go home. Alive."

"Don't you care if the communists take over here?"

"No sir. I care about my wife and children."

"We all have families. That's why we're here. We're protecting our families. If we don't stop the march of communism somewhere, it won't be long before it's on our own doorstep."

"Then we fight and die maybe. But not here. Not now."

"I guess it's my duty to inform you as to what will happen if you disobey my orders."

"Yes sir."

"If you disobey a direct command, you will be brought up on charges before a court martial and sent to jail."

"Do you know Lieutenant Fox got fragged in his hooch, sir?"

"Yeah."

"He very brave. He too brave. So he go home."

"What are you saying, Rodriguez?"

"I say if you too brave with us, you go home too," and he lobbed an imaginary grenade at Wilfred.

"You threw the grenade into Fox's hooch?"

"That's for us to know and for you to find out, sir."

Wilfred's eyes narrowed. "You don't scare me, Rodriguez. You wouldn't have the guts to frag me."

"Oh, no?"

"No. Not only that, it's a two-way street, Sergeant, and if you want to play that game, you'll be the one who'll end up on the paraplegic ward."

"Oh, Lieutenant. You are so tough. And so funny."

"I'm warning you."

"No. We warning you."

"Get the fuck out of here before I beat the shit out of both of you." Rodriguez and Matfield smiled at each other.

The two LPs left the perimeter at dusk and slipped into the woods. Wilfred lay in his hooch considering the challenge to his authority. He knew the deceptions and lies men use to achieve their ends and was ninety-nine percent sure Rodriguez was faking. The other one per cent made him toss and turn.

At two A.M., a wooshing sound. "Incoming!" a guard shouted too late for anyone to react. An explosion of light and matter, then others took up the cry. Troops froze in their holes, awaiting the next round, while one called "Medic!" into the darkness. Twenty minutes later landing lights flooded the center of the FOB, First Sergeant Biggs directing in the medevac with a flashlight in each hand. Men loaded the soldier—laughing and joking with him—and watched him fly away. For him the war was over.

CHAPTER 8

▼

COLONEL DAI

In the morning Wilfred walked to the perimeter and in plain sight of all, lifted a shovelful of dirt from the ground, lowered his pants, squatted over the hole, defecated and urinated, and replaced his divot, all in Asian privacy. You don't see if you don't look.

The company began moving up the mountain. Newcombe located a path, but the captain said it was too risky: "Too many booby traps and ambush sites." Newcombe was disgruntled. He had a good point man and wasn't afraid to make some contact, and he knew how they would spend the day if they didn't take the path.

"Machete," called the point man to the man behind him. "Pass it down," and back came the two-foot-long knife like a runner's baton. The day was spent with most soldiers languishing in the heavy air, rising to walk a few steps, falling to the ground again, swatting at a myriad of crawling and flying things. The battle was waged at the head of the line—slashing and tearing through the thickets and vines until strong arms lost their grip and replacements moved up to take their turn.

"Oh, what the hell. Light 'em up," Wilfred said, and out came the smokes. "They'll never find us in here."

The only gesture to security was that the men alternated directions as they reclined, and kept their voices low enough that the captain wouldn't hear.

The company would never surprise the VC with all this thrashing around, and the VC would never find the company, protected as it was by the crush of vegetation. Tactically it was a futile charade satisfying the combat leader's secondary imperative to protect his men, but sacrificing any possibility of accomplishing his mission.

At noon Simms reported to Colonel Clary that they were making very slow progress up the mountain and could not possibly reach the top and return to a new location on the plain by afternoon. Since they had only one meal of C's, the colonel gave them a new azimuth and told them to start back down after lunch.

Breaking the new trail down was not much easier. More men slipped, accompanied by sounds of pebbles rolling under foot, branches snapping, rumps and shoulders landing, voices cursing.

When they reached the plain, they set up camp as on the previous night, and darkness passed uneventfully.

The next day was more nerve-racking, albeit less strenuous for the men at the head of the column. The colonel sent them two kilometers along the base of the mountain, then up a stream littered with boulders. Reckert's men were in the lead, picking their way up through the rocks, looking for VC behind each one.

By noon the stream had narrowed, with vegetation closing in on both sides, and the heat and humidity grew stifling. When they crossed—thigh-deep water tugging at their legs—they held their rifles high above their heads. One man stumbled to his knees into the chilly current, but kept his rifle high and dry and came up laughing. Then others began falling, not by accident, and Reckert had to pass back word to "cut the crap."

They picnicked on the stream, reclining on the bank or perching on the rocks like gulls, and then continued up the hill.

Late in the afternoon they came to a small plateau. The stream meandered through a field of waist-high elephant grass.

Thunderheads had filled the sky, driven by erratic gusts and followed by a deep and sudden overcast. With the smell of rain, Captain Simms decided to make camp in the field, and the men hastily began forming their perimeter defense for the night.

They'd hardly begun digging-in when the storm began lashing them. Ponchos came out, and the soldiers crouched and waited. After an hour and a half, there was still a steady downpour, and the captain ordered them to continue digging in the rain.

By dusk it was a soaking drizzle. Guards were in muddy foxholes, others shivering endlessly in poncho tents. Everyone was soaked and hungry, but the weather was too severe for the chopper to bring food, packs, and poncho liners.

It occurred to Wilfred that since the helicopter hadn't come in, the VC wouldn't know their location and might stumble on them by accident. His only encouragement was thinking that the rain might keep the enemy from wandering around.

At one o'clock the sky cleared and the moon appeared. Shaking with cold, he walked the perimeter telling his men to be especially alert. His positions were only twenty yards from the wood line, an easy toss for a man with a grenade, and a deadly accurate range for a sniper aiming at the well-illumined targets. He'd put out one LP in the dripping woods, but this alone could not protect his whole section of the perimeter. In spite of his anxiety, the night passed without incident.

When morning came, the exhausted, famished, mud-caked troops faced a dense fog that again excluded the supply chopper. Retracing their steps to the valley would take three hours. By then the fog would have lifted. Two clicks ahead was a large clear area into which a chopper could drop rations, so Colonel Clary directed them to continue up the mountain.

Wilfred's platoon led. A few hundred meters up, Henry found a trail that crossed the water, and he elected to take it instead of hacking his way through underbrush that now nearly hid the stream. He moved up the trail more like a deer than a hunter. Stopping motionless. Listening. Looking. Treading without a sound. Eyes searching for trip wires and the glint of steel. Ears sifting the jungle sounds for the incongruous: the rhythmic crunch of walking, the vibration of the human voice, the clink of metal or glass, and the snapping of twigs under foot.

The column moved like an inchworm—bunching up, stopping, then leaping forward and almost running. Each man could see only the back of the man in front of him. At times an open hand, stretched down and back, would tell the follower to stop, or swinging over a shoulder, would motion him forward. One minute the soldier in front would disappear, and the man behind would panic and run forward, angrily whispering, "Slow it down!" or "Hold it up!" The next minute he would be crashing into the rear of the now-halted soldier in front who would hiss, "Don't bunch up!" or "Spread it out."

Soon the jungle was steaming. The verdant roof leaked pale yellow and screeched and howled with warnings from the tree dwellers. Shirts oozed sweat and insects buzzed flesh like taunting pilots. Shafts of light weakly pierced the hazy filter, eyes reached further, and fuzzy shapes came into focus.

"Lieutenant," whispered the rifleman in front of Wilfred. "Henry wants you up there."

Welbourne right behind, Wilfred passed three soldiers and found Henry on his knees, pointing at something with his thick black hand. "Careful," Henry said as Wilfred kneeled beside him. Then Wilfred saw it, glistening like a spider's thread across the trail. "The grenade's there. The other end's tied to that tree. You hold back this bush and I'll disarm the fucker."

Shit!

Steeling himself, Wilfred closed his hands around the branches and pulled them back, knowing that if they slipped from his grasp, they would strike the wire.

Henry said he wasn't sure how this trap worked. Pulling the wire could pull the pin or pull the entire grenade from a tin can enclosure allowing the handle to spring off and the grenade to detonate. Or the wire might be under tension; breaking it might release a spring that would pull the pin, so he couldn't just cut the wire. He had to see how the mechanism worked. The booby trap itself might be booby-trapped with punji pits or a compression mine. So he followed the wire off the path, probing the dirt with his bayonet wherever he put his knee.

Seeing the explosive shocked Henry. It was a claymore mine. If the wire was stretched half an inch, it would pull together contact points, close the circuit, activate the battery, and send thousands of steel pellets down the path.

"Claymore," he said. "Get down and pass it back."

Since he had no wire cutters, he disconnected the battery. He picked up it and the mine and handed them to Wilfred.

"They's gooks up there, sir. They wouldn't waste no claymore if they wasn't. Must be a bunch of 'em."

Wilfred sent a message down the file to be on alert and radioed a report to Simms.

"Roger that, Two-Six. Keep on going. Out."

Henry set out again with even greater caution, Wilfred and Welbourne right behind him. After moving twenty-five yards up a fairly steep slope, he stopped and motioned Wilfred forward. "I can smell 'em. Can you? Nuoc mam, smoke, an' shit."

Wilfred smelled his cologne. "Can you smell it, Welbourne?"

"Yes sir."

Wilfred took his rifle off the safe position.

As they came around a bend, the trail leveled out and they could see a splash of light ahead where the trail left the forest and entered a clearing.

"Stay here," Henry said. "I'll check it out," and he low-crawled ahead.

"Gimme a sit rep," the radio hissed. Wilfred took the handset from Welbourne and told Simms about the open area. Then, seeing Henry waving him forward, he and the RTO moved up.

"Ain't been long," Henry said, showing Wilfred a collage of rubber tire tread impressions left by sandals in a muddy spot at the edge of the clearing. "Must've been this morning, or the rain would've washed 'em out."

"Any sign around the outside of it?" Wilfred asked, looking at the waist-high grass, about the size of a football field, bathed now in bright sunlight.

"Can't see nothin'."

Simms told them to secure it, so Henry, Wilfred and Welbourne left the trail, followed closely by the company column, and began circumnavigating the field, meeting Captain Simms back at the starting point.

"Any sign of Charlie?" Simms asked Wilfred.

"No,"

"O.K. Clear the path through the clearing."

About halfway across, Henry raised his head above the grass and saw what he was looking for: two poles, twenty feet apart, tops barely visible above the grass. "Another trap," he told Wilfred. "This one's for choppers. There's a wire between those poles. The wind from the chopper blows the grass and sets it off. I'll get it."

Wilfred told everyone to get down and Henry disappeared into the grass. The group waited in silence for what seemed a very long time. Then Henry appeared with two more claymores and another battery, the gold cap on his right incisor revealing the white enamel NVA star as he smiled. "All clear, Lieutenant."

Wilfred radioed the signal to Simms who relayed it to the other platoon leaders, and then speaking in a low voice and glancing around to make sure no one could hear him, especially Rodriguez, Wilfred asked Simms, "You want us to check out the path ahead? They can't be far."

"Fuck this shit," Simms sibilated. "I'm hungry. Let's eat first. I'm callin' in the birds."

Not fifty yards down the trail, two NVA guards lay prone in the bushes, fifty caliber machine guns in hand, oblivious to the enemy in front of them. Farther back, two companies of NVA regulars camped under the canopy. Evening fires were quenched and many slept, some cleaned weapons, and one monitored a radio. Medics tended a dozen wounded, and a small group of officers planned strategy over a map and conferred with a VC guide.

Since the NVA were upwind of the clearing, they couldn't smell the cigarette smoke rising from the American ring of fire. It wasn't until the helicopter came wop-wopping down, nearly on top of their heads, that an outcry arose and the commander, Colonel Dai Anh Le, hastily ordered evacuation of the position.

Dai was unsettled. His specialists had carefully set booby traps utilizing reliable U.S. mines and had checked them that morning, but none had detonated. The most probable explanation was that they had been disarmed, evidence of an enemy force. But when the helicopter remained on the ground too long and was not followed by others, he concluded that the Americans were unaware of his presence. Also, the helicopter was of the type used to ferry food and packs to platoons or companies.

For a moment he entertained the possibility of attacking the Americans because he had superior strength and the element of surprise. Then he observed the confusion of the evacuation in progress around him and quickly dismissed the idea. His mission was to ready his wounded for travel and to join another unit to the south. Moreover, he was a cautious man who eschewed targets of opportunity, preferring instead to meticulously plan an attack following the general instructions of his superiors. If he attacked now, he might win a victory at the sacrifice of a larger victory later on. He also might get pinned under a hail of artillery. Even in victory, he might reveal the strength of his force and prompt a counterattack by a larger American force.

He sent a platoon to join the two guards on the trail in an ambush to protect his retreat. They could hold the Americans at bay long enough for the evacuation to be completed.

The rear guard proved unnecessary. The battalion trotted a mile down the trail carrying supplies and litters, and burrowed deeply into a new part of the jungle, stopping at an alternative camp, far off the trail.

The A Company perimeter was littered with boxes and cans when Henry began leading the company toward the first NVA camp. There they discovered lean-tos, defensive trenches, crocks full of rice, and medical supplies. Simms was disappointed that there had been no contact, no weapons captured, and no body count.

"The place was deserted," Wilfred told him.

"We could've had 'em," Henry said to Wilfred. "Those fires was still warm. They was here, right in our sights. They must've left in a hurry; look at what they left behind. Must've been scared off by that fuckin' chopper."

"We lost them for a can of C's," Wilfred said, awestruck at the size of the camp and secretly relieved.

They burned the rice and continued down the trail. Henry was sullen, but alert for ambushes. He stopped where the enemy had left the trail and showed it to Wilfred, but the captain ordered them to proceed. "We've got to think of the men," he told Wilfred. "They need a rest or they won't be worth a shit tomorrow."

CHAPTER 9

▼

THE DANCER

They left the woods after a few hundred meters, descended a gentle slope of chest-high elephant grass, and entered another barren rice paddy. Beneath some palms in the center of the field lay a tangle of charred beams, crawling with vines, scraped into a pile by the blade of a willful green bulldozer. The sole surviving structure in the former hamlet was a tiny walled graveyard harboring a one-room, bullet-pocked pagoda.

Wilfred hoped the VC would be less likely to mortar the home of sleeping ancestors than the adjacent paddies, so he led the company around the cemetery for the night.

He was burning over Simms' inaction, and when the captain arrived to check his section of the perimeter, Wilfred pounced on him. "I was just thinking how you let a fucking NVA battalion slip through your fingers today—twice. Congratulations."

"Stand at attention, Lieutenant."

"If you haven't guessed yet, I'm not a lifer, sir, and if you don't get off my back, I'll report your actions to Clary."

Simms smiled and his eyes began to wander. "Wilfred." It was the first time he had used the given name. "I didn't know they were so close to us. And the men were beat to shit. We hadn't eaten for twenty-four hours, for chrissake."

"And on down the trail?"

"You're such a hard ass. You want 'em that bad? I'll give 'em to you. Prepare your platoon for a night ambush. Back where they left the trail. You won't even have to recon it."

Wilfred managed to keep a steady gaze throughout his fit of panic until his anger returned. "You chickenshit sonofabitch. I'll go. But if you don't back me up, so help me God, I'll come back and blow your fucking brains out."

"You've got some mouth, Lieutenant. I won't forget that."

Wilfred regretted unleashing his animal.

Charlie Charlie deposited Colonel Clary and his RTO, Rogers, and roared away. "What happened up there, Simms?"

"We just missed 'em, sir. We'd no idea they were so close."

"Gotta be aggressive, Captain. Pursue. Eliminate. Never lag. Never quit. It's the only way to win."

"Yes sir."

"Any sign of them on the way down?"

"One of the men thinks he saw where they left the trail."

"What? And you didn't follow it?"

"I thought we'd stand a better chance tonight. I'm putting a platoon-size ambush up there."

"We can't let 'em get away."

"No sir."

"See that they don't. Tonight, send out your platoon-size ambush, but also put two squad-size defensive ambushes on these trails close to the LZ. Recon 'em this afternoon. And I want a fifty percent alert tonight. The NVA might attack you tonight. Tomorrow, go back up there and track 'em. I'll keep an LOH in the air to make sure they don't slip out onto the plain."

Sergeant O'Shaunnessey approached them as they made their plans. Simms glanced at him and asked, "What is it, Sergeant?"

"I have those medal requests you wanted on Lieutenant Carmenghetti and Sergeant Rodriguez."

Simms knew he was trapped. "Thank you, Sergeant."

"Let me see those, Simms," Clary said, and carefully unfolded the damp papers that O'Shaunnessey had carried for days in a plastic bag. He studied them with patient concentration, and then looked at Simms.

"Something stinks here, Simms."

"Sir?"

"You told me you captured the VC, Captain."

"What? No sir. I, uh…only assisted the lieutenant and the sergeant."

"You said you disarmed them."

"No sir. I said I grabbed their arms."

"Well, I guess I misunderstood. Get these soldiers for me. I want to see what heroes look like and shake their hands."

When Wilfred and Rodriguez arrived, Clary said, "Tunnel rats, eh? Glad somebody around here has balls. Congratulations." He shook their hands, amazed at Wilfred's diminutiveness. And Rodriguez' mixture of insubordinate apathy and hostile pride made him stiffen. "Keep up the good work, Lieutenant, Sergeant. Your courage honors yourselves and your country. You can go now."

As they were returning to their area, Rodriguez asked Wilfred, "Did you ask the captain to send us back up tonight?"

"That's no concern of yours, Sergeant."

"No. You right. It should be your concern."

It's time, Wilfred thought, and he headed for Reckert, as the Command Center lifted off.

"Gotta talk to you, Robbie. Private."

"Step into the confessional, my son."

"Father, my C.O. and two sergeants are giving me shit."

"Yes?"

"Simms's sending me up the hill tonight, out of revenge."

"Oh, my son. Did you put it in your mouth again?"

"He made me mad."

"I thought you liked to fight VC."

"And Rodriguez is still uttering threats."

"My son. My son. You must learn to get along with others."

"I have no power over my opponents around here. There are too many guns."

"All grunts are created equal."

"They don't fear me."

"What do you propose?"

"I need you to spread a little fib."

"And what might that be?"

"It goes like this. My family's New York Mafia. My dad's a big don. Numbers, dope, prostitution, protection. Connections in every city. Legitimate businesses. Politicians on the payroll. Bag men, soldiers, hit men. I need for you to tell everyone that you remember reading my name in the newspaper. You asked me about it and were unconvinced by my denial."

"Are you serious?"

"Perfectly."

"Oh, Wilfred. Do you have to do this? Can't you just lay back a little?"

"And let Charlie win by default?"

"Wilfred. This is no game out here. It's for real."

"It is a game. A high stakes game."

"I suppose."

"Does that mean you'll do it?"

"Play your silly game? I guess."

The hooches were up and soldiers lolling, letters and brews in hand. Wilfred found his pack. It had a dark, wet spot on the bottom and was reeking of cologne. He pulled out the bottle. It was three-fourths empty. He was irked. He had never felt so grubby. His first set of fatigues was mud-caked from the tunnel, the pair he had on was filthy and turning putrid with old sweat, and he had one clean set of underwear left. He would have paid dearly for a shower and a change of clothes, but he wouldn't get that for weeks. And now he had lost most of his cologne. Soon the stench would become unbearable.

The sun was going down when he instructed his men. "Don't forget. Fifty percent alert. Maintain sound and light discipline. No smokes. O.K. Jump up and down." They did so. "You. Tape those dog tags." He inspected their camouflage—leaves in their helmet bands and on their rifles and equipment. Straight lines broken. Faces and hands blackened and stinking of insect repellent. "Listen up. Let's make damned sure we get 'em all in the kill zone before we open up. One trigger-happy man can get us all zapped. Be patient. O.K. Move out."

Henry set a rapid pace. He wanted to be in place before all the light was lost. Nothing was darker than the jungle on a cloudy night. And he had to find where the NVA had left the trail. He'd marked it when he found it, in case they had to come back, but things looked different at night.

Thirty minutes later he found it, walked twenty meters past it and stopped. Wilfred came up, asking in a whisper, "This it?"

"Yeah."

Wilfred motioned the platoon off the trail ten feet. They reclined with a loud crashing sound that made Wilfred shiver, and aimed their weapons at the trail. Machine guns and claymores were placed at the ends and trained on the kill zone, wires run back to Henry on the left and Matfield on the right. Then everyone was silent.

He wondered if there would be contact. The NVA might lie low until A Company moved on or might try to change positions in case the Americans returned to search for them. They might have a scout watching them.

Colonel Dai's lookouts had watched two of Newcombe's squad leaders recon ambush sites where the other trails met the plain. At dusk, when Wilfred was preparing to leave, Dai's scouts had assumed that his platoon would be heading for one of the reconned sites and had returned to report to Colonel Dai without verifying this assumption.

The NVA needed food. A scout had returned to their former camp after the Americans had left and found the rice crocks destroyed. Consequently, Colonel Dai sent a platoon of porters back over the mountain on the same trail the Americans had traveled. He wanted them to be in position on the other side of the mountain to enter the plain at sundown. That would give them time to go to several villages, pick up provisions, and return soon enough that it could be cooked under cover of darkness.

At Wilfred's ambush site, the sounds of the night were deafening—chattering and howling of monkeys, chirping of crickets, calling of night birds, buzzing of mosquitoes. Be quiet; I can't hear, he shouted soundlessly. He was nauseous with tension and fatigue, but couldn't allow himself to sleep.

At about three o'clock, after countless negative situation reports, Wilfred began to believe that the night would pass in peace and felt himself beginning to drowse. Then Henry heard a change in the night sounds and reached over and shook the man next to him. Hands moved down the line until everyone was awake and slipping his weapon off safety.

Wilfred refused to believe what was happening until the first NVA soldiers trotted by with AK-47 automatic rifles. Then an electrical shock surged through his body. He knew that in seconds they would be surrounded by death.

They're breaking the rule, he thought. They're too close together; they're making a horrible mistake. His soul cried out a warning, but they would not listen. They were passing through in another realm and just kept coming—intent, oblivious.

The first explosion sounded from Matfield's right as a claymore mine flew apart. Hundreds of steel balls broadcast toward the backs of the first four in the column. The projectiles pierced leaves and twigs. Some stripped bark or became buried in the earth. Others tore through cotton fibers and soft flesh and continued in slow arcs to the jungle floor. Still others hit bone and ricocheted through organs and vessels, bouncing, ripping and lodging within.

Blood. Pulsing past shredded, oozing cells. Springs feeding streams forming rivers. Leaving their banks. Finding new channels. Flooding lungs and hollows. Rushing out new mouths to the endless airy sea beyond.

As the shadow of a man with a sack of rice on his shoulder stopped for an instant in front of Wilfred, he unleashed his machine gun. The horrible scream was reduced to an infant's bawl as the roar of torrential automatic fire reached its peak from all around.

The black of the forest night glowed intermittently with stroboscopic iridescence as muzzle flashes pierced the gathering cloud of smoke. Wilfred watched his target writhe in a presto dance macabre, jerking this way and that under the impact of each round. Head, neck, shoulder, chest, side, stomach, groin. A ludicrous bow, and the terpsichorean crumpled into the bushes under the weight of his sack.

As the fire receded into gappy bursts, Wilfred heard thrashing from his right front, rose to his knees and emptied his clip at the sound. A lull revealed silence.

He heard crunching thumps of running feet and a guttural growl, staccato cracking over his head, a thunderous shotgun blast, metallic sliding, eject and seat, and a second blast. Silence, save a purr of terminal moaning.

"Is everyone all right?" he shouted breathlessly to the darkness. Then the lunacy of the question hit him.

O'Shaunnessey responded from the void, "O.K. here, sir."

"Henry."

"Nothing but dead gooks."

"Rodriguez."

"O.K."

"Matfield."

"O.K."

"Washington."

"No one's hit here, sir."

He jumped up, the venom of hate pounding in him. "O.K. I want to see the bodies. Drag 'em out. Make goddamned sure the fuckers are dead and don't have any grenades under 'em." Sporadic fire erupted again as the soldiers performed coups de grace on the already dead, the bullets lifting the bodies like sizzling bacon.

"Lieutenant," Welbourne said. "Captain wants a sit rep."

"What's going on up there, Lieutenant?"

"They walked in and they're all dead. No friendly casualties."

"Nobody hurt?"

"No dead and no wounded."

"How many enemy?"

"Don't know yet. Call you back. Out."

"Lieutenant—"

Wilfred headed left toward Henry, stepping over bodies as he went. He found Henry pulling one onto the trail by the arms. "Is that the last one?"

"Last one we got. Claymore missed him. I ran him down."

"Is he the one that fired back?"

"Yeah."

Wilfred retraced his steps, flashlight lit, counting. The prostrate flesh was limp and warm, but pale. Various parts were missing or out of place. Intestines covered with dirt and decaying leaves. Half a face. Brains. An arm bent backwards at the elbow. Blood. Eyes refusing to back down. Jaws slack. Terror. Shock.

After viewing half of the bodies, Wilfred fell to his knees and threw up, dry-wretching long after his stomach was empty.

"You all right, sir?" Welbourne asked. He helped Wilfred up and they continued. Now his beacon counted pairs of feet, avoiding eyes and wounds.

"Captain again, sir,"

Wilfred took the phone. "Yeah?"

"How many did you get? Over."

"Twelve."

"Any wounded? Over."

"Negative."

"Weapons? Over."

"Four AK's, three grenades."

"O.K. You're done. Bring 'em in. I want to see them. Over."

"The bodies?"

"Affirmative. Bring the bodies here. The colonel will want to see them too. Over."

"Can't we even let them bury their own dead?"

"We'll bury them, Lieutenant. Over."

The radio hissed.

"Lieutenant?"

"You want to see the bodies, you come here."

"Listen, Lieutenant. We have to verify the count. Over."

"Fuck the count."

"What did you say?"

"I say again, sir, I have twenty-eight witnesses to the count."

"I don't care how many witnesses you have. I want those bodies. Either bring 'em down here or stay up there and guard 'em till 0800. Do you read me, lieutenant? Over."

"Say again, sir. I'm having trouble reading you. Over."

"You heard what I said."

"Transmission garbled, sir. I'm coming down."

"You're disobeying a direct order."

"Cannot hear you, sir. Out."

"You don't say 'Out' to me."

Wilfred turned to O'Shaunnessey. "Let's get the fuck out of here before they start pitching grenades at us."

"Leave the bodies?"

"You're goddam right. Bring the weapons and rice."

They ran down the mountainside, heedlessly thrashing and stumbling in the dark, fleeing a ghoulish nightmare. The attack had been too successful. They'd paid nothing, and they raced away like escaping robbers.

Wilfred couldn't dispel the vision of his dancing victim, and he could hear his sister Felicity's voice sobbing softly from the trees and bushes. He'd thought somehow that it couldn't happen to him. He was no killer. It went against everything he believed, felt, thought. But that's what he was now. He laughed out loud, long and maniacally, tears streaming down his blackened cheeks, jouncing blindly after the hurrying form in front of him, branches whipping and smacking and scratching his face.

CHAPTER 10

▼

WALKER AND JOHNSON

Two hours sleep, and they want us to return to our ambush site? The probability of walking into an ambush is a hundred and twenty per cent. Some of us will die today.

He called for O'Shaunnessey and his squad leaders and briefed them. "There was nothing I could do. The colonel wants us."

"Jesu Christe," Rodriguez moaned. "And I guess you want me to go first again?"

"I can't make you, Sergeant. But it's gonna be bad. And we need the best we've got up front. That means Henry. See what he says. Then make a decision and let me know. If you decide you don't wanna do it, I'll put another squad on point. But remember, whoever goes first, I'll be with him."

"That will help us a lot, sir," he said with muted sarcasm.

Rodriguez left and returned, reporting, "He says he wants to be first. I guess we do it."

Wilfred exhaled slowly. Henry. What the hell drives him? "O.K. Have everyone load up on coffee. We move out at 0900."

He found his pack, considered cleaning up, and thought, Fuck it. He smelled the faint aroma of his cologne and pulled out the bottle, eyeing the modicum remaining after the loose cap had sent it flowing all over the inside of his pack. A lifetime supply. Might as well use it up. Won't need it tomorrow. Oh, I'll make it somehow. Maybe I better conserve. He dabbed a drop onto his finger, held it to his nose, and breathed deeply. Nirvana. Then it struck him like a sledge. Why splash this stuff all over? One drop's enough. If everyone put one drop below his nose, the whole world would smell sweet to everyone. And think how much money it would save. Ha! Stench would disappear—sweat and shit and piss, rotting flesh, the reek of the animal. For a moment at least, it would be disguised. Screwing the cap back on tightly, he crammed it into his pack with new vigor.

He pulled out his cleaning kit, picked up his M16, and gave it the best care he could, stroking and caressing it with oil and pad. Will you save my life today, my friend? He slung it over his shoulder, picked up his empty magazine, grabbed a handful of bullets and pushed them into the spring-loaded clip, one at a time. And will you also kill today?

NVA lookouts had watched the platoons begin their patrol. Immediately they alerted the ambushes that Colonel Dai had placed on the blood-soaked trail to the camp and near the convergence of the two trails the American squads had ambushed the previous night; then they reported to the colonel. Simultaneously, another lookout at the top of a tree watched four helicopters disappear into the clearing at the top of the mountain and return to the sky.

When Dai received these reports, a feeling of entrapment seized him, until he looked at the forest. So many places to hide. And ambushes would give him time for an orderly move to the next bivouac if he wasted no time.

Immediately he gave the order to move. This time the soldiers and litter-bearers fanned out through the thick vegetation, each walking a different number of paces. Then they turned and moved south, regrouping on a new trail they had cut in the middle of the forest that ended in an isolated site three hundred meters from Captain Simms. Dai feared American artillery, offshore guns, and bombing and thought that his unit would be safest near the American commander. This location, close to the plain, would also facilitate a night escape should the Americans prove more tenacious than he expected.

Henry's shotgun was nestled in the crotch of his arm, barrel to the front, safety off. He walked low, bent at the knees and waist, ready to spring, moving gently at an irregular pace so the rhythm of footsteps was broken. His camouflage was fresh that morning. At times he heard footsteps behind him and knew he was being followed too closely. But he could not risk moving his hand from the trigger to signal the man to wait. Once he stopped, went to his knees, and motioned the man forward. "Walker," he whispered. "You're followin' too close. Stay back." But the eighteen-year-old from Buffalo was having trouble tracking the nearly non-existent trail and felt compelled to keep Henry's back in sight.

All Henry saw was the outline of a round pith helmet, thoroughly broken by camouflage, just off the trail, fifteen feet away. But it was all the point man needed.

The NVA soldier had already detected the platoon's arrival, but was holding fire to allow others to enter the kill zone, risking his own death to boost his pay-off.

Henry's gun roared as he sprang to the ground on the same side as his enemy, and although off-target, the outer fringe of shot tore into the head of the bush-whacker, entered his mouth, nose, and eye-sockets, and killed him instantly.

Deep, throaty, steady return fire from the NVA machine-gunner sounded behind the slain soldier. In quick revenge, bullets tore through Walker's chest, splintered the humerus of the man behind him, and ricocheted off the steel hel-met of the next man in line. Two men back, Wilfred heard the stutter of the gun and crackling overhead and dove to the ground off the trail.

Henry landed, rolled twice, grabbed a grenade, pulled the pin, and let the han-dle fly. After counting to three, he lobbed it at the machine gun, but it struck a branch, fell to the ground, and exploded a few feet away, deafening him. Every-thing stopped. Henry decided to lie motionless until he recovered his hearing, and the gunner decided to wait for visible targets.

"Medic!" screamed the man with the shattered arm, his lifeblood spurting to the ground.

"Who's hit?" Wilfred yelled.

"Me. Johnson. My arm."

"Anyone else?"

"I think Walker's dead. Help me."

"O.K. How's Henry?"

"Dead too, I think. Aaaaaaah."

"Can you get back here?"

Johnson began to move, but the gunner pinned him with lead. "I can't move, and I'm bleeding bad."

"Johnson," Wilfred called. "Hold the pressure point under your arm."

"Ooooooo."

"Lieutenant. The captain's on the horn."

"Fuck."

"Two-Six, this is Six. Report your situation. Over."

"Six, this is Two-Six. One friendly dead. Maybe two. One wounded bad. We're pinned down by machine-gun fire. Over."

"Pull back and we'll call in artillery. What's your position? Over."

"How the fuck do I know? I can't see twenty feet ahead of me. How the hell would I adjust it? Over."

"You put one round out there and walk the rounds in, just like they taught you in school. Over."

"It won't work. I won't be able to see 'em hit. I'll end up blowing up our own position. Over."

"Knock out the gun then. Over."

"Hey, Simms. This is your chance for a medal. Why don't you come up and knock out the gun? Over."

"Get that gun, Lieutenant. Out."

Johnson was sobbing. Rodriguez crawled up beside Wilfred.

"See if you can get the rest of your squad behind that gun. I'll send Washington around the other way." The sergeant nodded stoically, waved two of his men to follow him, and began crawling off into the bushes.

"Washington!" Wilfred shouted. The third squad leader came up. "Rodriguez is tryin' to get behind that gunner on the left. See if you can get your squad up there on the right and get a shot at him. Stay low, for chrissake."

"Yes sir," the sergeant said. He motioned his men to follow, and they began disappearing to the right, one at a time.

The gunner continued shooting. Bullets ripped past Rodriguez, whose steel pot was pressed against a tree trunk.

Henry's second grenade went farther than the first, but again was deflected by a branch.

"Lay down some fire!" Wilfred shouted. "Fire and maneuver. Cover each other."

The response was heavy and, although wild, served its purpose. The NVA gunner shied and ducked as rounds cracked over his head from three sides, and Rodriguez was able to lob a grenade with accuracy.

"Eeeeeeh," came the shriek of the wounded gunner, and Henry was on his feet, running low through the crossfire, pumping—explosion, eject and seat, explosion, eject and seat, explosion. The last shot, from six feet, decapitated the gunner. Henry raced past him in search of others, but they had slipped away long before, leaving the gunner to die his glorious death alone.

"Cease fire," Henry shouted. "They's gone."

"Medic!" Wilfred yelled, running to Johnson. He knelt over the body, sure that he was dead. Then he noticed a slight heaving of the chest and a slow pulsing of blood from the mutilated arm. The medic quickly applied a tourniquet.

O'Shaunnessey came forward and said, "You two. Find two poles for a litter."

"Where's Henry?" Wilfred asked.

"Here."

"I thought you were dead. Or at least wounded."

Henry grinned. "I am, sir. Got a little piece of frag under my skin here. From my own fuckin' grenade."

Wilfred found Walker on his back, his shirt soaked with blood, arms outspread, eyes staring at the canopy, mouth gaping in surprise. "Christ. He's just a kid." He began to feel dizzy and quickly looked away. Another soldier kept staring at the body in disbelief. "Close his eyes and wrap your shirt around him. Get somebody to help you carr—carry it down."

Two shirts were buttoned and bamboo poles slipped inside and through the sleeves. O'Shaunnessey and the medic lifted Johnson while others slipped the stretcher beneath him.

"Take off his belt. Strap him to the stretcher with it," the medic said.

"Captain again, sir," Welbourne said.

"This is Two-Six. Over."

"Sit Rep, Lieutenant. Over."

"One friendly KIA, one WIA. We're sending them down. What do you want me to do? Over."

"Any enemy? Over."

"Two KIA. One machine gun, one rifle. Over."

"Got him, did you? O.K. Send the KIA's, WIA, and machine-gun down with one squad. Then keep going. Who's the KIA? Over."

"Walker. First Squad. Over."

"Too bad. Find those bastards. Out."

Wilfred had decided that his first squad had been through enough, so he told them to go down with the litters. "Charlie's far-gone by now anyway," he said to Henry. "We'll make out. You need a rest. Sergeant O'Shaunnessey, you go too."

Wilfred took point now. The hike to the NVA base camp was uneventful. They found it deserted and located the mass grave. They saw tracks away from the camp and soon lost the trails.

"Johnson didn't make it," O'Shaunnessey said later. Wilfred said nothing. His first men dead. He'd known it would happen this day, and it had. "Could've been a lot worse, sir."

The next weeks crept by in tense monotony. Villages were searched and each mission seemed a repetition of the others. Smiling, begging children. Futile hunts and interrogations. A few detainees sent back for further questioning where more effective interrogation could be employed. Negative contact. A return to the mountain. Hiding in the woods at night. Silently stalking the paths, pursuing phantoms. Negative contact.

A service for the dead. Chaplain Stewart, young, sharing grief and dread, neither defending nor attacking the war, offering peace with God: Fear no evil, God is with thee.

"You've got them worried, Fred. They're beginning to believe your dad's a don."

"Oh, yeah?"

"Some are grousing that you're fighting to preserve the Mafia way of life."

"Well, Rodriguez hasn't said anything lately."

"The Cap'n's showing more respect too. You know what you need to clinch it?"

"What?"

"A fake newspaper clipping. I've got a friend who works for a printer. He could do one for you." Wilfred chuckled. Reckert sat him down and they began to concoct the story:

> **Son Of Don To Serve**, New York (AP)—Wilfred Carmenghetti, son of reputed underworld boss Carmen (The Knife) Carmenghetti has received orders to join the Airmobile Division at Onkay, Republic Of Vietnam.
>
> "I told him I could get him off," his father stated in an exclusive interview, "but he had his mind made up. I think he wanted to try some of that Vietnamese ass, so I tells him I can get him whatever he wants right here, any kind, size, color, shape, but he won't listen, and anyways, I figures it would be good for him, you know, to get a few hits under his belt, compliments of Uncle Sam."
>
> Carmen Carmenghetti denies any association with the New York Mafia, despite the fact that two of his brothers have been murdered in gangland-style killings and he himself spent five years in prison for extortion and attempted murder.
>
> "We've gone strictly legit," he claims. "Pizza parlors, construction, export-import, Vegas casinos. And it ain't gonna hurt us a bit for Wilfred to come back a hero."
>
> Mr. Carmenghetti says that he always hoped Wilfred would decide to come into the family business. "It's every father's dream, I guess," he says wistfully. "Carmenghetti and Son. Got a nice ring, eh?"

They wrote it funny and then wrote it serious, and Reckert stuffed it into an envelope with a note to his friend, the printer.

One morning Reckert saw Wilfred placing one drop of cologne under his nose. "What are you doing?" Wilfred patiently described his technological break-through in the application of cologne. "You've got to be kidding."

"Nope. If everyone did it, it would work as well as the conventional technique, and everyone would save. Everyone would fool himself and not worry about other people."

The next morning Reckert joined in the ritual, placing one drop between his nostrils. He spread the word, and soon others were aping Wilfred, their gestures founded in solidarity, respect and whimsy, and in revulsion to the stench of their own bodies. The cologne, of course, didn't last forever and Wilfred longed to get clean.

One afternoon, in desperation, he stripped naked and lathered up in a rain-storm, but as his luck would have it, the rain stopped, leaving him enveloped in suds. After spending the next day inside an itchy scum, he dove into a drainage ditch to alleviate his discomfort. The maneuver seemed efficacious until he noticed an old man defecating into the water upstream.

Wilfred and Reckert begged Simms to talk the colonel into sending them to the sea. They received their opportunity a few days later, assaulting a fishing vil-lage from the air. There was negative contact, but afterwards, they marched down the hot, wide, white sand beach, empty and endless, and spent the late afternoon body surfing, drinking beer, and taking turns at security duty in the grassy dunes.

"My God," Wilfred said to Reckert, gazing at the blue water and sky, white foam and sand, green paddies and hills, and deep purple mountains beyond. "What a gorgeous place."

"But it's wasted on an unappreciative people. Where are the cottages, board-walks, piers, and cotton candy? The sun-worshipers and sexpots?"

"They should be out surfing, not fighting."

CHAPTER 11

▼

TRANG AND CAN

"Welcome, Comrade Minh. Come in," Trang said, rising.

"The little whore will not return soon?" Mr. Minh asked with a sidelong nod at Can's bed.

"Every day at this hour she goes to a flame tree in town to wait for the lieutenant to deposit her wages in her outstretched bowl. She will be gone one hour, Comrade Minh."

"Good, for we must talk. Her whoremaster lieutenant and the black monkey he follows are doing great harm to our revolution."

"What harm?"

"They captured two guards and a vital store of ammunition at Phuoc Binh and in the mountains to the south murdered twelve of our patriots in a night attack when they were carrying food from the villages. The next day they killed two more soldiers."

"No! So what do you want me to do? Slip a blade between his ribs while he pillows the whore?"

"It might not be as easy as you think. He seems to be moved by the most evil of spirits. The captured comrades from Phuoc Binh say they were stalked by the black dragon in the tunnel. They could hear it growling and moaning and that is why they had to surrender. It had taken the form of the lieutenant."

"But he cannot always be thus protected. When his bad day comes, when the spirits are angry with him, or when he strays too far from them, then I could kill him. I am not afraid."

"Then the Americans would close the town, and we would be puncturing our eardrums and cutting off our tongues. No, we must try to bring him over to our side, and if we can't, then we will kill him away from town."

"Perhaps if I tell her my uncle was one of those killed by her whoremonger, she would pity me and remember her father."

"Your uncle was killed?"

"A useful lie."

"Clever. I must go." His eyes wandered over her body.

"Comrade Minh."

"Yes?"

"A starving man can think only of food." A cautious warmth came to her eyes as she spoke. "Feed on me before you go." They said no more. She stole his strength for a moment, and he left.

When Trang saw Can coming down the dim hallway, she flung herself face down on her bed and began sobbing. The footsteps quickened, but hesitated at the doorway.

"Trang. What is it?" Can asked, walking to the bed, sitting beside her roommate, and resting a hand on her shoulder. Trang sat up, threw her arms around Can, leaned her head on Can's shoulder, and let the water burst the dike. "Tell me," Can said.

"They killed my father's brother."

"Who killed him?"

"The Americans. He didn't even have a gun."

"How did it happen?"

"He was carrying food to some friends in the forest, and they killed him."

"Why?" Can asked.

"I don't know. He and eleven others were carrying food down a trail and the Americans just cut them all down like rice under the sickle, with no mercy or warning, and taking no prisoners."

"Horrible!"

"And the next day they killed two more. Fourteen men."

"No!"

"I loved him, Can. He was a good man, a farmer. He wanted to help our people, but he couldn't hurt anyone himself."

Can remembered a big, gentle man picking her up and hugging her, and her mother saying her father would never return. Then a horror swept over Can. "What Americans did this?"

Trang was silent.

"Tell me!" Can demanded, more fearful with every moment. Trang's weepy red eyes looked into those of her terror-stricken prey and she shook her head and refused to answer. "No! It cannot be. Wilfed could not do such a thing!"

Trang's eyes fell and she whispered, "Do not blame him, Can. It is not his fault. It is war that turns good men into killers. It is cruel, evil old men, and their misguided followers who send their young men to kill ours, and sent Wilfed to kill my uncle."

"But how do you know it was Wilfed?"

"No one knows for sure. All we know is that his platoon murdered our countrymen, and that an officer's men are in his command, like extensions of his body. He could have prevented the butchery if he had tried."

"I can't believe it."

"It is true, Can. But it does no good to blame Wilfed. I like Wilfed. I like you. And I know you love him. So we must try to help him to see what his country is doing to us and how evil is the government in Saigon. They put Catholics into power in the villages. Support landlords and foreigners who enslave us. Dance on the strings of the foreign puppeteers."

"You are Vietcong!"

"What does that mean, Can? Only that I love my country and hate the evil that infests it, just like your father did."

"But Wilfed thinks he is helping us."

"They all do. They are fed so many lies from the time they are babies that they come to believe them."

"I am so confused. I know so little of these things."

"You are still a child, Can. A sweet, lovable child. But every child must become an adult and discover what is true, learn correct beliefs and how to see and act on those beliefs."

"Will you help me?"

"Yes, Can. I love you like a little sister. And…I…"

"What?"

"I-I fear for Wilfed's life."

"So do I. He is a soldier. But is there something else?"

"He is a soldier who has been doing his evil job too well, killing fourteen in the forest and capturing two and a year's supply of arms in a tunnel at Phuoc

Binh. He is hurting us too much, and some want Lieutenant Carmenghetti dead."

"No."

"So, you see, we must help him, save him, and quickly."

"Oh. What can I do, Trang? Tell me."

"Teach him, Can. Make him understand that what he is doing is hurting our country. He must stop his killing."

"But how can I open his mind?"

"Womanly guile. You must use his love for you. Make him think if he continues his actions, he will lose you."

"But I may lose him if I do that. And I love him no matter what he did."

"You must take that chance, if you love him, or he may be lost to everyone forever."

The men of A Company found their seats under the rushing blades of the Hueys and took to the air, beginning another sabbatical leave from the war. This time they would spend a week on security duty at LZ German, the division's forward operational base on the other side of Sang Tran from the bridge.

From the open door of the chopper Wilfred watched as the sprawling city of tents and bunkers came into view and tried to throw off his battlefield tension, the compulsion to alertness inspired by fear—eyes roving, ears straining. But something inside would not let him to drop his guard. At the same time, he began to resent the security of the tent-dwellers below and a concurrent wave of arrogance swept through him. He was fighting the war, not those straphanging sonsofbitches down there. He tried to think of Can, but she was a stranger.

The company went about its security duties and gradually began to adjust and relax. The afternoon brought trips to the shower tents, clean uniforms, mail, beer, hot chow, and sleep. By evening many were able to consider matters of importance, such as which girl they would have in town the next day and which they would invite to the bunker bang.

Wilfred had little time to relax. After checking his defensive positions, meeting with Simms and the platoon leaders, and O'Shaunnessey and the squad leaders, he barely had time to clean up before leaving for battalion briefing with Newcombe and Reckert.

At the large sandbag battalion briefing bunker, prickly with antennae, they descended a few steps, turned a corner, passed a neatly dressed guard with an M-16, and entered a brightly lit room full of folding chairs. A raised wooden platform across the opposite side was regaled with maps, charts, flags, and a large sign that promised "Can Do," the battalion motto. Groups of officers in starched fatigues and spit-shined boots chatted loudly and laughed boisterously over the muffled hum of the generators. The atmosphere is positively clubby, he thought.

"There he is, gentlemen," Colonel Clary boomed over the din. "Our new tunnel rat and assassin extraordinaire. Gentlemen, may I introduce the biggest little man in the battalion, Lieutenant Wilfred—that's Wilfred!—Carmenghetti." Wilfred was flabbergasted. He'd never seen this lively side of the colonel.

"Tearin 'em up out there, are you?" a burly blonde major said, followed by handshakes and kudos from two captains and three first lieutenants: "Not bad for a wop," "Good going, Lieutenant," "Wish I was out there with you—some guys have all the fun," "Keep it up and we'll all be home for Christmas."

Newcombe listened to the hullabaloo with friendly envy. Then Reckert was introduced to the group. Simms and Lieutenant Fierden entered in the midst of the colonel's ovation accompanied by Lieutenant Lorde who was not really with them.

"Well, let's get this thing started," Clary said, and a hardened squint returned to his eyes, which just before had sparkled with joviality.

The briefing was a repetition of all others with time checks, intelligence reports, and battle plans. The only surprise was when the colonel questioned a plan for a daylight combat assault on a village: "Lieutenant Crock," Clary said, addressing the S3 operations officer. "We keep getting these reports that Thach Long is a hotbed of enemy activity, and we keep hitting it and coming up dry—twice in the past three months. What makes you think we'll catch them this time?"

"We just haven't had any luck, sir," the lieutenant said. "If we keep trying, one of these times we'll get them."

"Luck, huh. I hate to depend on luck." The generator hummed, and Lieutenant Crock shifted his feet and felt perspiration beginning to bead his forehead. Clary began looking around the room and his eyes stopped on Wilfred. "Lieutenant Carmenghetti. How do you think we should run this operation…to improve our luck."

After a stunned silence during which he sorely regretted his new prominence, Wilfred let loose. "I'd say we need to regain the element of surprise. I suspect that many of these villages have an escape drill that starts when they hear our artillery prepping the LZ. I also think Charlie gets used to our routine of morning attacks. Maybe we should attack in late afternoon, skip the prep, land all our birds at the same time on three LZs around the village, and move in at double-time."

"Comments?" the colonel asked the group.

Fierden rose. "Sir. Lieutenant Fierden. I believe such action would be reckless and ill advised. Our normal combat assault techniques have proved effective in both destroying the enemy and in protecting our men and equipment. What Lieutenant Carmenghetti proposes would vastly increase the probability of getting friendlies killed and helicopters shot down."

"Other comments."

"Sir. Captain Simms. I agree with Lieutenant Fierden. Our responsibility is not only to accomplish the mission, but also to conserve our capacity to fight. Lieutenant Carmenghetti's proposal would place this capacity in needless jeopardy."

"Care to rebut, Lieutenant Carmenghetti?"

"Yes sir. I don't believe the risk of losing men and equipment would be much greater. Charlie will be panicked and in flight, so his reactions will be off-target and uncoordinated. Chances are, he'll throw up his hands and give up."

Colonel Clary was sold on Wilfred's suggestion. The lieutenant's fighting spirit reminded him of his own a decade earlier. But now he had to think of his career, and he became cautious, deciding that before he committed himself to the plan, he better clear it with the Brigade commander. And he heard a small voice saying, When in doubt, do it by the book.

"Take note, gentlemen. Awards ceremony tomorrow, 1400, A Company CP. Officers required. Anything else? O.K. Rise."

"Can Do!" the officers shouted in unison.

The blonde major approached Wilfred and said, "Lieutenant Carmenghetti. The colonel requests your presence at his table at brigade officers' mess tonight at 1800."

"Thank you, sir. I'll be there," Wilfred said, riding the crest of his own celebrity.

The meal was heady. Wilfred was the only lieutenant. He sat between Lieutenant Colonel Clary and Lieutenant Colonel Kemp, commander of the other battalion in the brigade. Colonel Wheatley, Brigade Commander, faced him from the other side of the table. Captain Simms was the only other representative from A Company and sat distantly at the other end of the table.

During the banquet Wilfred was invited to discuss the tunnel action and ambush. By now he was able to describe them vividly. He had relived the actions so many times during the past weeks that the horror and guilt had worn thin.

In response to an accolade from Colonel Wheatley, Wilfred said, "I was just doin' my job, sir. Got lucky, I guess."

"You made your own luck out there, Lieutenant, with guts and heads-up leadership," Colonel Wheatley said. "Your actions are an inspiration to us all. Keep it up, boy."

"Thank you, sir. I'll try."

Expectations, he thought. Will I meet them next time?

CHAPTER 12

▼

CAN AND WILFRED

The scent of cologne drifted into his nostrils as he approached the stranger in black pajamas and coolie hat at the flame tree. "Can?"

"Wilfed," she said, and she pressed into his arms.

A shock passed through him as he journeyed light-years. Then he was with her and she was real, and instantly he was in love again and certain that she loved him. His arms grew strong and he held her tightly and whispered, "I love you, Can."

"Love Wilfed," she said, her soft brown eyes glistening.

He felt his tenseness draining away and his body refilling with a joyous lust for hers. They walked to her room, ever touching, his arm around her shoulder, hers around his waist, oblivious to the glowers of Vietnamese passers-by.

They loved each other with abandon and lay twined together in naked peace, on the edge of sleep, hoping never to awake. But gradually the world crept between them, dragging in its chilling bag of dangers and duties, refusing to leave them alone. He felt her stiffen, and unbelievably, he found himself mentally checking the position of his pistol. Then she sat up, her body shaking, and when he looked at her face he saw bitter tears.

"You kill bookoo Vietnamese."

"What do you mean?"

"Wilfed kill bookoo Vietnamese!"

"I did not."

"Do not lie to Can." She sat up and pushed him away.

"I'm not lying," he stated legalistically: he hadn't personally killed bookoo.

"Again you lie! You think Can dinky dau. You think Vietnamese have no ears, no eyes, no tongues?"

"You're wrong, Can."

"You kill fo-teen. They cally lice."

Wilfred was astounded that she was so close to the truth. How did she know? It was Trang! And in his confusion he blurted out the words that confirmed all that Trang had said. "I didn't kill fourteen, Can. I swear I didn't. I-I only killed two."

"Only two! You kill only two!"

He tried to sit up, but she pushed him back down and began pounding his chest with her hard little fists. "You numbah ten! You kill two, you G.I. kill twelve, so you kill fo-teen."

"They just kept coming. They wouldn't stop!"

"Snake! Numbah ten. Ba here, you kill Ba!"

She kept hitting him and eventually clipped him with a blow that split his lower lip. Blood gushed down his chin into the black curls on his chest. "Oh!" she gasped when she saw the red, and the hammers stopped, suspended in air. "I hurt Wilfed." She jumped off the bed, seized a silk scarf from a drawer in the dresser, and with maternal solicitude, began dabbing his lip.

"Can you get some ice?"

"Oh, yes." She jumped up and flew through the curtain.

"Can!"

"Yes, Wilfed,"

"Put your clothes on."

"I fo-get." She slipped on the black slacks and long, tight blouse, and padded down the hall. "Can so solly," she said when she returned, handing him a chunk of ice picked from a block, gazing at him with temerity.

"It's O.K., Can. It's just a little cut."

"Can numbah ten."

"No, Can numbah one." Especially the right cross, he thought. She ought to be in the ring, with hands like that.

"Wilfed love Can?"

"Yes, Wilfred loves Can."

She patted dry his chest and chin, and then disrobed again and climbed up beside him, pressing her soft, warm flesh against his. But soon he saw terror in her eyes. "What's wrong?"

"VC want kill you. You, Wilfed," she said, pointing at him.

"Who says? Did Trang say that?" Can did not speak. "It was Trang, wasn't it? Trang VC! Trang number ten."

"Trang no numbah ten. Trang wants help Wilfed."

"I bet." Help me to my grave.

"Wilfed. French kill bookoo Vietnamese. G.I. kill bookoo. *Ba, má, bébé.* War make Wilfed kill. G.I. help Saigon, but Saigon kill bookoo Vietnamese. Take bookoo land. Give land to Catholic. VC want give land Vietnamese. Stop war. Help people. I want G.I. help VC, no help Saigon. Want Wilfed help VC."

"Did Trang tell you to say this?"

"Trang speak numbah one."

"Trang number ten, Can. VC number ten. VC kill number one Vietnamese. VC take land. VC make Vietnamese work for no money. They number ten, Can. Number ten!"

"Wilfed. VC kill you. Wilfed help VC."

"I no help VC." He sat up angrily and began dressing.

Can's entire body was shaking. "Wilfed no kill Vietnamese."

"I kill VC!" he barked.

"No!"

"VC number ten. I will kill VC!"

"No," she sobbed. "Wilfed love Can, Wilfed no kill."

"I will kill VC. I will kill VC because I love you, Can. Because I love you and Vietnamese."

"No, no. Wilfed kill, Wilfed no love Can."

"That's enough!" The first thing I'll do will be to blow the whistle on that little cunt, Trang.

"No kill, Wilfed. No kill."

He recalled some stories about ARVN interrogations, and his resolve weakened. "You tell Trang to di di mau. In two days I tell Army Trang is VC. Two days!"

"You...you di di mau."

"All right, Can, if that's the way you feel." He threw aside the curtain, and stomped down the hallway.

"Di di mau!" she screamed through her tears.

"I won't be back, Can."

"Num ten G.I."

Wilfred halted, pulled out his wallet, took out two one hundred dollar bills, crumpled them up, and threw them at her. "Here." Then he turned away, his hand clutching his pistol.

"Oo, di di mau."

A radio blared Vietnamese love songs in another room a few blocks away. A banner on one wall crowed, "Can Do." An NVA helmet, pistol belt, and machete decorated another wall, and a crudely lettered sign proclaimed, "Meanest Motherfucker In The Nam." On a small table was an open bottle of rice wine and a wet empty glass. Joshua Henry was sprawled facedown on the bed. His girl, Quan, was kneading into somnolence the thick muscles of his massive back. She was squat and thick-limbed with dark tan skin, flat nose, and heavy lips; her eyes were transfigured with black lines, and her hair swirled up into a beehive.

Surreptitiously her fingers left the drowsing form, assembled and straightened, rose into the air, and descended on the buttocks with a fearful smack.

"G.I. turn over now," she said, chortling.

In one motion the great back lurched upward, the body twisted, and the arms grabbed the girl and pulled her on top of him.

"I going teach you to slap me on the butt." He grinned and coiled and crushed her like a snake.

"Let go me, black boa." It was one of their jokes, a pun she herself had discovered when he was teaching her the English names of snakes. "Boa," she chirped. "You boa too!"

"Don't call me no boy, lil girl."

Now he bartered. "What you going do for me if I lets go?"

"Oh, I make you feel good, G.I.," she said, sheathing his penis in her hand.

"Well, go to it, baby," he said, loosening his hold on her.

Three fourths of A Company stood at attention in four orderly rows, grouped by platoon. The uniforms were neat, rifles slung vertically on backs, steel pots level. Officers from Brigade faced them in review. Colonel Wheatley, followed by Lieutenant Colonel Clary and Captain Simms, moved down the line and stopped in front of Sergeant Rodriguez.

"Sergeant Jesus A. Rodriguez. By order of our Commander-In-Chief, President Lyndon B. Johnson, the honorable Secretary Of The Army Stanley R. Resor, Commander of the Airmobile Division Major General Grant Powers and myself, for your heroic actions in service to your country and our brave Vietnamese allies in the A Company tunnel action at Phuoc Binh 3, I award you the Silver

Star. Your valorous actions bring honor to God, your nation, your family, and yourself. Congratulations, Sergeant Rodriguez." They shook hands, and the defiant sneer on his face was replaced by awe, insubordinance by stiff pride.

Now the procession moved down the line to the tiny lieutenant. All eyes looked straight ahead, but ears strained to hear. The words were repeated verbatim, the same award conferred, the same pride instilled. "Congratulations, Lieutenant Carmenghetti," Colonel Wheatley said.

"Thank you, sir," Wilfred said, resolving at that moment that if Fate again should call him to heroic action, he would embrace the opportunity once more; and though his insides were rent by his severance from Can, he would harden himself and forget her, and concentrate his energy on doing his duty.

He didn't return to the flame tree the next day. Can wept in despair, and reading his absence as an ominous signal, hurriedly warned Trang.

"Thank you for telling me, Can. It's too bad the lieutenant will not help us. Now he must die."

"No. He spared you. You must not kill him."

"Forget him, Can. He kills your people. He is evil. He is already dead. Forget him. But now I must leave. You must take my place. You must be the eyes and ears and tongue of your people."

"I-I don't think I can."

"You must! He will not be back. He is dead. Look to your father, Can. Obey him. You must return to the men. You must learn to talk and make the G.I.'s drink and talk. Learn to whisper in their ears. And use your body to make them weak."

"I can't do it."

"You must. It is your duty. You must. Your life is at stake," she added threateningly.

"What?"

"And the lives of us all. We are at war, and you will do it. Mr. Minh, the man with one arm and a limp, he will come to you soon. Listen to him and obey. Now I must go."

"Where will you go?"

"I will join the men in the jungle. I will get a rifle and fight. If necessary, I will die like my brothers have died and like my father died against the French, for the freedom of my country and the honor of my ancestors. Death to the American swine, Can. Good-bye."

CHAPTER 13

▼

HENRY AND SERGEANT RODRIGUEZ

At a stream at the base of the mountain, Henry spotted something white—a bandage stained with blood—and heard faint voices drifting down from rocks above him. He motioned everyone down and called for Wilfred.

An area the size of a football field was strewn with boulders, some as big as a car, turned this way and that on a gentle upward slope, as if a temple of rocks on top of the mountain had teetered and fallen and tumbled down the mountainside into a crotch of earth at the floor of the plain. There were no bushes or trees, no sign of any kind of life, no sounds, just the pile of rocks. Near the highest part a stream cascaded over a boulder in a miniscule waterfall, barely taller than a man.

O'Shaunnessey told Wilfred they should check it out, surround the rocks, and form a perimeter facing in and out. As they were doing so, Rodriguez saw a helmeted head disappear into a hole, and shouted, "Charlie!"

"Frag him," Wilfred said, and Rodriguez pulled a grenade from the front of the shoulder strap holding his pistol belt, yelled, "Fire in the hole" twice, released the handle, counted to three, and lobbed it. A scream of death knifed through the late morning air.

Wilfred waited until his encirclement was complete before checking the hole, wanting to be prepared in case the platoon was attacked. Then he, Rodriguez, and Henry set out. They hadn't gone far, walking and jumping from boulder to boulder, before Wilfred realized the extent of their danger. A Charlie could be in any of the holes, lying in darkness, rifle pointed upward, invisible to their constricted pupils as they approached in bright daylight, and could fire unseen to their front or rear and slip back into the protection of the rocks. They were treading on a nest of rattlesnakes. Wilfred was about to start for the perimeter when he was jolted by rifle fire. Rodriguez was emptying half a clip into a crevice to their left.

"That one dead, sir."

"Let's beat it," he said, and they leaped from rock to rock to the edge.

Wilfred caught sight of two of Rodriguez' men, Louis King and Ed Michaels, on the other side of the rocks, waving and pointing at a hole near them. He made a lobbing motion to them, and they tossed their little bombs at the place where they had seen the movement.

"Check it out. Be careful."

Michaels led the way, one rock ahead of King. As they neared their target, rifles pointed down, eyes searching every hole, an enemy soldier appeared ten yards above them and fired. One round spun Michaels around. He lost his footing and tumbled into a hole. King flattened himself, and all weapons spun toward the assailant who had disappeared.

"Hold fire! Hold your fire!" Wilfred shouted, fearing his men would unintentionally send bullets ricocheting off the rocks at each other. "Michaels! You O.K.?"

"It's my arm."

King lobbed three grenades down holes near Michaels to keep any VC away, yelling "Fire in the hole" each time, and then pulled his friend out. Michaels clambered off the rocks ahead of King. His torn shirtsleeve was soaked red, but the wound was oozing, not pulsing. Medics dressed it and called for a medevac.

"Why don't we drop one in every so often just to keep their heads down," O'Shaunnessey suggested, "and move the grenades around so they don't know where to expect 'em." Wilfred agreed and passed word to start dropping grenades, one every minute, into a different hole each time.

The company had filed in by now, and Captain Simms called a platoon leaders meeting. Simms asked how many enemy soldiers there were. Wilfred said, "Could be five or six or a whole fuckin' platoon of 'em."

Simms asked how to get them out of their holes. "What do you think, Lorde?"

"Wha?" Lorde said, blinking in shock.

"How can we get them to come out?"

Lorde puzzled a moment and then said, "Ask them."

"What?" snapped Simms, his right eye twitching.

"Ask them to come out." The flight of a faraway bird caught Lorde's attention now, and he turned away with interest.

"Jesus, Lorde. You really are fucked up. Engraved invitation, huh?" Simms laughed, alone.

"He might have an idea," Reckert said. "Get a Kit Carson with a loud speaker and see if he can talk them out."

Newcombe said it would take more than talk. "We'll have to frag them to death and scare them out." Wilfred suggested doing both: "Hot and cold. Punish them and then offer them a chance to get out safely." They agreed on the plan.

Wilfred brought up the difficulty of guarding the rocks at night, and Simms said he would get some illumination rounds for the mortar. "We can pop one when we think we see something."

"And we better run some land lines up there so we can get the illumination without a lot of radio noise," Newcombe said.

They had grown accustomed to hearing the grenades thud at one-minute intervals, when two went off in quick succession near the top of the pile.

"I think we got another one, sir," Rodriguez shouted.

"Christ," Simms said. "What the fuck are we sittin' on? Maybe we better stick your whole platoon up there, Newcombe. Keep one down here, plus weapons, one around the rocks, and one on top. We'll rotate for tonight. Newcombe, you take the rocks. Carmenghetti, move down here. Reckert, go up the hill. You and Carmenghetti each put out two LPs. I don't want any surprises. Another thing, when we think we've got Charlie's head down, let's get those bodies and weapons out of there."

When Wilfred returned to the rocks, he found that his men were gaining confidence. "How'd you get that last one?" he asked Rodriguez.

"A little game of cat and mouse. We sit by his hole and listen. When we hear him moving, we frag his ass."

"Great. You think we can get those bodies out any time soon. They'll be stinkin' before long. It's getting hot."

"I think so. It's getting real quiet now. I think, sir, if I was Charlie, I get as far in my hole as I can. Then I pretend I wasn't there and hope the G.I.'s go away."

A stone vault sixteen feet high with no right angles, impregnable surfaces lying in deformed curves and precarious tilts, as though crushed in the fist of a giant, connected to a labyrinth of tunnels. Shadows of three men shook uncontrollably in the light of a kerosene lamp.

The small, lean man with intense eyes sat in a canvas chair, pen in hand, completing details of his planned attack on a nearby American artillery base. The nails on his slender fingers were more than an inch long, the sign of a man who works with his brain, not his hands. Two others guarded entrances.

The shock wave arrived first, chased by the echoing thud of the explosion and diffused by its fragmentation into a thousand contorted paths. Then, a muted shriek of agony and death.

Colonel Dai jerked upright in his chair. *An accident, or are we under attack?* The chunk of the second grenade echoed and rifle fire ensued. "Damn evil gods!" he cursed. "How did they find us?" Addressing the soldier who guarded the doorway, he said, "Ask Captain Vo and Captain Dung to come here. And pass the word to make no sound and fire no weapon."

A distant foreign shout was followed by one thud, and another. The first guard scrambled in. "Colonel Dai. It is the Americans. And one of us sleeps."

Curse the gods. Only a five-day supply of water. But if we are silent, we can hide our strength. Then when we attack, they will be surprised and frightened by our numbers. But how can we attack? They are all around us. They have infinite numbers of grenades and limitless bullets. We are a hundred men strong, but only twenty or so can rise from the holes at one time. We are blood in a bottle with a tiny neck. When we hit the air, we will coagulate and cap the bottle ourselves. We must get outside assistance. Tonight I will send my best man, Captain Dung, and two of his men to get help.

Wilfred's platoon spent the afternoon in the queasy task of finding and removing the dead. Three men would crouch on the rocks, facing out, searching black pockets. When a body was found, three other men would retrieve it, two pulling while the third aimed his rifle down the hole. The bodies weren't heavy, but each had to be disengaged from boulders that gripped them like dinosaurian jaws, and the dead gave no assistance.

Rodriguez told Wilfred that grappling hooks and ropes would be useful. *Fishing for bodies,* Wilfred thought. *Drop down a shiny barbed hook, jerk the rope, puncture the skin, tear the flesh, and pull the boy up.* He quickly squeezed the vision down into his boiling mass of unthinkables.

The platoon carried down two corpses that afternoon, along with three AK-47 rifles. Wilfred gritted his teeth and examined the bodies. They were NVA invaders, not local VC guerillas: they had complete uniforms and were well armed and well fed.

The body of the soldier Rodriguez shot was wedged in its crevice. Simms asked Wilfred, "Can't you get most of it out?"

Wilfred giggled nervously, then clarified the question: "You mean, dismember it?"

"What's wrong with that? It's just a dead gook."

"Well, it'll be harder to count if it's in pieces, sir, but I guess if we turn in more than half, they'll still have to give us a new one."

"What?"

"Nothing. Listen, why don't we wait a few days. It'll be easier to dismember after it's cooked and rotted up in the sun. Why it'll be so tender then it'll just fall off the bone like barbecued chicken. Mmm, good."

"You're sick, Carmenghetti."

The evening food flight arrived, and the platoon leaders sent half the men from each squad to chow so the defenses would never be at less than fifty percent strength.

When Wilfred and Reckert arrived at the main course, they gazed at the lump between the server's tweezers. "Oh, shit," Wilfred said. "Barbecued chicken." They laughed hard and felt closer than they had for a long time. Ever since they'd arrived at the field, Wilfred had felt that Reckert was growing more distant, as if he was critical of Wilfred's success in combat and lamented his breakup with Can.

"Boy, I'd sure hate to be in their shoes," Reckert said, gazing up at the rocks.

"Yeah. We've really got 'em by the balls this time."

At mail call Reckert received the newspaper article from his friend, the printer, and showed it to Wilfred.

"Great," Wilfred said. "It might come in handy."

"I'll let my RTO borrow it. He likes to gossip. I'll tell him I think it's best if everyone knows what we're dealing with."

The platoons shifted positions for the night, Reckert on the hill, Newcombe on the rocks, and Wilfred on the plain. LPs were sent out. Illumination rounds were readied, and cases of grenades hauled up on the rocks. Then the silent vigil began, punctuated by lonely cries of "fire in the hole," deadly thuds, and puffs of smoke rising into the cloudy, moonless sky above.

At 0200, immediately after a grenade explosion, Captain Dung and the others crept to the surface. A corporal from Newcombe's third squad thought he heard something and searched the dark mounds for distinguishable shapes, looking past the sound to gain a few more rays of black light with his peripheral vision. He saw nothing, but brought his rifle to the ready.

After several minutes the trio emerged from the valley of rocks, adroitly climbing with two feet and one hand, the other hand grasping a rifle, finger on the trigger, weapon steadied by a strap over the shoulder, butt jammed into the armpit.

Now the corporal caught the glint of steel and the movement of humped backs coming toward him. "Gooks!" His finger slipped the safety, and still not looking directly at his foe, he squeezed. Twanging ricochets sprayed the sky. The sound shook everyone. Another soldier caught the motion of the escapees, now leaping toward the perimeter, and he opened up. Then a third.

The nervous hand of Newcombe's first squad leader ground the handle of the landline telephone, but the mortar platoon sergeant, having heard the rifle fire, bypassed the phone and reached for an illumination round. "Thunk." The round burst from the tube, soared upward and popped, releasing its parachute and igniting the flare. As it drifted down, the light swung back and forth on its cords, casting a vacillating white glow over the area, the dim light displaying three dead NVA soldiers on the rocks.

Jolts of anger hit Newcombe's men as the flare went out, leaving them in blackness again. But in another second, another "pop" sounded and the sky was light again.

"Keep those flares comin'!" Newcombe roared into the phone. "No interruptions." To his men he yelled, "Let's frag the fuck out of 'em and get those bodies. When I say 'Fire in the hole', hit every hole on the pile."

Fourth of July Grand Finale. Sky lit up and a score of explosions in rapid succession.

It struck Newcombe that the flares were defensive as well as offensive. Light seeping into the caves would keep the enemy from coming out. He called Simms and discussed the possibility of keeping constant illumination all night. Simms checked and found they could only shoot four an hour.

"Let's do it," Newcombe said. "It'll make the men more alert too."

The rest of the night was a mixture of wavering lights and exploding grenades. The mood of the troops on the rocks shifted from calm assurance when a flare popped to lonely fear when the light went out. Night crept by with maddening sloth to the lazy but benignant dawn.

"They did not make it, sir," Colonel Dai heard the guard say. The rock walls seemed to inch in on him from all sides. He stared ahead and made no reply. Captain Dung would have been a general some day. Damn the gods! They could have sent a night bird to distract the eyes of the enemy. Or sown sleep in the night air. But no. They themselves slept instead. Cursed gods!

"We must try again," Colonel Dai told Captain Vo. "Get me three good volunteers for tonight. They can try another exit, another group of soldiers. If we keep our heads down today, perhaps by tonight the Americans will be lulled enough to be careless, and the guards we test this time won't be alert."

"Yes sir," Captain Vo said, hiding his doubt.

"Make sure there is nothing to give us away today—no sound or chatter, no cooking fires. And have you put the water under guard and begun rationing as I instructed?"

"Yes, Colonel."

CHAPTER 14

▼

SERGEANT COY MATFIELD

Simms ordered more grenades, enough flares to provide constant illumination, and a Kit Carson and loudspeaker to try to talk out the enemy. Since no one had seen any enemy soldiers since the night before, Clary told Simms to stay another day and if no more came out, to send in some tunnel-rats to look around.

Reckert's platoon took the rocks after breakfast, and Newcombe led his tired group to the paddy. Wilfred took his men to the hillside above the rocks, directing some to face the scrubby woods to the sides and rear. In the distance they looked out over the sweep of paddies, clusters of hamlet palms, and the immense blue of the South China Sea. Directly below was the rolling boil of rock. Soldier dolls on boulders enacted a still-life drama against the backdrop of toy tents in the field beneath. Bits of conversation flew about the hillside like swallows, mingling occasionally with muted shouts and boring "chunks" of grenades.

After an uneventful morning, the Kit Carson arrived, and at 1300, the grenade shelling halted and the first cold period began. The interpreter took the bullhorn and began asking them to come out: You will be helped and will receive food, water, and medical attention. You will enter the Chieu Hoi training program and then join the Army of the Republic of Vietnam. I myself am from Hanoi and went through the training. Now I have a good life and want you to have the same. For the next three hours you may come out without being harmed. Just call out "Chieu Hoi" and come out with your hands behind your head. When three hours are up, we will begin dropping the grenades again, so come out now and save yourself. It is a beautiful day. The message was repeated throughout the afternoon, but no one responded, and the hot period was renewed.

After supper, Wilfred's platoon moved to the rocks for the night. A dead animal smell had begun to mix with that of the gunpowder and chipped rock, and as dusk gathered, the flare rounds began popping, continuously, save brief seconds of darkness between each round. Now, night was day.

"They have captured darkness," Captain Vo said to Dai. "Our friend escapes for but a moment and is locked up again."

"They have endless supplies too. But perhaps they will run out near morning. Arrange the escape for three A.M."

Many of Wilfred's men had decided there were no more enemy. Half were asleep by right, and the others, on the very edge, mesmerized by the sinking, rocking light of the flairs.

Underground, two groups of three men twisted and turned, pushing and crawling toward the dim light.

The first team emerged near Sergeant Matfield's section. The big, quiet mountain man had found shade and slept most of the day, preparing for the night's hunt. Now he sat in his rocky blind, rifle cradled in his arms, one of the few still alert. After a fresh flare exploded the darkness, he saw the shape of a man on a boulder twenty yards away. Slowly he brought his rifle to the front and slipped off the safety. Knowing he had nearly thirty seconds of light, he waited for others to appear. When the third man came into sight, he took aim and fired three shots, each of which found its mark.

Everyone awoke. Shouts burst forth from Sergeant Kaslovski's section. Two rifles and a fifty-caliber machine gun opened up on full automatic at the second NVA team in a wild flurry of fire, joined by the thunks of two grenade launchers, aimed point blank.

On the opposite side Matfield dropped behind his rock and listened to American bullets cracking over his head.

Just before breakfast, Wilfred inspected the corpses. Those killed by Matfield had holes through the chest, but Kaslovski's dead had huge cavities opened by explosive rounds of grenade launchers and limbs torn off by the machine gun.

Near the front of the chow line, Wilfred spotted Matfield. "Don't you know you can put your rifle on automatic?"

"That wouldn't be fair. Where I come from, if you miss on your first shot, you gotta let 'em go."

Colonel Clary arrived after breakfast in Charlie Charlie, his command center helicopter. Simms and Wilfred led him to the pile of carnage and weapons. "Good going, Lieutenant."

"What do you want us to do now, sir?" Simms asked.

"Sit on it, Captain. If there's a dozen here, there's a whole platoon of 'em. Sit on 'em and wait 'em out. What we have here, gentlemen, is an old-fashioned siege. They're inside and can't get out, and we can't get in."

"Sir," Wilfred said to Clary, "One thing that worries me is keeping the mortar tied up at night with illumination rounds. What if we get hit down here or on the hill and need some explosive rounds? Then we lose our light."

"Good point. I'll see if there's a Spooky available—a.k.a. Puff the Magic Dragon—a World War II C-47 twin-prop. They're outfitted with flare kickers and three mini-guns that put out fifty-four thousand rounds a minute—nearly a thousand a second. Better not count on getting it tonight, though."

Wow, Wilfred thought, but you can't kill a man more than once, can you? Dead, deader, deadest? Spooky makes 'em deadest.

Simms was barely controlling his rage. Who the fuck do they think is running this company? He leaped into the gap. "Sir," he said. "Why don't we just get the Air Force to bomb it! You know, drop some big ones. Then we can go look for some gooks."

"Captain. The enemy is here, and we need to take as many alive as we can for intelligence. You know that."

The NVA concealed themselves all day. Only one sign attested to their existence. Near the end of the cold period, when the interpreter was making his final appeal, a scuffling sound was heard in the rocks followed by a muffled pistol shot.

"That traitor who talks to them over his loudspeaker is beginning to convince some to surrender," Captain Vo said.

"That is not good," Dai said. "If we fail tonight, we must stir them into an all-out attack tomorrow during the lull."

Only two days of water left, thought Dai. But if we lose half of our men, we will have four days of water. The fresh food and U.S. Army food are gone. Only rice is left. And without fires to cook, everyone must chew their rice dry and take a sip of water so the stomach pains are not too great. And odors! Urine and excrement from a hundred men, dried blood, gunpowder, dead bodies. We are imprisoned in a cesspool. Captain Vo says the men's bodies suffer from lack of exercise, jammed into crevices, muscles cramped, bones aching from ungiving rocks, running sores and abrasions, metal slivers under the skin of many. And their minds suffer from being without light for so long. They lie in darkness, day and night. Day is the same as night. Time is unmarked, as though it does not pass. Oh, for the certainty of the sun. The men grow desperate. One can see it in their eyes. They know we will have to do something soon, surrender or fight.

The boulders on the mountains above the rock pile were farther apart than those below, eggs resting in nests of grass and thin brush. The slope was steeper here and each outcrop offered a dominant vantage point over subjacent terrain. Below each rock, however, a blind spot existed that could only be observed by leaning out over the edge.

It was from one of these coverts that tunnelers had made enough daylight to wriggle through to the surface. The lead digger was followed by a chain of conveyers passing helmets full of dirt back and empties forward. Taking turns digging, they had followed the curves of the bottom of the rocks, dipping and climbing, tracing the flinty ceiling, searching for a crevice.

For Wilfred's men the day had been tedious, and boredom was whittling away their caution. Safe in the heights, their minds wandered to Onkay, girls, R & R, and home. They no longer heard the explosions below and sat enthralled as the shadow of the mountains slowly spread across plain and sea. Twinkles of light appeared from hamlet fires and fishing boats, and the burdensome heat of day began to loosen its grip.

The reverie began to collapse when Sergeant Washington saw the shapes of five men lurch from behind a boulder toward another on the way to thick brush on the north side. The NCO had shot no one during his four months in country, and a torpor gripped him like a strait jacket. Then panic set in as he watched the evaders disappear behind another rock. "Charlie!" he shouted, leaping up and pointing at the rocks. Another second passed as the numb platoon looked up, stunned. "They're getting away. Stop them." He sprayed six rounds at the fugitives, but the bullets ricocheted harmlessly. Then his rifle jammed.

The weapons platoon sergeant looked up when he heard the rifle burst, but a feeling that it was too early for an escape attempt, too early for his night of work to begin, lay in his mind like a rock and immobilized his body.

"There they are," Kaslovski shouted, pointing them out to the gunner on his right. "Get 'em!" He aimed his rifle and dropped one of the fugitives as the others disappeared into the waist-high bushes. The machine-gunner had glimpsed the movement. He picked up his tripod, repositioned it, swung the barrel down the hill, and let loose a steady line of bullets at the heads and trunks bobbing and weaving down the hill. The luminous tracer rounds cut through the dusk like a searchlight, wire-thin and intermittent, showing the gunner himself where to aim and drawing the fire of the entire company to the same spot.

Wilfred's grenadiers stood on boulders and sent their explosives on high arcing flights toward the targets. Rifles chattered and parachute flares popped and drifted insouciantly.

As the heavy fire poured down, the enemy disappeared. After five minutes Simms ordered a halt and told Wilfred to "find the bodies." The search located four. Night passed in a tense cease-fire, and at first light, Newcombe led a patrol in search of the fifth soldier. They followed a faint trail of blood for a hundred meters, then lost it and returned to the FOB.

Wilfred's platoon moved to the rock pile that day, and by early afternoon the rocks had grown hot to the touch and the smell from the decomposing carcass saturated the still air. Thank heavens, Wilfred thought, for one drop of cologne.

Soon the cool period arrived and the Kit Carson again began to speak. The only new information was that the previous night all five escapees had met gruesome deaths. "Resistance is hopeless. You might as well come out." And come out they did.

At the sound of the bullhorn, Lieutenant Ho scrambled up, fired his automatic rifle into the air, and began leaping for the south side, shooting as he went. Heads appeared from twenty other holes, and the Kit Carson dove and hugged the ground.

Rodriguez crumpled Ho with a quick burst. Then the whole perimeter opened up with a roar, and Newcombe's men on the hill began raining fire onto the pile.

The NVA fired back fiercely, but their traverse over the infinitely variant facets of stone made accurate fire impossible. In an instant their bodies were twisting all over the rocks as lead struck them from every side. A few G.I.'s took cover to escape the projectiles of their friends and enemies.

As the first wave of enemy fell, Wilfred decided grenades might be more effective and a heck of a lot safer. "Frag 'em," he screamed, and he threw in the first. Soon the sound of automatic fire was joined by scores of explosions in rapid succession and a cloud of smoke engulfed the rocks.

"Cease fire!" Wilfred shouted into the bedlam, repeating it till he was nearly hoarse. Slowly the firing died, replaced by a terrifying silence. "Be ready for more," he warned.

As the pall lifted and drifted down through Reckert's perimeter and out over the paddies, it revealed the first battlefield scene most of the men had ever seen. Bodies were everywhere, bleeding and moaning. Shredded uniforms. Perforated helmets. Amputated limbs. Disfigured faces.

Wilfred polled his squad leaders. None of his men were killed and only one was wounded. My God. One man wounded. Dozens of dead gooks. And we're sitting on a fucking battalion.

Newcombe and Reckert each sent a squad to remove the bodies while Wilfred's men kept aim on the rocks. Seven wounded were evacuated and two with minor wounds were interrogated. This time the exhumers used grappling hooks to raise the dead. Thirty-two bodies were dragged down and laid out in the grass alongside thirty-four rifles. Photos were taken, and the arrival of Colonel Clary eagerly awaited.

His Charlie Charlie dropped in several hours later. Gazing at the display he asked, "Where is that amazing lieutenant?"

Wilfred arrived, proud and elated.

"Let me shake your hand, Lieutenant, again. You've done one helluva job here." They shook, and Simms grimaced.

"I tell you what, sir. I give all the credit to my men. They hung in there in the thick of it and really gave 'em hell."

"They're under your command, aren't they?"

"Yes sir, but—"

"No buts, Lieutenant. You deserve a tremendous amount of credit. What's your kill ratio now, Wilfred?"

"We've killed sixty-three and lost two, sir."

"Thirty-one and a half to one. Not bad."

He looked at the bodies again. "We'll have to get a Chinook in here to carry that load." The colonel left and soon the green boot-shaped insect settled down in the field with every soldier on the perimeter crouching and shielding his eyes. Men loaded the bodies, weapons, and prisoners, and fifteen minutes after touchdown, the chopper reared up on its hind wheels, raised its great bulk straight up, and roared away.

After a supper of steak and potatoes, Wilfred replaced Reckert on the paddy. As they passed, Wilfred noticed that his friend's eyes were red and watery.

"What's the matter with you?"

"Nothing."

"What do you mean, nothing?"

"Well, if you really want to know, I've been thinking about their wives and kids and parents and friends and—"

"What? They're commie pigs. They came after us with rifles blazing and they deserve everything we gave 'em."

"They're men, Wilfred. Human beings."

"They weren't shootin' at you."

"Most of them were boys, eighteen or nineteen years old."

"We gave 'em their chance to give up and they wouldn't do it, so fuck 'em."

CHAPTER 15

▼

LE AND STORP

That night Spooky made its debut, banking and gliding in great vulturous circles over the rocks to kick out a flare, then leaving, but returning before the first light expired—droning in crescendo and diminuendo as it came and went.

Three times in the night Newcombe's men heard movement below as the NVA retrieved dead and wounded that had crawled back down their holes. At each sound, they sent grenades bouncing after them, and death begat death.

In the morning, after three more bodies were pulled out, Reckert's platoon sergeant suggested, "Let's really rattle their bones. Let's drop in a little C-4. O.K.?"

Reckert's tormented silence gave passive assent, and the sergeant began preparing the charge. He peeled back the clear wrapper, pushed the fuse into the doughy white mass, tied the wire around it, lowered it into a crevice, and uncoiled the other end to a battery twenty yards away. Twice he called "Fire in the hole." Soldiers crouched lower than usual, fearful that boulders would roll or large chunks of rock would come flying at them. He connected a wire to one battery pole, and then touched the other wire. The sound shook villagers all over the plain.

Inside the rock pile men were knocked down, trembling, many temporarily deafened. Those closest to the top were unconscious. All began crawling frantically, like frightened animals, deeper into their abysmal cave.

Two NVA soldiers surrendered—Le, a sixteen-year-old from Haiphong, and Ta, a nineteen-year-old from Hanoi. "Chieu hoi!" they said, arms upraised. A medic examined them, treated minor abrasions, and offered them C-rations and water. When the cold period was over, Trinh, the Kit Carson, began his questioning. He assured them that they would not be tortured if they cooperated. They, like himself, would be retrained, get a nice job, and go home to the North when the Americans left. Ta remained silent, but Le cooperated, giving his guesses as to the number of soldiers in the rocks—about forty—their physical condition, and the remaining amount of ammunition, food, and water. Trinh asked which of them loved their brothers enough to save their lives—to go back in and convince them to come out. Le volunteered.

Night passed calmly and the next morning much larger charges of C-4 were detonated. When time-out came in the afternoon, the G.I.'s watched Le fearlessly disappear into the rocks. They waited, fearing the sound of a pistol shot, and when he emerged an hour later with three new Chieu Hois, he was an instant hero. They nicknamed him G.I. Lee and showered him with C-rations, candy, cigarettes, smiles, and pats on the back.

Wilfred's platoon sat around the rocks, bored. The company had been there a week, and everyone was itching to move on. The corpse of the man killed on the first day and left in the rocks was issuing flies in great abundance, the stench masked by a hundred drops of cologne. Thousands of flies roamed and buzzed the rocks in search of blood donors and homes for new generations of offspring. Men held contests to see who could kill the most flies. Bets were placed, and storybook claims bantered from rock to rock. But on the whole, it was sordid business since they knew the pests emanated from human flesh.

The heat was intolerable and the men suffered in filthy uniforms, many soaked with blood. Now that the danger had abated, they looked to the waterfall above the rocks for cooling ablution. Simms gave permission, and lines formed for the chance to press against the boulder and feel cold water sliding over their shoulders. They lathered up and danced in the chill, hooted and laughed, genitals flying, and came away refreshed.

That afternoon Le brought out five more soldiers to the enthusiastic cheers of the Americans, and a Huey brought in a generator and searchlight to shine on the rocks. Brigade had determined that Spooky was too expensive for this operation.

Wilfred's platoon had duty in the paddy that night, and the lieutenant went to bed early, floating on air under his poncho tent in the shallow hole Reckert had dug a week before. Not bad duty, he thought. Sit around all day. Plenty of chow. Two beers a day. Showers. No holes to dig. Not bad.

At 0100, a mortar round landed in the middle of the paddy: Wilfred tore out of his hooch screaming, "Stay down! Is anyone hurt? Did anyone see where it came from?" A clamor of shouting answered. Then he heard the whistle of another round.

"Incoming!" He dove to the grass and covered his head with his arms. This round exploded twenty yards away.

The weapons platoon sergeant said, "Get me some high explosive, Willy." He dropped a round down the tube and it bounced out, sailed away, and shook the ground when it exploded. They waited for the next incoming round to hit, but it never did. The weapons sergeant spread five rounds on the target and quit. "If we got 'em, we got 'em. If we didn't, we didn't."

Trang and the four other VC had fired their only two rounds and had quickly disassembled their mortar and hurried away.

By the next morning a sullen mood had settled over the camp. Peace had been ripped away.

That afternoon, G.I. Lee convinced six more NVA soldiers to surrender, but they told Trinh that hope still lived below.

Screaming down out of the blue in all its glorious fury, a supersonic silver F-4 Phantom fighter from its carrier home ninety miles away, dived toward the rocks at 1000 hours, rear wings tipped down, main wings folded up at the ends. Breathlessly, A Company watched from fifty yards away, necks craned, as it came at them, growing bigger and bigger. Then a white sausage-shaped canister separated from its belly: it had laid an egg in flight. And just as the bird of prey was about to crash into the mountainside, up it pulled in a death-defying display of power, shot straight up, contracted into a tiny speck and disappeared. The egg, however, continued downward, struck the base of the rocks, burst, careened up the hillside, ignited, and splattered into an inferno of burning jellied gasoline. The entire rock pile was consumed with yellow-orange flames, twenty feet high. And just as the fire began to recede beneath a cloud of smoke billowing skyward, the screeching thunder returned, diving down and down, unleashing its heinous hell-fire once again on the innocent rocks below. Four more times it came and went. Then it was gone, and slowly the men's exhilaration vaporized.

"Boy, it must be something to fly one of those things," Wilfred told O'Shaunnessey.

"Those flyboys love to put on a show especially when no one's shootin' at 'em."

"Do they still get to go home after they kill so many enemy planes—you know—like the old aces did?"

"I guess so, but there aren't too many enemy fighters to knock down around here."

"We oughta have a system like that, you know, zap thirty gooks and you get to go home. Might end the war sooner."

"They'd have to make kids, women, and old folks off limits, or there wouldn't be any Vietnamese left."

They headed back to the smoldering rocks, and Wilfred said, "I guess that's the end of the 3d of the 106th."

That afternoon, Le brought out eighteen NVA. From what Trinh could grasp, they'd been deep in the cave, fearing the Americans would repeat the previous morning's blasting. A tornado roared through from all sides to the top, and they felt mysterious warmth from above. The great mass of the boulders had absorbed most of the heat, and heat that radiated downward was picked up by rising air and carried away.

"Only eight of us remain," Captain Vo told Colonel Dai. "What do you want us to do?"

"What do the others want?" Dai said.

"They are determined to stay with you to the end."

"How much food and water remain?"

"For eight men, a week, sir.

"Half of us sleep, and nearly half have surrendered. It is over, Captain Vo. I have been ignominiously defeated."

"We can make them fight in here, on our terms."

"They can wait longer and dream up some new way to finish us off. Face it, Captain Vo. I have lost. I have been defeated!"

A grim silence gripped the tomb. Then Colonel Dai looked up at Vo with withering ferocity. "Tomorrow, captain, you will lead the others to the top and surrender to the Americans."

"And you, sir?"

"It is not your concern!"

C-4 blasting resumed in the morning with Wilfred in charge. As they moved to the rocks, he noticed white spots of unburned napalm around the periphery, the consistency of old chewing gum. The flies were as bad as ever, rising now from excrement in the cave. The rotting corpse that had been sleeping in his open grave for ten days had been partially cremated in the air war, its charred bones jutting through pieces of crispy black skin.

A newspaper reporter came in with Colonel Clary late in the morning. He was tall and wore camouflage jungle fatigues, floppy hat, and handlebar moustache. We're going to help them increase circulation, thought Wilfred. That's what war is for.

After lunch Trinh climbed back onto his rock and began to talk again. Le smiled as G.I.'s shouted, "Go get 'em, tiger," and he slipped between two rocks. Soon, the muffled crack of a pistol shot was heard, and everyone on the surface grew tense. A quarter of an hour passed. Then Captain Vo emerged, and with an authoritarian, "Chieu hoi," ordered the Americans to take him. Six others followed, faces sullen and proud, but not Le.

In the bowels of the cave, Colonel Dai sat in his chair alone. He hadn't moved in twelve hours—to eat, stretch, urinate, or empty his bowels. The lamp provided only the faintest flicker, its wick charred short, thirsting desperately for oil.

In near darkness his slender fingers with jutting nails held up to his eyes an American grenade, pin pulled, handle in place, as he tried to peer through the patterned steel skin to the mechanism inside.

Are you what you claim? Or is there a defect within that makes you an impotent imposter? And what of you, Colonel Dai? Is a colonel with dead and captured subordinates still a colonel, or a silly masquerader? And what future do you have, little bomb, if you cannot do your job? To become a lump of rock that no one respects? You will not tell me, will you, naughty child. Not unless I loosen my grip and let you cast off your little handle. Then you will tell me? But perhaps not even then. Perhaps a god will interfere and keep you silent. And what do the gods think of me? Do I deserve to sleep, to be consumed by flies in this catacomb? Or do I deserve to live? Life without help of the gods is futile. If they had helped me here, I would be victor. And if I continue to exist without their aid, what hope have I? It is not up to man; he cannot succeed alone. It is in the hands of the gods. So why not ask them? Demand an answer. Let the handle fly, and they will be forced to speak, to act, or sit by—to determine my future. They will decide if I am worthy of their favor. And if I am not, I shall prefer to sleep.

The moment has come, my ancestors. Speak now. Let me live, with your help, or let me come to you. Speak!

He released the handle and waited in puzzled silence. Fascination. Terror. Then they spoke—with a deafening explosion of energy, shrapnel, and light.

The rear end of the Chinook opened, and out flowed VIP's: Major General Powers, Division Commander; Colonel Wheatley, Brigade C.O.; Lieutenant Colonel Clary, Battalion C.O.; and a gaggle of aides. With them was a network TV crew: Frank Storp, war correspondent, and Lew Lance, cameraman. The officers wanted TV exposure for career advancement.

"Rocks, fuck," Storp said. "Who the shit cares about a pile of rocks? For that matter," Storp muttered to himself, "Who the shit cares about generals?" He noticed Wilfred and asked, "Don't you have any bodies around here, for chrissake?"

"We shipped them all out." Storp's repugnance intensified.

"Well, can't you get us some fresh ones?"

"We don't even know if there are any more in there."

"This place sucks. There's no story here," he told Lance. "We should've stayed home and played with dollies."

Wilfred was annoyed. "We killed thirty-three NVA here. Captured forty-nine, and had only one man wounded."

"Congratulations, little Louie. You got yourself a shutout. That'll make a fantastic filler in some AP summary. But listen, man. We're the visual medium. We gotta put on a media event to reassure folks at home that we're winning so they won't get tired of watching and make us all go home. We gotta have action— gore and tears and terror—'cause that's what people want, and if they don't get it, our ratings'll drop, the advertisers won't pay, and the producer will start screaming at us."

"How 'bout naked soldiers taking a shower in a waterfall?"

"That'd be great, except they don't let us use that blue stuff on the air. According to the rules, corpses aren't pornographic, but live nudes are."

Powers, Wheatley, and Clary lined up facing Simms, and the lieutenants. Lance panned the rocks, then zoomed in on Powers' face as the general read words of the II Corps commander congratulating A company on "finding, fixing, and systematically destroying a sizable and determined enemy force" and praising the company's "alertness to fleeting opportunity, rapid response, resourcefulness, sustained application of firepower, and undisguised pride in carrying out the assigned mission in the highest traditions of the Airmobile Division."

The ceremony lasted three minutes. Powers, Wheatley, and Clary shook hands with Simms and the lieutenants, and the group dispersed. An aide to the general handed Simms a stack of badly mimeographed copies of the commendation for distribution to the men. Lance and Storp began packing their gear, and Powers and Wheatley hustled to the chopper to get out of harm's way.

Wilfred thought the company was being cheated out of its deserved immortalization on the six o'clock news. "Storp. Don't you want to take some shots of the men in the rocks?"

"Would you like to tell me why?"

Wilfred led him and Lance to the last remains.

"Disgusting," Storp said. "Now you've got something. They'll love it. They dig horror, man."

Lance let his camera roll. Mike in hand, behind a rock next to Wilfred, Storp began. "This is Frank Storp," he said in hushed tones. "I'm at a rock pile in Vietnam, where the valiant troopers of A Company, First of the Thirteenth, Airmobile Division have been waging a fierce fight against a whole battalion of seasoned NVA veterans. The enemy is in those rocks right now. This is Lieutenant Wilfred Carmenghetti, the platoon leader in charge of the battle at the moment. Lieutenant Carmenghetti, can you tell us what's happening?"

"Sure," Wilfred said. "We're guarding the rocks. Any minute enemy soldiers may appear from all those holes between the rocks and come at us, rifles blazing, like they did a few days ago."

Lance panned the rock pile, zooming in now and then on the worried countenance of one or another of Wilfred's men. They were delighted to be on TV, and since they wanted to preserve the respect of those at home, they were all business.

"What are you doing right now?" Storp asked Wilfred.

"Watching and listening. If we hear movement in the rocks, we'll toss in a grenade and frag 'em."

"Is that why you have that grenade, Lieutenant?"

"Yes. We have to be alert and ready to—shhh. I hear something." Eyes wide, he pulled the pin, shouted, "Fire in the hole," and tossed the bomb, which burst with a boom.

"Do you think you got him?" Storp asked Wilfred.

"Don't know. We'll have to go see." The camera followed as Wilfred led the way to the corpse. It recorded Rodriguez, Henry, and Wilfred pulling at the charred body to retrieve it for display, and caught horror on Wilfred's face as he watched the arms come apart from the shoulders and the blackened skull fall off and bounce down the hole. His cologne was overwhelmed, and the lifting of his upper lip, uncontrived. And when he turned, doubled up, and nearly puked, the camera was there.

"Fantastic!" Storp chirped. "O.K. Bring it back to me, Lou," and the camera stopped, turned, refocused on the correspondent, and rolled again. The clear blue eyes narrowed and fogged. "Not a pretty sight, war. This is Frank Storp…with A

Company…in Vietnam. Cut. And print. Great. O.K., let's get out of here. This place stinks." He started packing up.

"So we gave you a good story, huh?" Wilfred asked.

"Yeah, now all I need is a hundred more like it."

"Because people watch them every night?"

"Yeah. That's the trouble with chronics. That's what we call them. They're like chronic ailments or serials or soaps. We scare people and make 'em think the world's ending, then say, 'Hold on, folks. Maybe not. Tune in tomorrow to find out.' But then we have to have another story."

"Can't you use crime stories and natural disasters? And political campaigns?"

"Yeah. But nothing beats a good war. It gets good audience ratings, pulls in big advertisers, and goes on and on."

"And it's cheaper than covering the whole world."

"Sure."

"And you can reuse the same war footage over and over."

"We do that."

After another silent night, A Company woke refreshed. Lieutenant Fierden jumped out of the morning chow bird, and Lance and Storp climbed on. Fierden was miffed that he had missed being on TV the day before.

Simms asked for volunteers to go in and check out the cave. "I'd go in myself, men, but a commander has to stay with the majority of his men, and that's on top of the ground. We could be attacked at any time." Wilfred volunteered with eleven others, including Rodriguez and Lieutenant Newcombe, and noticed Reckert looking at him with a worried expression.

Lieutenant Fierden was infuriated by Wilfred's display of courage. "Y-you can't go in there."

"Why not, Fierden," Wilfred called loudly, silencing the group. "Would you like to go in instead of me?"

"No, I wouldn't."

"But it's your chance for a medal. Down in the rocks. In enemy territory."

"You're a psychopath, Lieutenant."

"No, Lieutenant, but you're a…oh, well. We don't need to go into that now." Some men smirked, and a few even snickered. Fierden's pale, pimply face turned blood red.

They began their descent into half a dozen scattered holes. Newcombe stayed with Wilfred. Some spaces between the rocks were so tight that Newcombe had to push with his feet and compress his rib cage to get through, and Wilfred wasn't sure he himself could make it. The deeper they went, the more anxious

Billy Joe became. The boulders seemed to be pressing in on him from all sides. He wanted out. But there was no place to turn around. At last the passage opened up into a large room where Rodriguez' voice said, "Red."

"Suspenders," Newcombe replied.

The company spent the rest of the day clearing the cave and found weapons, radios, documents, and the body of Le, which had one shot through the forehead.

CHAPTER 16

▼

CAN, QUAN, AND HENRY

"*Dung lai!* (halt)," a woman's voice commanded through the mist. Wilfred dove to the ground off the trail and began crawling forward through the bushes, rifle shots cracking over his head and Welbourne following. Henry's shotgun roared. Then thrashing sounds as Henry charged forward. Again it exploded. Again. And again. "Chieu Hoi!" a voice pleaded. A final blast brought silence.

"All clear," Henry called menacingly. "All dead."

Wilfred followed the bodies to Henry. The lieutenant's shocked eyes burned Henry's with respect and not a little fear. "That makes fourteen for you, if I'm not mistaken."

"Yes sir."

"You don't have to win this war all by yourself."

"Self defense, sir. Just self defense. There wasn't nuthin' else I could do."

He noticed the opened chest on the last corpse, a rifle and mortar round in the bushes, and remembered hearing "Chieu hoi" cries. "This one too?"

Henry's eyes glared. "He's one gook'll never kill no more of us. Right?"

"Right, Corporal," Wilfred said, turning his back on the situation and instantly promoting the private, not condoning as much as understanding. You can't just turn off fear and anger like water from a tap.

Wandering back through the carnage, he saw that one had a mortar tube strapped to his back, and another was crumpled under a base plate. As he looked closer at the body of the female leader, recognition hit him in the face. "Trang."

Every day Can went to the flame tree, and after a week, when she heard that A Company was gone, she went into mourning. Another week crept by. She'd sent most of the money to her mother and was beginning to wonder what she would do if Wilfed did not come back. I will have no money for my family. But I must have money for my family. Maybe I should go home to Onkay again. But what if he returns and I am not here? "He is dead," kept ringing through her brain, but she would not believe it.

She passed the days in lingering despair, loving and pounding G.I. backs, pretending each was Wilfred's. At times she was angry with Trang for making her say those things to Wilfred. Then in her mind she watched him killing Vietnamese and thought of her father and felt righteous anger. In one breath she cursed the war; in the next she thanked it for bringing Wilfred to her.

One day she went to her room, and there was Mr. Minh. "It is time you began to work. Tomorrow you will begin renting your body to the Americans again. And you will find out for me where C Company will go when they leave LZ German."

She felt chilled by the words. But she also needed money and could no longer depend on Wilfred, so she obeyed.

Her first attempts at gaining information were crude and unsuccessful. She didn't like deception and found it difficult to pretend she loved someone to gain his trust, especially when she still daydreamed about Wilfred. Then Minh returned.

"Have you found out what I asked?"

"No. They would not tell me."

He slapped her, knocking her down. "Do not fail again."

She wanted to run away, but felt she had to stay, so she began trying harder. Usually the G.I. didn't know where he was going or would not say. But a few unwittingly babbled and she guiltily passed on the words to Mr. Minh.

When A Company returned to guard the bridge, Can heard of their arrival and for three days went to the flame tree and waited in vain. On the third day she returned to her room and found Mr. Minh. He slapped her again, forehand and backhand. "Now he has killed Trang. Blew her head off with a shotgun."

"No!" She fell keening onto her bed, pounding her fists in agony on the love that was not there.

And now she heard Minh, as if he were in another room, telling of the massacre at the cave. "He and his soldiers trapped a battalion from the north in rocks near the sea. Killed thirty-four. Captured forty-eight. Think of their families."

"I swear I will never try to see him again."

At the bridge, Wilfred was thinking of finding Can and attempting reconciliation. He wanted to be with her, to talk with her and enjoy her love again, but he still was angry with her for defending the VC and was worried that she'd somehow found out about Trang. If she had, she might be more deeply committed to the VC than ever. It might even be dangerous for him to go back to her now. He kept hearing her say, "No kill VC!" and "G.I. num' ten!" Finally he decided, the hell with it. Some day he might go back and try, but not yet. Maybe absence would make her heart fonder. And make her listen to reason.

Henry, meanwhile, had gone to Quan's room the first day A Company returned and greeted her with his usual, "Hey, baby," arms open and face grinning.

"Josha Henly!"

"What you say we get it on?" he asked and he scooped her up and took her to the bed. They performed for each other with gusto, and when he rolled off, she grabbed his huge hand and held it to her belly and said, "Josha Henly. You son. Here."

He leaped at the wonder of it and felt new warmth and responsibility for the mother and child. He hugged her and laughed and said, "Well, I be fucked. You going be a mama."

"You papa," she said, cheeks flushed in a hopeful smile.

Then he grew silent as the implications began clubbing him. Will he have no daddy, like me, or will I be his daddy? Will I take him home? Will I take her? Marry her? And what'll they think back home? Will they accept her? She ain't black. Then he thought of the neat black chicks he had made in the world and felt their certain scorn.

Questions kept coming. Can I really dig a child that ain't black? Will I still dig Quan when I get back to all that sweet black meat? Oh, baby, come to your papa. And then will I run off and let the government keep them? And fuck. What chance does a half-black half-gook kid have of makin' it back there anyway? What chance does he have here? And how can I fight for black with a gook wife? And hell, she won't understand none of it.

"Josha. What's long?"

"Nothin', baby. I just gotta figure something out."

Two days later, he was still trying to understand and decide. "You sure that baby's mine?"

Her eyes grew wide. "Baby you! You no love Quan, no love baby." She turned away and began weeping and moaning.

"Hell, baby. I loves you. It's just that you don't know what it's like back there. It's bad bein' black. But least if you're black, you're somebody."

He thought of growing up black. Poor. Afraid of whites. Momma telling you places you can't go, and how you was supposed to talk to white folks. He thought about the projects. Brick towers. People getting robbed. A murder down the hall. Gangs. Cops scared to come. Welfare workers looking around. That man Momma knew who was afraid to come by too often. Always being hungry at the end of the month. And how bad could it be for his kid? And for Quan? She ain't even black. White folks don't mind gooks 'cause they stays to themselves and don't make trouble. Might be O.K. for her. But does I love her enough? If it weren't for the world, I know I'd be happy with her, her skin, and her strong body. It might have a chance. Least she ain't white.

On the day before A Company left, he said, "Hey, Quan. You wanna get married?"

"Oh, Josha Henly. Yes!" and she threw her arms around him and cried.

"Let's do it, next time I comes in," he said.

"Oh, I love you, Josha Henly."

Birds lifted A Company to four small bridges on the coastal plain about fifteen kilometers from Sang Tran. The bridge assigned to Wilfred's platoon was close to the base of the mountains and near no village. During the day a few ox-carts and bicycles passed. At night all traffic ceased.

Separated from the rest of the company, Wilfred felt vulnerable. The VC would rarely attack a company. But a platoon? His insecurity was exacerbated by O'Shaunnessey's departure to Onkay to correct an error in his finance records.

He planted his defense of the outpost with rifles covering the stream and machine guns and claymores, the road. They cleaned out existing foxholes, pitched tents, passed out C-rations and mail, and ate alone in silence.

Rodriguez ran up to Wilfred. "Sir, Henry left."

"What do you mean?"

"He just left. Andrews see him reading a letter. Then he picks up his rifle and pack and walks down the road."

"What?"

"Andrews say he mad and sad."

"Fuck. That's all we need."

Wilfred spent the night worrying, and in the morning they left for security duty at LZ German.

The men in the platoon they were to relieve were wandering in a trance, each carrying a sandbag. Near the center was a rectangle of sandbags within which some torn and broken bags lay scattered. Not far away three half-full bags, sides wet and red, rested on the ground. Wilfred noticed a platoon sergeant with a bag in his hand looking all around the area. "I'm Lieutenant Carmenghetti. We're relieving you."

"You'll have to wait."

"What happened?"

"The mortar bunker blew. We're picking up the pieces."

"Where's your C.O.?"

He spread his arms, looked around through a screen of tears, and shrugged. "Out here." Then he pointed at the three red bags and shook his head.

"How many were killed?"

"Don't know. Five maybe."

"Was it incoming?"

"Don't know. Don't think so."

"Need any help?" The sergeant shook his head no.

A deuce-and-a-half pulled up and the sergeant told his men to load the remains. Some were in bags, others in ponchos.

"It's all yours, Lieutenant," the sergeant said. Wilfred assigned his squad leaders to different areas and told them to send two men back to help Kaslovski rebuild the mortar bunker.

Two M.P.'s pulled up in a jeep and a burly sergeant in a white helmet told Wilfred, "We've got your man. He was with his girl, all right, and he got violent when we took him. There were four of us, and we still had to bang him up and get him down and pin him and get him in a strait jacket, and he's still in it, the fucker, and he's gonna stay in it too. He just won't calm down."

They drove to the military police bunker, and the MP led Wilfred down a sandbag corridor past several guards to a stout wood door. "He's in there," he said. Then he unlocked and opened the door to the dimly lit room. "Be careful, sir."

Henry took a second to recognize Wilfred. "Get the fuck out, you asshole honky, or I swear to God I'll kill your motherfucking ass." His head was bandaged in two places and the white jacket bulged and strained.

"You want that thing off?"

"I's telling you, you takes it off, and I'll kill you."

"The hell you will. You know I can beat the shit out of you whenever I feel like it."

"I ain't buyin' your fucking jive this time either. I swear to God, I'll kill you."

"All right, then, kill me. Sergeant. Take that damned thing off." Wilfred reasoned that if Henry really wanted to kill him, he wouldn't warn him.

"He's still too dangerous to—"

"Take it off!"

"O.K. It's your funeral. Harry. Joe." The sergeant untied it while the others aimed pistols at Henry's head.

"This corporal is the best point man in Vietnam. He's killed seventeen gooks all by himself. Earned a silver star."

"Fuckin' animal," the sergeant said.

"Lock us in."

"You're as crazy as he is, sir."

"Get lost."

"Fine." The three M.P.'s backed out and locked the door.

"O.K., kill me."

"Shithead."

"Talk, Henry. What's going on?"

Henry stared away, and his body grew rigid. He struggled to hold in tears, his chin fell, and he couldn't speak.

"Well?"

"My sister!"

"What about her?"

His head flew back and his eyes looked up as he gasped back a sob and gritted his teeth. "She was looking out the window and one of your motherfucking po-lice-men killed her."

"What? Why?"

"Said he saw her move and thought she was a sniper."

"A sniper? Why did he think that?"

"It was in one of those riots, man. Those fucking honky cops shot some dude they said was robbing a store, and everybody got mean and tried to get the cops, and then it all blew up and they was running through the streets—hundreds of 'em—and fighting and taking shit from stores, and then they rolled over the cop's car and burned it, and then a whole shitload of cops came in, and there was more fighting and shooting, and then…they shot her."

"Oh, god. Was it near the projects?"

"No, man. Momma moved out of there a couple of months ago 'cause it was getting too bad for Miranda. Momma was afraid she'd get raped or into dope or something, so she moved up town into a nice apartment over a store. Me and my brothers been sending her bread to help her make it. But now this. They just ain't no way to get away. Momma should've just stayed where she was. Least Miranda'd be alive."

"But what were the cops supposed to do? Let those people take everything and burn down the town?"

"You white mothers can't know what it's like. You ain't nobody's slave. But I tells you what: this's just the start of it. We gonna burn down the country; you wait. They're gonna be real snipers in them windows, and I'm gonna be one of 'em, and they ain't no fuckin' honkies gonna make it through our town alive. We're gonna have our own black police in our own black cities, and ain't no whites coming in telling us what to do."

"Was anyone else killed?"

"Motherfuckers killed forty-three people. Forty-three! I swear to God, man. This is the beginning of the war. I just wish I was there now. I'd get that fucker that murdered my sister. I'd cut out the fucker's heart and nail it to the fucking wall."

Wilfred pictured his sister, Felicity, lying on the floor beneath the window, and said, "I'm sorry, Henry. I'm sorry."

"Ain't good enough. Ain't near good enough. Too motherfucking easy. You gonna pay. All you fuckers gonna pay."

"I didn't do it, man—"

"You all did it! Every goddam one of you."

Wilfred felt powerless. "Let's get out of here. Let's go back to the platoon."

"I ain't going."

"Why not?"

"Why the fuck am I killing gooks for you whiteys?"

"We're fighting for our country, for freedom."

"We ain't got no freedom. If you ain't got bread, you ain't got freedom. No, man. I'm gonna start fightin' for the commies."

"What? You don't know what they're like. They take everything you have, and you do what they tell you to or they'll kill you or put you in prison. Talk about slavery."

"We ain't got nothing to take. Whitey takes it all. That's the difference. With the commies, everyone works, and shares what they makes. And it don't matter what color a man is."

"That's not how it is. If a man wants to work hard and get ahead, they won't let him. Don't you want the chance to get ahead?"

"All we gets is the sure thing of staying behind. I've been fighting on the wrong side, man. It's time I joined the colored folk here. It's the same war here as in Detroit, only somehow I got conned into fightin' for the enemy. Well, no more. I got a kid coming here, and I'm gonna start fightin' for him."

"A kid?"

Henry blinked. "Yeah. Me and Quan."

"Wow."

"Anywhere I takes him it'll be the same."

"That's not true. You take him back to the states and make sure he gets an education and learns to work hard and work with other people, and he'll make it, man. But leave him here, and he won't have a chance. A half-black kid. And you watch what happens if we ever leave here. There'll be the biggest bloodbath you ever saw. There'll be refugees leaving in droves. Don't tell me about the wonderful communists."

Henry was quiet. He was trying hard to figure it all out, but nothing was right. "Why'd the fucker have to kill her?"

"It was a terrible, horrible accident. He wasn't shooting at her. He was shooting at a ghost. He was just scared."

"It's all fucked up, man."

"I know it is. Every square inch of this god-forsaken world is fucked up."

"Aw, fuck, man." Henry seemed to wilt, and he began to cry. "She was just a pretty little girl. Ten years old, man. Ten years old." He broke into sobs.

CHAPTER 17

▼

CAN AND FIERDEN

Wilfred decided to walk back to the perimeter. He was in no hurry to get there. The thought of the bleeding, woven plastic bags was overwhelming. And his satisfaction at having talked Henry out of his fury was evaporating with every step. Had he told Henry the truth, or just more white lies? How would he feel if he were Henry? An even deeper rage, he was sure.

He walked down a hill on the dusty road past bunkers and tents and gazed at a similar mélange across the little valley in front of him. Then his eye picked out an irregularity—a spot of dark green a few streets back from the main road. Out of curiosity he watched it grow as he came closer. When he neared the bottom of the hill it disappeared behind bunkers and tents. He jogged to the left, drawn down a side street toward the mystery. Then he passed a big tent, and the mass of dark green leaped out and slapped his face. Fifty feet away stood stacks of plastic body bags, two deep, ten high, and twenty or thirty long, each stuffed with the refuse of battle and neatly tagged for shipment.

Are the sacks of flesh from the bunker here yet? Have they sorted it somehow? Shit, no. They got the names and tagged the bags and dumped some in each one. "Hey, Larry. Put a little more in this one, will you? It's a little bit shy."

Again the smell of death overcame his cologne and the magnitude overwhelmed him. War's a giant killing machine. March 'em in one end, blow 'em up, grind 'em up, fill up the tubes, and ship 'em out. They're free, everybody. All you pay is your taxes. And the military officers at the doors say, "It is my duty to inform you..."

"Where's Henry?" Simms asked. "In the klink?"

"I gave him a pass to town."

"You what?"

"He'll be back."

To his relief Henry returned at four o'clock. Wilfred could tell from his expression that he was in a state of relapse.

"You gonna bust him again for going AWOL?" O'Shaunnessey asked Wilfred. "That's what Simms wants."

"Fuck Simms. You can't hit a man when he's down. You gotta pick him up."

"I was afraid you wouldn't see it that way."

Can found Mr. Minh in her room, his back to the door, examining a photo on her bureau. "Greetings, comrade. I have a new assignment for you."

She shuddered imperceptibly. "How can I assist you?"

"As you probably know, A Company, First of the Thirteenth, is at LZ German now and will leave in a few days. I want you to find out when and where they will go."

She froze. It was the first time he had asked her to get information on Wilfred's company.

Minh noticed her hesitation and said, "Ah, your lieutenant. I had forgotten. You are still hoping he will fly to your side and carry you away to his palace in America where you will live like the wife of an emperor and forget your poor mother and the sleeping father who gave his last breath for your freedom."

"I have no such dreams."

"Can't you remember how many of your countrymen he has murdered? Have you forgotten Trang so soon? He is a demon in the body of a man. He has captured your mind with his wickedness. How many more must he kill before you can see what he is?"

"Why do you want to know where A Company will go?"

"You are a traitor. Perhaps you should be treated as such."

"Will you kill him?"

"Will we kill him?" he repeated in disbelief. "Will we kill the spirit of evil? And will we also drink the entire South China Sea? No, Can. It is for our own safety that we must know. We must not allow him to kill any more of our soldiers. We fear him. We wish to avoid him and save ourselves for fights against lesser foes. But we must have your help. Without your help, more and more of us will sleep. Please help us."

Twenty-one hours before A Company departed, Lieutenant Eric Fierden left the battalion officers' briefing with all the information concerning the move. He was still bristling from words he'd had with Wilfred that morning about demoting Henry. Carmenghetti lacks respect for authority and self-respect. Lets his men walk all over him. Never takes advice, even from someone like me with so much more command experience. Hell, no, because he's a fathead know-it-all. And someday I'll get the asshole for making a fool out of me at the rocks.

The sun was hot and he needed a beer and some female companionship. Downtown he stopped at a few bars and then sauntered into the Paradise massage parlor where as luck would have it, he drew Can. He thought he remembered her from the barracks at Camp Vassar.

"What's your name?"

"Can. Please take off clothes and get on table."

"You're from Onkay," he said. "How did you get here?"

"Lutemma Cahmehgehee."

"Carmenghetti."

"You know him?"

"He's in my company. I guess he brought you here, huh?"

"Yes. We were fliends."

"Brought you with him on a plane?" He removed his shirt.

"Why you wanna know?"

"He's a friend of mine. Number one. Very funny. I like to hear stories about him. Brought you on a plane. That's funny

She sighed and said, "Yes, but we no fliends now."

"What happened?"

"He no like me now."

"That's 'cause he's a number ten motherfucking asshole."

"Pants."

"Oh, yeah." He removed his pants.

As he relaxed under the toil of her fingers, he began to think how much fun it would be to fuck Wilfred's girl and tell him about it later.

"You vely nice, G.I. So stong. I like you. What you name?"

"Lieutenant Fierden."

When the massage was over he followed her upstairs, and they engaged their working parts, and for him she had three orgasms. And after he had spat his spit-

tle, she told him "Oh, you better than Wilfed. I love you, Lieutenant Fielden."
She lay beside him for an hour asking questions and doting and opening his
beers. She cursed the VC and praised the Americans and told him of VC concen-
trations throughout the area.

"You no go there?" she asked hopefully.

"Naa," he said, feeling drunk and contented.

"You tell me where company go, I tell if VC there."

A red flag unfurled in Fierden's brain. If she's VC, that could be trouble. They
might ambush the company. But if A Company gets hit, maybe Carmenghetti'll
buy the farm. And Henry. Second platoon'll be the first one in. And maybe
Simms'll get zapped. And then I'd be the new C.O. I hope she is VC. "Sure.
We're going to search Quin Loc..." and he proceeded to tell her the details of the
operation.

"I cannot fail," said the colonel with protruding nails to the stocky young captain and the one-armed man in the quivering light of the village hut. "The gods
are with me now, since they pried back my fingers and jerked the grenade from
my hands in the rocks and sent it clattering into that crevice!" He recalled Wilfred's face in the sergeant's flashlight. "I only wish I had killed him there. But
they gave me no light to find a gun."

Mr. Minh was not at all sure that divine intervention had saved the colonel
instead of a last second decision to live. He was certain, however, of the strength
of Dai's desire for revenge against this lieutenant who had wounded his battalion
in the forest and annihilated it at the cave. Moreover, the intelligence he had
received from Can, in her moronic attempt to save the lives of Wilfred and her
countrymen, was in much greater detail than usual and seemed more reliable.

For this mission the Vietcong command put a captain and one platoon under
Dai's command, so instead of the large operation, which Dai had hoped might
destroy A Company and complete his revenge, he would have to settle for a quick
thrust and immediate retreat and hope he at least could kill the lieutenant. And
although far beneath leading a battalion, the command would be the first step
back to his former status.

The captain sent runners to outlying hamlets with orders directing several
teams of soldiers to report to Dai at Quin Loc (2) at 0400. Dai himself took three
of the captain's men who were in the village at the time and went to Quin Loc,
arriving two hours early to familiarize himself with his surroundings and recon
his positions and escape routes.

The hamlet consisted of sixteen thatch huts with dirt floors beneath dozens of shading palms. A dirt lane ten feet wide wound between the houses. Thick, high hedges surrounded the village and lower ones defined yards, vegetable gardens and livestock pens. The hedges and thatch walls and the curve of the street protected residents from evil spirits, which move in straight lines, like bullets, and are impeded by matter.

As Dai neared the sleeping village, his approach was announced by barking. People stirred, and an old farmer, the hamlet chief, rose. "*Lai day.*" Dai ordered, and the old mayor approached him in the darkness. His face displayed worry and fear as he listened to the colonel's plans, but he knew he had no choice but to aid Dai, so he asked a ten-year-old boy to show Dai around. Then he left, and Dai knew he would warn the villagers. They could not flee into the paddies and risk getting shot from the air, so they would have to get into the hand-dug pits in their huts to escape fire. Then the chief would go to the altar in his house, burn a stick of incense, and pray.

The sky was clear, the moon nearly full, and Dai got his bearings quickly. He found the paddy to the south where the Americans were to land and located the drainage ditch beside it, a gully about four feet deep and twice as wide with water a few inches deep and waist-high hedges at the top. He followed its curves for two hundred yards around and past the village to where it emptied into a shallow stream that wandered across the plain past many other villages. The stream lay beneath banks more than head high with brush and trees on both sides. Dai was pleased; the banks offered excellent protection from fire, and the hedges and bushes would conceal their escape. Next, he circumnavigated the hamlet and planned alternate sites in case the intelligence they had received was inaccurate.

When the soldiers arrived at four A.M., the colonel was disappointed. They were a motley lot—some young, some old, in mismatched uniforms or just shorts and shirts. Their weapons were similarly varied—AK-47s and SKSs, Russian and Chinese, an ancient French submachine gun, two M16s, and an old American M1. There were six grenades among the nineteen men, and most had only one magazine, which could be emptied in ten seconds on full automatic. In contrast, the colonel himself carried a pistol and an AK-47 and had four clips of thirty-five rounds plus two grenades. Yet, as he talked with the men, he grew more confident. They were grim-faced and tough and several bore scars from previous battles. Although the attack would be brief, he grew certain that these men would provide a lethal punch.

He showed them the escape route, the paddy into which he expected the Americans to land and the alternate ambush sites on the other side of the hamlet.

"The Americans," he told them, "will give us time to get to the alternate sites when they bring in their artillery on their landing zone." Then he placed them in their primary positions in the drainage ditch and reminded them, "I will be first to fire."

They cleaned and loaded their weapons, camouflaged themselves with branches and leaves, spread out in the ditch, found firing ports in the hedge, and waited. Now, thought Dai, if only our intelligence is correct. He prayed that it was and that the gods would let him begin his new life in honor.

At daybreak, the first round hit, fifty yards to their front. They dropped into the ditch beneath the spray of fragments and clung to the side while the villagers scrambled into the holes in their huts. After twenty artillery blasts, they heard the gunship propeller and the cracking sound as it showered the ditch with lead, which thudded into the bank behind them. Next came the beating of wings as four huge green dragonflies lit on the field to their front. "Up!" Dai shouted, and his men rose and took aim. Green fleas holding sticks hopped from both sides, and Dai aimed at one next to a large one with a single antenna protruding from its back. He fired, and the entire line began spraying the infesting swarm. The skittish helicopters leaped away, exoskeletons riddled with punctures.

The first shot was four inches too high on Wilfred's moving figure and tore the steel helmet off his head. "Get down!" he yelled, falling prone and watching in horror as others spun, jerked, and crumpled on buckling knees. He saw flashes and smoke to the front. "They're in the hedge line!" Then he pulled his rifle into firing position—his elbows and belly a tripod—and began squeezing bursts at the flashing smoke. As the rumble of firing swelled, mixed with a chorus of screams and moans, he tore a can of red smoke from his suspenders, pulled the pin, and flipped it behind him. Deep red poured from the can, rose, swelled, and faded to pink. He saw Welbourne lying face down in the grass and crawled toward him, fearing the worst, till he heard a voice whispering, "Deep Sky Six. Deep Sky Six. Come in Deep Sky Six."

"Gimme that thing," he said, snatching the handset away. "Six, this is Two-Six. LZ hot. Repeat. LZ hot. Over."

The captain's voice rushed out. "Roger Two-Six. We're keeping back. Where are they and how many? Over."

"Looks like thirty or forty in the hedgerow next to the LZ. We've got friendly wounded. Need a medevac, quick. Over."

"Did you get that, Smokey Bear?" Simms said. "Over."

"Roger," the gunship pilot said. "We'll work 'em over for you." But as it raced down the line of the ditch, pumping off 40mm grenades and spewing rockets like dragon's fire, Colonel Dai stood up, partially shielded by the curves of the ditch.

CHAPTER 18

▼

DAI AND THE OLD WOMAN

"Shoot it down," Dai shouted, and raised his rifle in the face of the oncoming missiles. Half of the men followed his command, while the others cowered.

Some rockets found their mark. One soldier was flung nearly out of the ditch by the force of an explosion. But as the monster approached, Dai unleashed his rifle, turned to fire again as it sped away, and watched it lose altitude and explode into flames just beyond the village.

Wilfred seized the opportunity of the helicopter attack and jumped up, shouting, "Get 'em."

Racing a zigzag line toward the hedgerow with many men following, he saw the chopper explode and a rifle barrel poke through the hedge. "Hit it!" He yelled and dropped to the ground and renewed his bursts of fire.

When the VC saw their comrades falling and the charge of Wilfred's platoon, most began splashing down the ditch, over the bodies of other soldiers and toward the stream, but not Colonel Dai.

"Shoot them," Dai shouted, and he and three others began returning Wilfred's fire in single, well-aimed shots.

"Six. We're pinned down. How 'bout putting in a platoon at each end of the village and letting them work their way to Charlie. Over."

"Negative, Two-Six. We've got men down, a chopper down. I'm calling in artillery. I'll direct it from up here. Over."

"Six. My men are dying, and the VC are dug in. The artillery won't touch 'em. And you'll hit the village. Over."

"The hell with the village. It's commie. We'll see how they like our artillery. Out."

"But my wounded don't have time. Gimme some men. Over."

"Good money after bad, Two-Six. Stay down. Out."

The first round of artillery hit behind Wilfred's platoon. He couldn't believe it. Simms was going to walk the rounds through his platoon. "Six. That was behind us. What're you trying to do? Kill us all? Over."

"Keep calm, Two-Six. I won't hit you. Out." He called in the adjustment to the firebase. The giant gun shot again and recoiled from its deed. Seconds later Wilfred heard the round whistle, watched straw and bamboo from a hut in the village fly in all directions, and heard the huge crunch of the explosion.

Colonel Dai was shaken, but decided that unless there was a direct hit, they would be safe enough in their ditch.

They would only need to drop below the surface whenever they heard an incoming round, so he urged his men to continue firing.

The third round landed between Wilfred and Dai. "Simms!" Wilfred screamed into the handset. "That was right on our heads. Cease fire. I say again, cease fire. Over."

"Must have been a short round. Out."

Soon the rounds were hitting the village every few seconds. One hut after another blew apart with a crunch. The VC fire became sporadic, but continued. After each round hit, they rose, fired a shot or two, and dropped back down.

Wilfred was furious. "They're still shooting at us," he announced to the handset.

Some of the men behind him had crawled up to try to help their wounded friends, but Wilfred noticed that the volume of the screaming had waned amid the clatter of gunfire.

"Lieutenant," one man yelled. "We gotta have a medevac right now. He's gonna die if we don't get him out of here."

"Six. My men are dying. We need a medevac. Now. Over." There was no response.

Wilfred looked up. In the distance he saw the twelve Hueys suspended in a giant circle. *That sonofabitch isn't going to help us.* Then he saw flames rise in the village and heard screaming to his front. "Let's crawl in and frag 'em. Now."

He started sliding forward, grenade in hand. Behind him men fired cover and others began moving up with him.

When Colonel Dai saw the determined advance, he tried to stop it with rifle fire, but had to duck for the next artillery blast, and when he arose again, Wilfred's men were beneath his line of fire. "Retreat," he ordered. Two VC moved, but one was slumped over his rifle. As they splashed down their escape route, Dai counted five more who had given their lives for their country.

Wilfred sensed a trap when their firing stopped, but kept on crawling and when within range, threw the first grenade. To his right he saw Rodriguez tossing his, and to his left, Matfield and two of his men. When the grenades exploded, it grew quiet in front except for the snapping fires and wails from the village and the pounding, pulverizing blasts of the artillery.

"O.K.," Wilfred shouted. "Let's throw one more, then go over the hedge. Ready. Now." The missiles sailed and boomed. The six rose and ran, pausing only when they saw the ditch that lay beyond the hedge. Over they went with a splash as another artillery round shook the village. Wilfred looked around, saw two dead soldiers lying in the ditch, then shouted, "Cease fire," and took the handset. "Six. This is Two-Six. They're gone. Stop the artillery and bring in the medevac...Rodriguez. Take your men up the ditch and sweep the village. Matfield. Take yours and clear the ditch the other way."

G.I.'s were standing or kneeling in six little bunches, hovering over the dead and wounded. Wilfred ran from one to the next to get the status of the casualties. "It's Murph, sir."

"Sucking chest wound. Looks bad. Keep that bandage tight. Come on, Simms. Get that medevac!"

"It's the new guy, Samuelson. Got it in the head."

"Dead?"

"Gotta be, sir."

"Louis King."

"No. Is he—"

"He's gone, sir."

"No!"

Wilfred asked Welbourne who else got hit as O'Shaunnessey supervised loading the bodies.

"Clifford got his arm shot up, and Mendoza got it through the neck, but they think he'll make it. Jonesy's dead."

Wilfred made no response.

The confusion over evacuating the dead and wounded had delayed the patrols through the ditch and village. When Rodriguez and Matfield were finally lined up to go, Wilfred shouted with sudden venom, "Rodriguez. I'm going." He stood up, snapped a fresh magazine into his rifle and swaggered over to join them with Welbourne following.

Henry read the rage in his eyes. "You O.K., sir?"

"I'll take point," Wilfred snapped.

"You know, those people in there might not of had nothin' to do with this. Charlie could've forced 'em into it."

"They could've stopped it and they didn't. They could've given us a warning."

Henry heard the implied, "they gotta pay." "Don't matter what they did or didn't do. They already been punished."

"Lieutenant," Welbourne said. "Captain's comin' in. Wants to see you."

"Fuck the sonofabitch. Move out!"

They crossed the ditch, split from Matfield and entered the hamlet. It was devastated, Wilfred noted with satisfaction. As they rounded a high bush, he saw a dozen people wandering, wailing, bleeding, searching the rubble for survivors; others lying here and there on the ground, some mutilated, some moaning and moving slowly. But Wilfred saw enemy who had killed his men and his friend. Over his shoulder, he bellowed, "Finish 'em off!" and he raised his rifle and began to fire.

An old woman fell down, holding a bleeding arm and screaming, and the people began to scatter—an old man hobbling, an infant grabbed under the arm by a scurrying mother. At the same time, two black arms surrounded Wilfred, lifted him, threw him down, and jerked away his weapon. He was up in an instant, charging Henry like a rabid dog, but a hard stiff arm put him in the dust, and a knee on the chest held his squirming body to the ground. Then Wilfred saw a blur and felt his head snap to one side, then the other, as Henry tried to slap him into sanity.

"Welbourne," Rodriguez said, taking over the patrol. "Tell the captain to get more medevacs. Tell him we got—I don't know—tell him we got maybe fifty wounded."

Henry unsnapped Wilfred's holster, took his pistol and pulled his grenades off his web gear. "You does anythin' else, I's going slap shit outa you."

Wilfred appeared to have listened, so Henry let him up, but told Rodriguez, "Put a guard on him." Then he shouted to the rest of the squad, "Y'all better get out there and save some lives. Anyone that wants do any more killin' is going get it from me, you hear?" He went next to the woman Wilfred shot, saw that she was bleeding heavily, ripped a strip of cloth from the bottom of her blouse, and made her a tourniquet, while others in the squad began gathering people, examining wounds, and applying first aid. Then, looking up from his work, Henry shouted, "Another thing. Anyone say anythin' to anyone 'bout this thing with the lieutenant, they's in trouble with me. Hear?"

Colonel Clary came in just after Simms. Simms approached Clary, and they stood near Wilfred as they spoke, but didn't see him. "The VC were in the village," Simms said. "I thought we'd lost enough men. That's why I called for artillery."

"You did this to get a platoon of VC?"

"I don't think we did that bad, sir. We got six of them, and they only got three of us."

"Four. Corporal Murphy didn't make it. Plus four more in the gunship. Plus what, thirty or forty civilians?"

"It was an accident. I didn't know all these people were in here. Anyway, the important thing is, we killed six VC."

"What do you want, a medal?"

"You're blaming me for this?"

"The man monitoring your transmissions said Lieutenant Carmenghetti tried to get you to put more troops on the ground because the artillery would hit the village."

"I was trying to protect my men."

"You protected them, all right. Congratulations, Captain. Now. How are we going to report this thing?"

CHAPTER 19

▼

CAN AND LIEUTENANT NEWCOMBE

Wilfred had the night to recover from his pain and fury, but awoke with his head pounding and body trembling.

At the officers' meeting Simms described the plan for the day. They would move up the stream five clicks on a search and clear mission, then cordon and search a village. "Notice I said 'search and clear'. Colonel Clary says word's come down that all operations formerly known as 'search and destroy' are now called 'search and clear' or 'search and hold.' The words 'search and destroy' are verboten, out. And he says if we wanna burn down a hooch, we have to get his personal permission. Got that? O.K."

He was mystified by this semantic sleight of hand. Nothing had changed but the name. Must be for the press or the public. But maybe not. He says we're supposed to stop burning villages.

"Now. About yesterday. I want to read you the official report that's going in. Make sure your men get the message. Here it is: 'At 0632 A Co. was air lifted to village vicinity QB421783 for a cordon and search operation. The 2-6 element in the first lift landed on a hot LZ, received heavy fire from the village, and returned fire. A UH-1 gunship was shot down and destroyed by enemy fire. Artillery was adjusted on the enemy. Results: 15 KIA (VC), 11 WIA (VC), 3 AK-47, 2 SKS, 1

M-1 carbine, and 40 rounds of ammunition. Friendly casualties: 4 KIA, 4 KIA (helicopter crew), and two WIA.' Any questions?"

The platoon leaders had listened in amazement, except for Lorde who spied a tiny beetle climbing a blade of grass and watched breathlessly to see if it would make it to the top.

"That's a lie," Wilfred said. "We only killed six, and didn't capture any, and we murdered twenty-nine innocent civilians."

"Come on, Wilfred," Newcombe said. "What do you mean, 'innocent'? Did they oppose the VC or try to warn us? Hell, no. They got what they deserved."

"Old men and women? Children? Babies?"

"You know those kids are spies. They'll even sneak up and frag you."

"That's another fucking lie. How many G.I.'s have been killed by children?"

"O.K., O.K., simmer down," Simms said. "It was an accident, and there's nothing we can do about it."

"An accident?" Wilfred said. "You slimy motherfucker. I told you you were gonna hit that village, and you said, 'The hell with it.' You said it was 'commie.'"

"Yeah, and you wanted to put more of us on the ground and get more of us zapped."

"So you brought in artillery for fifteen minutes while my men bled to death. You killed them, you sonofabitch."

"Maybe you'd like to make the life and death decisions. You'd sing a different tune then."

"It's water over the dam, Wilfred," Newcombe said.

"Not the report," Reckert said.

"You mean the cover-up. What's the matter, Simms? Don't want your actions evaluated? What are you afraid of?"

"Don't make waves," Simms said.

Wilfred pressed on. "How come you only listed fifteen VC KIA instead of thirty-five? I mean if all those old women and kids were VC, we ought to get credit for them too."

"Not enough weapons," Reckert said. "It would look suspicious."

"We only counted the most probable VC," Simms said, "the ones that should have warned us."

"Thirty-five VC," Reckert continued, "but only five rifles. That wouldn't look right. The VC are better equipped than that."

"And if we counted all thirty-five," Wilfred added, "hell, we'd have generals and reporters crawling all over us."

Wilfred was remembering the woman he shot. *I'm such a hypocrite. Maybe I can accept a cover-up.* But another part of him longed for disclosure, punishment, expiation, and release.

"And according to the report," Reckert said, "the other dead and wounded non-combatants just don't exist."

"That is correct," Simms said.

"I understand your feeling that dead people don't exist," Wilfred said to Simms, blinking away the face of Louis King.

"History is always rewritten," Reckert said, "which is why it's so important to understand the biases of the historian."

"We gotta keep from becoming numbers. Louis and Jonesy and Murph and Mendoza. They're all numbers now."

"Do we have to include the chopper crew in the reports?" Newcombe asked Simms.

"I'm afraid so," Simms said.

"That's too bad," Newcombe said.

"It doesn't seem to matter who we count," Wilfred said to Reckert.

"O.K., weirdo," Simms said to Wilfred. "Keep it down."

"It's kind of hard on our kill ratio," Newcombe added.

"But do we count with the accountant in the sky? That's the question," Wilfred said.

"Yeah, I know," Simms said. "Let's see. It's only about two to one if the chopper crew's included. That stinks."

"That's right," Newcombe said. "But if we didn't have to include the crew, it'd be almost four to one."

"A better blood balance," Wilfred said to Reckert.

"O.K., you guys," Simms said. "Knock it off."

"Can't you talk to Clary about it?" Newcombe asked. "I mean those guys weren't even in our unit."

"I did. He won't have it."

Lorde was slouched on his elbows watching the morning sun pierce the fog and emblazon the dark mountains to the rear when, in barely audible tones, he began singing the opening notes of "On The Trail," the third movement of Ferde Grofe's Grand Canyon Suite, "Dum dee, dum dee, dum dee, da da da…"

"We can count on the government to keep us counting, on and on," Reckert said.

"He doesn't care because it wouldn't affect the battalion ratio any," Newcombe said. "But he could have given us credit for more of the villagers."

"He was pissed off at me for using the artillery."

"That's just great," Newcombe said.

"And he really was afraid those press guys would come out here," Simms said.

The "dum dee, dum…" in the background was rising in pitch and intensity.

"Shut the fuck up," Newcombe said to Lorde, who quaked and quickly rested in peace.

"Great Presidents don't lose wars," Wilfred said, "and they're not quitters. Especially when we're doing the fighting."

"Those bastards," Newcombe said. "They probably would try to hang this thing on us."

"And counting," Reckert.

"O.K. O.K. Shut up, I tell you," Simms said. "I've had it with this shit. I'll ship you all to the fucking loony bin if you don't shut up. Now about this incident. Get out the word: It's senseless to dishonor our colors and our country over what was at worst an unfortunate mistake made under difficult circumstances. The report stands as read. Now. Let's eat."

Reckert collared Wilfred and said, "Are we going to let him get away with it?"

"I guess I am," Wilfred said, and he told him about his shooting the woman.

"But that was different. You must have been temporarily insane or—"

"There's no difference."

"But you didn't kill anyone."

"I would have if Henry hadn't stopped me. In fact, I'm the one who committed the atrocity, not Simms."

"What?"

"That colonel at Vassar. He told us that atrocities are committed in anger on the spur of the moment…and without any rational justification or blessing of a legal authority, and…and real close up."

"So Hiroshima and Nagasaki were not atrocities."

"Right," Wilfred said. "They were done without passion and were carefully planned…and were justified by saving the lives of American and Japanese soldiers. And they were approved by the president."

"And done by pushing a button way up in the sky."

"Yeah. Here we pull back and call in the artillery. But I did something different."

The company finished eating, the bird took off with their packs, and as they lined up for the patrol, Henry approached Wilfred. "I told Rodriquez I ain't taking point no more."

"What? What's the story?"

"I told you, I ain't killing for whitey no more, that's all. I ain't killing no more Vietnamese, no more VC."

"You gonna…kill any of us?"

"Nope. I'm done with killin'. Least over here. Unless you starts shooting brown babies and old men and mamasans. Then I'm gonna stop you any way I can. That goes for that captain. You tell him that. He starts dropping any more bombs on villages, I'm gonna zap his ass. You gonna tell him or you want me to?"

Wilfred hesitated, then said, "I'll tell him. Rodriguez. Put someone else on point."

Can heard about the incident at Quin Loc hours after the first medevac came in and grew extremely agitated. Minh tricked me! He said the soldiers would avoid Wilfred's company, but they attacked it instead. Oh, the lying pig. And the attack must have hurt the Americans badly or they would not have killed so many in the village. Oh, so many people. Did Wilfred do it? He couldn't have. Oh, Wilfred. Are you still alive? Ooooh.

She went to the market to buy rice and vegetables, and when she came back, there was Minh.

"You lied to me," she said. "Tricked me. You said the VC would stay away from Wilfed's company, but they attacked it."

"I did not lie. We were unable to get word to the village militia. A helicopter killed our messenger as he crossed the paddies in the moonlight. The Americans pounced on the village and your courageous brothers tried to defend it, but the foreigners overwhelmed them and cut them down, and then butchered all the people—mothers and babies, honorable grandfathers and grandmothers. That, my dear Can, is the truth."

"Is Cahmehgehee all right?"

Minh was furious. She would not let go of her murdering lieutenant, no matter what. It must stop, he shouted to himself, but only death will end it, so he killed Wilfred with a word.

"Lieutenant Carmenghetti was killed by the militia."

"No!" She leaped at him in a blind fury, attacking him with a flurry of little fists. "It is not so. It is another lie. It—"

He threw her against the wall behind the bed with a mighty shove, and then followed her, grabbed her throat, and squeezed until she was nearly unconscious. Then she felt her assailant inside of her, stabbing her again and again. "Ooh," she screamed, her head straining to the side. "Pig. Get off." She sunk her nails into his sides, pushed, and tried to bite his neck and his arm, but he was too strong.

And when he was done, she leaped at him in his weakness. He knocked her down again, and she felt her face swelling.

"Slut. Never have you offered yourself to me. Only to your fornicating lieutenant. Well, now I have taken. And now you can fuck the spirit of your lieutenant. For he is dead. Forever. And you have received what you deserve for your disloyalty. Thirty-five people he killed this time. Women, old men, babies."

She disintegrated into a choking, shuddering mass of tears, and Minh left, anxious to turn his lie into truth. He sent an order to Colonel Dai: "Eliminate Lieutenant Carmenghetti immediately. Highest priority." Dai showed it to the VC captain and asked for a high-powered rifle with telescopic sights. The captain complied and gave him the latest intelligence on the location of A Company, and Dai left on foot.

Lieutenant Fierden lay on a bunk with his hands behind his head, mulling the Quin Loc results with chagrin. Wilfred was alive and Simms in command. They ought to relieve him for committing an atrocity; then I could take over. Phooey.

He got up and went to town. He would at least have the pleasure of fucking Wilfred's girl again. As he entered the Paradise, he wondered: if she loves Wilfred, how could she have given me the information that could have gotten him killed? Maybe she's stupid, or doesn't care about him anymore. Maybe she likes me. And what's so hard to believe about that? He found Can sitting on the edge of her bed, red-eyed, bruised, and morose.

"Oh, Lutemma Filden. Oh, you tell me. Please. Wilfed no' dead, is he? Is he?" His delusion evaporated. She still loved Wilfred. But he would show her, her and that stinking asshole.

"Can, I don't know how to tell you this. I have number ten news." Her heart fluttered. "Wilfred was killed this morning."

"No...no...no..."

He sat beside her and tried to put his arm around her to comfort her, but she jumped up and pointed to the doorway, crying, "Di di mau...di di mau...you num ten...you—"

"Well. If that's how you feel, I'll go. I only thought you'd want to know."

"Di di mau!" Fierden left, smiling in triumph.

That evening Can received a package, neatly wrapped in brown paper, tied with twine. Opening it, she gasped in horror. It was a small fatigue shirt, riddled with holes and soaked with dried blood; the nametag screamed, "CARMENGHETTI". That night she packed and the next morning left for her family in Onkay.

"What is your fee?" Minh had asked the tailor at a shop where rear area officers went to eliminate bagginess. The couturier had selected the smallest size shirt, shortened the sleeves, printed a nametag, and affixed it and patches of an equine head, crossed rifles, and brown lieutenant's bar.

"For you and the cause, I charge nothing."

Next he went to the meat shop, which supplied restaurants with USDA-inspected meat. "I have an unusual request," he told the shopkeeper. "I need blood." The butcher took him into the back where a pig was hung up to drain, wrapped in a swarm of flies. Minh dipped the shirt into a pan of blood, took it into the stockyard behind the shop, threw it into the dirt, drew his pistol, screwed on his silencer, and fired eight shots into the shirt. This ritual impressed the butcher, and when Minh asked him to bundle it up and have it delivered, he was compliant in his terror and took care that his part of the ceremony was perfectly executed, again at no charge.

The company left the village and followed the drainage ditch to its outlet, turning upstream toward another village, and walking on the exposed silt bottom next to the rolling brown water. Trees and bushes lined the sides above them. Newcombe was third man from the front of the column.

As the stream curved one way, then the other, the dry bottom path kept changing sides, necessitating numerous fordings. The curves were too small to be on Newcombe's map and he frequently stopped the march and climbed the bank to get his bearings. When he did so, he and the captain were always disappointed at their progress.

At Wilfred's position near the rear of the column the combination of Newcombe's recons and the accordion effect turned the march into a series of splashing sprints alternating with irritating halts. The stops were too short to eat or sleep and ended abruptly. Men would begin to move ahead, rapidly, and on a seconds' notice, would be dashing through the water again. They were soaked from head to foot, but in the late morning when they lost the shade of the trees on the banks, the wetness felt good.

Just before noon, Wilfred froze at the sound of an explosion, far ahead. He grabbed the horn and listened as the confused dialogue slowly crystallized into yet another horror. In climbing the bank, Newcombe had tripped a wire detonating an artillery round, an American dud rearmed by the VC. Newcombe and his RTO were dead, and three others gravely wounded.

Wilfred withheld an urge to run to the scene, and collapsed uselessly against the bank. He really didn't want to see.

The column moved up, Wilfred with it, as Reckert's platoon secured the medevac landing zone. Wilfred heard the chopper come and go. Then they were moving again as if nothing happened; only now it was Reckert who talked to the captain on the radio.

Eventually he came to the bend where the bank was caved in and saw bloodstains and hundreds of footprints in the soft silt. "Oh, my god." He stumbled past as quickly as he could.

When the company arrived at their village, it was deserted. They found cooking fires, food in bowls, and other signs of hasty departure. As the company left the village, Newcombe's men, at the rear of the column, kicked coals from the fires into several of the hooches, and when Simms saw the smoke, he called Newcombe's platoon sergeant and asked how the fires started.

"I don't know. I guess the wind picked up sparks from one of them fires. You want us to go back and try to put it out? Over."

"Negative. Out."

CHAPTER 20

▼

STEWART AND O'SHAUNNESSEY

He received a letter from Felicity in the afternoon mail telling of her antiwar activities at Columbia and the slogans they were chanting: "Hell, no, we won't go," and "Hey, hey, LBJ. How many kids did you kill today?" "Madge and Mike are fine, but Madge seems to be putting on weight. I think she's worried about you. Robert's been sailing off Long Island with some other Yaleys for the past two weeks (lucky boy!). I think I have him talked into going to Canada if his number comes up. Please!!! Don't kill anyone. And be careful. Love, Felicity."

Wilfred loved her, but with smoke rising in the distance, friends dying around him, and the atrocity of yesterday still stuck in his throat, he somehow despised her happy little peace movement and wished his damned brother would get drafted. If they only knew what it was like, they couldn't be so goddamned happy. Then he guessed he was just feeling sorry for himself, he who wanted to see war.

Dinner was spaghetti. He left the line and wandered toward Reckert, thinking of ground flesh swimming in blood. He squatted and without noticing Reckert's depression, said, "I'm getting sick of this war, Robbie."

"You?"

"Yeah, me. Why not me?"

"Sounds kind of strange, coming from the great warrior."

"Why're you coming down on me?"

"I'm just disappointed in you, that's all. I never thought you'd let this thing beat you."

"What thing?"

"The war. The military mind-bender. Oh, you laugh at it sometimes, but the truth is you've let it completely take you over."

Chaplain Stewart held services for the dead that night. To Wilfred, it was too soon: say the words quick, get rid of them, and forget them. But the souls were beginning to pile up. Stewart is getting behind in his work. If he doesn't get started soon, another shipment will arrive and he might never catch up.

The group was quiet and much larger than usual. Over half the company was there, even Captain Simms. Wilfred was afraid they made too good a target. One mortar round and they all might buy it. They sat on the grass facing the standing priest. Tonight he had donned a long black robe, which fluttered in the breeze and clung to his legs.

Wilfred looked past Stewart toward the sea and saw thick black clouds rolling in. The sun over the mountains was reaching back to expose every shape, desperately warning those it was leaving behind. He scanned the crowd and picked out Reckert and Lorde but couldn't find Newcombe. Absent without leave.

Stewart began: "John says, 'By grace are ye saved through faith.'"

They'll get him. They'll bring him back, court martial him, and lock him up. The army won't let him get away with it.

"All we have to do is believe and we will be rewarded with eternal life, no matter how many villages we burn or mothers and babies we murder. We can sin all we like."

The congregation began to fidget. What's he leading to? He sounds angry.

"Can this be true? I think not. James tells us, 'Faith without works is dead.' And John says, 'He that loveth not, knoweth not God; for God is love.' Put another way, if you don't love, you don't really believe in God."

Love. How novel.

"Jesus says, 'If ye forgive not men their trespasses, neither will your Father forgive your trespasses.' So don't depend too heavily on faith if you want to get to heaven. Your actions are important too.

Shit.

"We must obey God's laws. What are they? One says 'Love your enemies, bless them that curse you, do good to them that hate you, and pray for them which despitefully use you and persecute you.' Another is in our Lord's prayer. 'Forgive us our trespasses, as we forgive them that trespass against us.' Here and now, that means we must love the VC and the NVA, forgive them, and not kill them."

Not kill them?

"If that's not clear, look at the law God gave Moses. It's strange. Radical. It's this: 'Thou shalt not kill.' Plain and simple. The law is not diluted with exceptions. It doesn't say, 'Thou shalt not kill anyone except your enemies or except the enemies of your country or except in revenge or except in self defense or by some negligent accident or as a means to some glorious end like stopping communism or winning democracy. It says, 'Thou shalt not kill'—anyone, anywhere, for any reason."

Wilfred couldn't believe what he was hearing. Telling soldiers not to kill!

"That's it, boys. That's Christianity. It's not practical or realistic. If you want to get to heaven and avoid eternal punishment, you better tell the Army and that Godless country of yours to stick it. I'm not at all sure your dead friends are with God. They were disobeying the law of Love, and I don't have much hope for them, or for you either, for that matter."

Simms was on his feet. "That's about enough!"

"It is said there are no foxhole atheists. But I say to you the opposite, there are no foxhole Christians. Throw down your weapons before it is too late and beg for forgiveness—"

"Stupid idiot!" cried a corporal.

"You," Stewart yelled, pointing at the soldier. "Man!" he bellowed, sweeping his finger over the crowd. "If you're so smart, why can't you stop your God damned killing? You can't do it, can you? You're too feeble-minded, aren't you?"

Wilfred heard the other men growling. He felt the wind press harder, heard it howling through the palm trees, and watched it rip poncho tents from their stakes, sending one high into the air. He saw it blow the sun over the mountains, and he was afraid. The cloudbank was nearly upon them, looking like a giant mass of phlegm.

Simms turned to the group and said, "This service is over. You're all dismissed." They began walking away. Wilfred heard one shout, "Communist!"

The deluge pounced on them. Wilfred ran to his hooch and arrived just before Welbourne. It was gone. They stood together and surrendered to the downpour.

Through the dark torrent, Wilfred thought he could see Stewart kneeling, arms raised toward the sky, and went to him. "You all right, sir?" he shouted through the drum roll of rain.

"No."

"What's wrong?" Wilfred asked, squatting and bringing his face close to Stewart's.

"What, in the name of God, am I doing here? Comforting men so they have strength to kill again? Promising them eternal life if they get killed? I'm as guilty as Simms. Worse. I do it in the name of God."

Someone came up now, his shiny green skin rippling in the wind, head tucked anonymously into his hood. Close up, Wilfred recognized him. It was O'Shaunnessey, bringing them spare ponchos. "Here, sir. You need to put this on. Here's one for you, too, Lieutenant."

It rained hard for most of the night, but quit before dawn. The weary men rose, shivering with wet, regarding the sun as an insensitive intruder that was prying into their gloom and demanding their return to normalcy. Gradually they yielded to habit: the day must proceed, and life, go on. But their heads throbbed with residual grief and guilt and anger.

Wilfred shunned his cologne. The thought of its sweetness seemed repulsive and inappropriate.

He was worried about Stewart and wanted to talk to O'Shaunnessey about him. He found the sergeant, bent at the waist, filling his sleeping hole with mud. "Morning."

"Good morning, sir," O'Shaunnessey answered brightly.

"You seem chipper. Did you get much sleep?"

"Oh, a little. I think I was a good bit drier than you, though. What's up?"

"I was just wondering what you thought about the chaplain last night. He didn't look too good. What do you think we can do to help him?"

O'Shaunnessey paused at his work and looked at Wilfred. "If you ask me, sir, I think he's got battle fatigue. He's seen too many people get zapped."

"You mean you think he's going crazy?"

"I don't know if I'd use that word. But I don't think he can take too much more."

"What'll happen?"

"I don't know. Maybe he'll crack. He's only human."

"Well, last night he was talking like he isn't even sure there's a God. And he doesn't believe in this war anymore."

"Who does?"

"Humph. Well, we sure haven't been winning many hearts and minds lately, have we?"

O'Shaunnessey pointed with his head to a figure behind Wilfred's back. "He's comin' now."

Wilfred turned and saw Stewart. Then he heard a snap like a tiny firecracker. As he turned back, he saw O'Shaunnessey falling down, hitting the muddy ground, head bouncing, and blood spraying from a small red hole to the left of his nose.

"Sniper!" a distant voice sounded, and Wilfred sprawled next to O'Shaunnessey, put his hand over the hole, and looked into eyes. Inanimate. He saw blood soaking the grass beneath the sergeant's head, and he rolled the limp head to the side. A patch of hair was missing, the size of a silver dollar. A strange gray and white substance bulged out, and a finger-sized stream of brownish-red fluid poured from the stringy center. Wilfred covered this hole with his other hand, trying to make it disappear.

"Don't worry. You'll be all right. You'll make it." Then he yelled, "Medic!" He looked up at a shadow and saw Stewart kneeling down, his eyes crystals of ice.

"My God. O'Shaunnessey," Stewart said.

"He'll be all right," Wilfred assured him, his hands soaked with blood.

"He's dead."

"No. He's all right."

"They killed him," he said, and he lurched to the side and began vomiting.

Small arms fire erupted from Wilfred's sector.

Wilfred shook his head. "No. Not O'Shaunnessey." He looked again at the pale head and unfocused eyes and felt the warm liquid slipping through his fingers. He sat up, pulled the guilty hands away, looked at them with a shudder, held them up to see them better, and began to wail.

The medic arrived, closed the sergeant's eyes, and told Simms, "Better get him out of here." The medevac came. Blurred figures rolled the body onto a stretcher, and then he was gone.

Reckert sat down by Wilfred, put his arm around him, and said, "It's all right. Come on. Let's get you cleaned up." He poured water from his canteen into his steel pot and kneaded Wilfred's hands with a washcloth. "It's all right."

The supply bird came in, disrupting the grief with a rush of activity as the mermites were unloaded and the chow line set up. Reckert continued to kneel by Wilfred, and a small group clustered around Stewart.

The chaplain had spoken his last word. They asked him if he was all right. If he wanted to get up. If he wanted to eat. If he wanted anything to drink. If he wanted to go back on the supply chopper. If he needed anything. He only sat and stared. They told him it was time to go now. To please get up. He had to hurry. "Are you all right? Chaplain?" Two men tried to help him up. Four men carried him and strapped him in. Then he vanished like the others.

Reckert got Wilfred to drink some coffee. "He got my bullet, Robbie. If I hadn't turned to look at Stewart, I'd be dead. I'm the one who oughta be dead."

"It's too soon. You're not short yet."

Reckert led a march around a mountain because Newcombe had deserted and Wilfred was sick. Nothing happened except that Welbourne was jolted in the back, and his radio quit working.

Wilfred spent the day seeing ghosts—bloody sandbags, the stack of body bags, Louis King, the wounded woman, Newcombe, the holes in O'Shaunnessey's head, the procession of litters, the dancer, performing in the light of Wilfred's gun. Bodies were piling up all around him now, surreptitiously crawling up and dying. A human trash-dump. Bulldozers heaping them, until he was buried in them. And who would be next? Matfield? Welbourne? Rodriguez? Henry? Reckert? Who?

Words darted through the bodies like rats. Stewart reciting the law: "Thou shalt not kill." O'Shaunnessey asking: "Who does?" believe in the war. Felicity begging: "Please!!! Don't kill anyone." Henry announcing: "I'm done with killing." Can ordering: "Wilfed no kill Vietnamese." Reckert censuring: "You let it take you over." He kept asking, why did Stewart come up just then? Why did O'Shaunnessy nod? Why did I turn? Why him instead of me? He got my bullet. It should have been me. He thought of O'Shaunnessey's wife and son. Newcombe's wife. And King's. And all the others, lost and angry, weeping into rectangular holes.

He thought of freedom and democracy and heard the machine-gun clatter of falling dominoes hitting each other, knocking the next to the tabletop. Then he remembered Robert Kennedy's comment: "We're killing innocent people because the communists are 12,000 miles away, and they might get 11,000 miles away." How could that justify the killing?

At dinner it seemed like people were shying away from him. Then he remembered that O'Shaunnessey and Welbourne had been standing next to him when they were hit. As he examined the dent in his helmet he wondered, can someone really be taking pot shots at me, me in particular?

That night in his hooch the clamor of voices grew higher, and the images of death lashed him relentlessly. He saw artillery rounds disintegrating the village like specks of black falling on cities of children in roaring, exploding storms of fire, pushed out of bomb bays in endless chains by rational men, packs of animals, warring tribes. The Vietnamese woman stared at him. Henry stood by with sullen force while Reckert chided, Stewart preached, and Felicity and Can begged for mercy. Then the leaking face of O'Shaunnessey appeared and grew larger and larger, filling his screen. The holes became hydrants, and his blood gushed out of them with terrible force, flooding the earth, gathering around Wilfred's feet, bubbling and boiling, rising to his knees, his waist, his chest, his—

"Noooo!" he screamed, and he sat up sweating, shaking, and panting. He turned and reached, fumbled blindly in his pack, pulled out his cologne, tore back the netting, slithered out of the poncho tent, leaped up, ran away, and sent the bottle hurtling into the sky over the camp.

PART III

▼

THE PEACE

If you want to change reality, you've got to change the illusion of reality.

—W. B. Carmenghetti

CHAPTER 21

▼

SIMMS AND TRINH

"Incoming!" Simms bellowed, smashing the crystalline silence of night. Soldiers in foxholes slipped to their knees, steel pots returned home, frightened lips formed supplications. Then began the eerie, loathing wait for death and disaster.

Wilfred scrambled back into his sleeping hole. Fucked by the fickle finger of fate. The instant I get out, we come under attack. He lay with the others in dread until it occurred to him that he was the aggressor. Then he rolled in laughter, crawled back out of the hooch, and walked crisply to Reckert's tent.

"Hey, Reckert. You awake?"

"What do you think? First screams and hollering, and now you. Did we really have incoming? I heard Simms shout, but I didn't hear any explosions."

"I threw away my cologne. I pitched it as far as I could. It must've hit him or near him and scared him."

Reckert snickered. "Why did you throw it away?"

"I decided I want to smell war the way it is. It stinks, Robbie. I stink. You stink. We all stink."

"Thanks a lot."

"There's no point deluding ourselves any longer. This is a war, not a police action, and Johnson didn't start it because five little North Vietnamese PT boats in the Tonkin Gulf attacked one of our destroyers with two torpedoes that missed by football fields."

"Not exactly Pearl Harbor, was it? But why did he want to go to war? To teach the savages a lesson?"

"Another delusion. There are so many. We're not helping the Vietnamese. We're punishing them. We're not fighting communists, we're fighting nationalists, and they all want the foreigners out. And the war won't be over in a couple more years. And the kill ratios don't prove we're winning."

"Well, at least war stimulates the economy back home."

"The hell if it does. Deficit spending does, but we could stimulate the economy just as well by building things that last instead of by taking them out and blowing them up."

"So war sucks. Is that what you woke me up to tell me?"

"No. I wanted to tell you I've decided we've got to stop the killing."

"Great. And how are we going to do that? Lose and go home?"

"The United States has never lost a war."

"Quit and go home?"

"Americans are not quitters."

"Destroy everything and kill everyone and then go home?"

"We have to stop the killing."

"So what do we do?"

"We have to pretend to win and go home."

"I thought you threw away your cologne."

"Reckert. If good is to survive, it has to be sneakier than the devil."

Wilfred went back to his hooch, tore it down, picked up his entrenching tool, and departed the perimeter. As he cleared his bowels into a little slit in the ground, he looked across the paddies and noticed an old farmer similarly occupied, squatting on a dike. Wilfred felt a sudden affinity for the old man. I'm no shit-burner, he told the man in his mind. From now on, I'm for you, old man. No more killing. Wilfred felt proud.

He stood up and as he bent over to pull up his pants a crack sounded over his head. "Fuck!" he yelled, diving to the ground. Across the paddies he saw the old farmer running away, rifle in hand. He returned to his hooch, steaming. That's no way to treat someone who loves you.

He dropped by to see Henry. "I'm gonna talk to the captain now and tell him what you said."

"You ain't done it yet?"

"I'm doin' it now," he said, looking Henry in the eye. "I want you to stand here, hold your shotgun at the ready, and look my way while I'm doin' it."

"Whatever you say."

"Captain Simms, I want to talk to you."

"Whadyou want?"

"You see that man over there, Captain?"

"Who, Henry?"

"Yep."

"What about him?"

"He's getting ready to blow your head off if you don't listen to what I say."

"What?"

"You heard me. He doesn't like the way you've been running the company, and neither do I. We're tired of you letting people get zapped and killing innocent civilians."

"I told you. That was an accident."

Simms turned and began to walk away. "Captain, I mean it. He'll kill you. There are others too."

Simms turned back. "Who?"

"The 'who' isn't important. But if you want to live, you better hear me out."

"Are you threatening me, Lieutenant?"

"I'll make it perfectly clear for you, so there can be no misunderstanding. Yes sir, I'm threatening to kill you and put us out of your misery. You and I are going to make a little deal. The first part is that I'm taking over the company."

"Mutiny!" he shouted, louder than Wilfred liked.

"That's right. In exchange for your command, you get the following. First, you get my silence on this thing. Second, I will allow you and your mother and father to live."

"You slimy gangster creep. You won't get away with this!"

"Shut up. You think that bottle of cologne this morning was an accident? It wasn't. You would be very wise to consider it a grenade that didn't go off. Now, I'm gonna sweeten the deal. The third thing you get is the best kill ratio in the division."

"How're you gonna deliver that?"

"Don't worry. I will. Fourth, you get your silver star."

Simms was flooded with gratitude. "You'd do that for me?"

"It's part of the deal. But you mustn't renege on your part. That would be extremely unhealthy for your mother." Simms grew quiet again. "Well?" Wilfred said, looking over his shoulder at the black rock, Henry. "Do we have a deal?"

"I guess I don't have a choice."

"Right. Now what are we doing today?"

"We hump four clicks and cordon and search a village. I call in a gunship to zap anyone that runs."

"O.K. I'm gonna make one change. When we get near the village, we're gonna stop and bring in artillery between us and the village for ten minutes, just like we prep our LZs."

"If we do that, all the VC'll get away."

"Yep. Just like when we prep our LZs."

"You've gone over to the other side, haven't you?"

"Nope. I just want to stop the killing."

"Well, tell me this. How will I get the colonel to go along with prepping our departure point? That's ridiculous."

"You don't tell him that. Tell him we're under attack."

"I don't think I'm gonna like this."

"I promise you, you'll like the alternative less."

Wilfred told Henry about the conversation, and the point man laughed out loud for the first time in weeks. "You jive."

"It's all true. Are you with me?"

"Sure thing."

"Good. I need a little muscle on my side. How about taking point for me again. Sure would make things easier."

"O.K., man, but don't expect me to kill no one."

"It's against the new rules, Henry."

"Now let me get this straight," Reckert said later. "You're going to put out a contract on his mother in order to stop the killing. That's unique. And you're going to improve our kill ratio by not killing. Are you sure you're all there?"

"Never fear. That's the beauty of ratios, man. If no G.I.'s die, you reduce the denominator to zero and the value of the fraction goes to infinity."

"Only if you kill at least one VC. Who gets sacrificed?"

"Maybe no one. Maybe not even one."

The company moved out with Henry in the lead. That was about all that was normal. Wilfred replaced Welbourne with a new RTO, himself, so he could keep up with everything on the air, and took second place in the column, right behind Henry, since lieutenants almost never get that close to the front.

When they neared the departure point where the platoons would split off to surround the village, Wilfred turned and started firing into the air over his own platoon while Henry began blasting away with his shotgun in the other direction. Then he took the handset and pressed the button. "Six, this is Two-Six. We're under attack by some Charlies in a hedgerow. We're pinned down and returning fire. Bring in the artillery. I'll direct."

It was the first time Wilfred had directed artillery in combat, and he found the experience exhilarating. By any standard, he did a professional job. He walked the rounds into the hedgerow and completely demolished it. In ten minutes, when the battle was over, not one VC was alive—or dead.

He leisurely inspected the hedge, called in a report of "Negative casualties: the bastards got away," and proceeded with the cordon. When the village was secure, he was confident that any VC who'd been in the village before the barrage had escaped, so he was disappointed when Reckert's men pulled two strong, young, sullen men from a concealed hole in the floor of a hut and two rifles from a dung heap.

Hearing Reckert report his find to Simms, Wilfred immediately called the captain, using Reckert's call sign: "Six, this is Three-Six. Over." Reckert was amazed to hear himself talking when he was pretty sure he wasn't.

"This is Six," Wilfred said. "Over."

"This is Three-Six. That's a negative on the weapons. The report was erroneous. We have no weapons. Over."

Simms decided to speak. "But—"

Wilfred pressed the transmit button, and the static overrode much of Simms's transmission. When Wilfred released the button, Simms was saying, "Over."

"Six. This is Three-Six. You heard me. No weapons. Out."

Reckert took the two VC to the interrogation point along with several dozen other villagers. Wilfred joined him there and asked if he had the rifles. "Yeah. I wrapped them in a poncho. "One of my men has them."

"Great. They're indisputable evidence that a dead man's a VC. We need as many as we can get. We can get at least two confirmed body counts for each weapon. Hell, Simms and Clary got fifteen KIA's with only six weapons at Quin Loc. But those rifles sure won't get us any points here. No bodies. And we sure don't need to prove those two are VC. You can just look at them and tell. And they were down in that hole, hiding. No, we've got to save those guns till we get some bodies."

"But where'll we get bodies?"

"There are bodies all over Nam. Be patient."

Simms arrived. "What did you tell Clary?" Wilfred asked.

"Just that we had two VC suspects."

"Good for you."

"I don't see how all this is gonna help our kill ratio. It would have been smarter to zap those two."

"There ain't gonna be any zappin' unless I say so, Simms. Understood? You'll get your kill ratio. I'll see to that."

Wilfred returned to Reckert where Trinh was questioning the VC. They watched for a while, and then the VC got up and left.

"Wait a minute," Simms yelled to Trinh, and he, Reckert, and Wilfred hustled over to the Kit Carson.

"Yes?" Trinh said.

"Those men you let go are VC," Simms said.

"No VC. Farmers. Numbah one. Like Amelicans vely much."

"Did they look like VC to you?" Simms asked Reckert.

"I don't know, sir."

"But didn't you find them hidden in a fucking hole?"

"They sleep in hole. Ground much cooler."

"Now wait a minute," Simms said. "Farmers work during the day and do their sleeping at night."

"They take baby buffalo last night. Vely hard work. Men vely tired."

"I believe him," Wilfred said to Reckert. "Do you?"

"Sure do. They look like farmers to me."

"You see?" Trinh said to Simms. "Farmers."

"Farmers," Reckert said.

"Remember your mother," Wilfred said. Simms stomped off.

"Thank you," Trinh said to Wilfred. "They farmers."

"If they were farmers, my mother is Ho Chi Minh. They are VC, and now it's nice to know that you are VC."

"Oh, no sir. I no VC. Not me."

"The fuck you aren't, Charlie. From now on, you will do exactly what I tell you, or you're gonna have a little accident." He inserted the barrel in Trinh's ear. "Got that?"

"Yes, yes. I do you say."

"Good. Come on, Robbie. Let's go."

As they walked away, they noticed that Simms had watched and listened in bewilderment. But having heard Wilfred's shouts, the edge was off his temper. Trinh was exposed.

"Make sure Trinh stays with us," Wilfred said to the captain. "He'll be useful."

"R-roger," Simms said. "He's VC, the sonofabitch."

The next morning Wilfred discussed the day's operation with Simms. They were to walk six kilometers and cordon a village near a big lake. Wilfred said, "I have a revolutionary tactical strategy. I want first platoon to take positions from 9 to 12 o'clock on the perimeter, third platoon, from 12 to 3, and fourth platoon, 3 to 5. My platoon'll do the search."

"But that leaves from 5 to 9 open."

"That's what's so revolutionary. It will take two thirds as much time to get into position. Now that's quick: a thirty-three percent improvement in our performance. The brass will be ecstatic, and boy will Charlie be surprised."

"He'll slip out between 9 and 5."

"That's O.K. It's a 9 to 5 war, anyway."

He discussed his plans with Rodriguez and Matfield. "We're gonna stop the killing. Can I count on you two?"

"Sure," Rodriguez said. "We was going to come talk to you again. Too many people die. We're getting a little short now, and we'd like very much to make it to the world alive."

"That's what it's all about, men. See if you can get some others to join us. But make damned sure they have tight lips."

The cordon and search was uneventful. As Wilfred expected, the encirclement went faster than usual, especially since the platoons didn't have to waste time finding each other. No VC were found in the village, just an old man who had been killed the previous night by a chopper. The pilot was heading home on a supply run, saw the figure standing alone in the middle of a paddy relieving himself, and zoomed in to investigate. Surprised at the sound of approaching blades, the old man was felled by a heart attack. An old woman poured out the story as Wilfred gazed at the body and listened to Trinh explain. "Tell the woman I must borrow the body, but will bring it back." Trinh's eyes widened, but he did as he was told.

Henry and Rodriguez took the body out while Trinh restrained the screaming woman. They carried it to the northern end of the village and placed its stiff form on its back in some bushes. Reckert's platoon brought Wilfred one of the rifles, and he laid it beside the body. Then he fired a few bursts into the air and called Simms. "Six, this is Two-Six. We got a VC KIA here. Call it in."

Charlie Charlie was on the ground in five minutes. Simms met Clary, and Henry walked them to the body.

"That's the oldest Charlie I've ever seen," Clary said. "You never know, by God." Then he looked a little harder and said, "Sure did get stiff quick. Now that's peculiar."

Wilfred jumped into the breach. "That's the way it is with old people, sir. They're kind of stiff to start with."

"Hmm. I didn't think of that."

"Rifle fire sounded from the opposite end of the village followed by an explosion.

"What's that?" Clary asked.

"Six. This is Three-Six," Reckert called. "Got another one, sir. KIA. He tried to frag us. Over."

"We're on our way," Simms said. "Out."

Matfield led Clary and Simms on a tortuous journey through the village. At one point Clary said to the sergeant, "Haven't we been here before?"

"Nope," was all that Matfield said.

Meanwhile, Henry, Wilfred, and Rodriguez were running the body to Reckert. "He was suspicious," Wilfred said.

"Yeah," Henry said. "What if he recognizes the body?"

"I don't know. We gotta change it somehow."

When they got to Reckert, they found him alone except for a young boy who was practicing a little begging on the lieutenant.

"Reckert, Henry," Wilfred said. "Put the boy's shirt and shorts on the old man. And put the body face down." They pulled off the boy's clothes and sent him howling to his mother. The old man was so gaunt that the clothes fit perfectly.

Wilfred noticed a swayback pig in a nearby yard. "Sorry, people. It's pork chops for dinner tonight." He shot the beast dead with one round, and he and Rodriguez carried it back and laid it on the body.

Wilfred asked Rodriguez, "Got a knife?"

"What are you going to do?" Reckert asked.

"Clary is suspicious. We gotta freshen up the corpse."

Rodriguez pulled a switchblade from his pocket and snapped it open. "Those things ain't legal, Sarge. Against Army regs."

"You want it or not?"

"I want it. Slice open its belly. Gotta get the blood on the body." Rodriguez obliged, and they held the dripping carcass over the old man. The red glistened in the sun.

"What if the colonel turns the body over?"

Wilfred puzzled a second. "I got it. Put the pig down for a minute and gimme your knife." Wilfred slit the pig, reached inside its belly, pulled out the intestines, cut them off at the ends, and stuffed them under the old man's belly. "There.

Clary won't give him a second glance now." They tossed the beast into some bushes and left Reckert with the body.

Simms, Clary, and Matfield arrived two minutes later, and as Wilfred predicted, gave the remains one fleeting glance. Reckert delivered the epitaph: "When we shot him, he couldn't get rid of the grenade. Blew his whole belly open."

"Carry on," Clary said with a quick about face.

"That's what we're doing," Reckert told Wilfred. "Carrying on."

Reckert and his men cleaned up the body meticulously and then redressed it in its original garb. It wasn't easy. The man refused to bend his arms.

After Clary left, Wilfred and Reckert returned the corpse to its rightful owner. She had a wild look in her eye. "Dinky dau num ten G.I."

CHAPTER 22

▼

MATFIELD AND SIMMS

They sat in the twilight watching wisps of fog rising from the glassy lake. "It's becoming clearer to me now, Robbie. What we need to create is the functional equivalent of war: everything except the killing."

"You mean the illusion of war."

"Yes," Wilfred said, astounded at Reckert's clarity. "But I'm not sure I should've used that old man's body. The look in that woman's eyes. I don't think I could do that again."

"You'll think of something else. There are bodies all over Nam. That's what someone told me, anyway."

"It's not the bodies that worry me. It's the guns. Where will we get enough of them?"

That night Can came to Wilfred in his sleep. She snuggled up and forgave him. "Wilfed love Vietnamese. Wilfed no kill Vietnamese. Wilfed numbah one. Can love Wilfed." He felt her hands caress him and then slip off her pajama bottoms and unbutton her top until her warm breasts pressed against him. Then her hands unbuckled his belt and pants, reached inside, and gripped his penis. On top of him now, she guided him into her, and he felt the rising and falling and heard the sweet smack of flesh on flesh. He wanted to be closer, and he thrust upward and gave her all that he could—in and out, up and down, the dance of the gods. As he rolled over on top of her, the beat grew stronger and louder and more insistent, demanding, obligatory, imperious, and virulent until he could no longer withstand it and his mind succumbed in toto and let his body have its way. It grabbed and held and crushed and shouted, "Oh…oh…oooooooooh!"

"Sir. Sir! Really, sir! I-I…Will you please get off of me, sir. Please!" Wilfred was all over Welbourne. He awoke embarrassed and wet and cursing the war that made him sleep with men, squeezed together in a hole under a net and rubberized canvas, and he vowed that as long as he was changing other aspects of the war, he would change this too.

"Robbie! Robbie! I figured it out," Wilfred cried. The sun was flooding the plain, and Reckert had toothbrush in foaming mouth and canteen cup in hand.

"Bwoo?" Reckert asked, lips closed to hold in the froth.

"I couldn't sleep last night, and I lay awake and figured out why we have to have a war every ten or twenty years."

Reckert spat onto the ground. "Why?"

"Two reasons. First, so we don't have to fight a war without veterans. Can you imagine fighting without veterans?" He held an imaginary microphone to his mouth. "'This is Daniel Dud at the Pentagon. I'm talking to General Malaise. Sir, can you beat the Russians?' 'Gee, ah don't know. Ah've never fought anyone before, and neither has anyone else in the armed forces. We haven't had a war in fifty years, you know.'"

"'Don't you think that's a little…dicey?'"

"'Oh, ah don't know. Ah'm sure we can beat 'em at war games and maneuvers. Ah always beats the Red Team at them.'"

"'Good, sir. We'll all sleep better knowing that.'"

"I get it. We have to fight a war every ten years or we won't know if our personnel are good enough to win. What's the other reason?"

"Back to Daniel Dud. 'I'm talking with Howard Lose, CEO of General Munitions and Armaments Corpse. Mr. Lose, sir. Can your new F3001 fighter beat the Ruskies' new MIG 2973?'"

"'I've got to hand it to you, Dud. You really know how to ask the hard ones. The truth is, I don't know. They've never been in a dogfight before. All I can say is that the F3001 exceeds all possible specifications. It's even blown away our new MEF2538, the most advanced mock enemy fighter we've ever developed.' 'Thank you, sir. That's comforting. This is Daniel Dud, returning you now to ABM Central.'"

"So the only foolproof way we can test our weapons systems is to use them in a real war. Everything else is conjecture."

"That's it, Robbie. For reasons of personnel and ordnance, war is essential to our national security. The only way we can be sure we can keep the peace is to remain at war."

"A sobering thought, Will. But we need a better war than this one if its going to do the job. We can't test nukes or gas or chemicals or missiles or anything good in this dumb war."

"We need to attack Russia real bad, Robbie."

"You bet. And here I thought we had wars to win Presidential re-election campaigns."

"To have streams we can't change horses in the middle of?"

The company cordoned yet another village this day. The operation was a replica of the day before except that Wilfred couldn't find a body. Undeterred, he went to Trinh who was sitting with detainees at another interrogation point.

"Hey, Charlie," he said. "Come here."

Trinh reluctantly complied.

"Today you die twice." Trinh shuddered. "But not for long,"

It was an easier operation than the day before, since Trinh was self-mobile and Wilfred had the foresight to steal the gallon can of ketchup from the mess line the night before.

"Hey! Where's the ketchup?" growled the soldier, his franks nestled in their buns like fresh bodies in caskets.

Wilfred and Henry led Trinh and two old Vietnamese men wearing shorts and shirts to a secluded part of the village, ordered them to disrobe, fired a burst into their shirts, and soddened them with ketchup. He dressed Trinh in one shirt, ordered him onto his belly, hid the amazed old men, and called in Captain Simms and Colonel Clary.

"Now this one looks more like a Charlie," Clary said as he kicked Trinh in the ribs. Trinh quaked, let out a grunt, and stiffened in pain. "He's not dead!"

"I can assure you he is quite dead, sir," Wilfred said. "Haven't you ever seen a chicken run around with his head chopped off. It's the same sort of thing. Involuntary reflexes."

"Every time I come to this company, I learn more about bodies," Clary marveled.

Shots rang out again and this time Henry led Simms and Clary through a maze. Wilfred ordered Trinh up and ran him to Reckert, the Kit Carson clutching his bruised ribs all the way. Wilfred dressed him in the other clothes, had him lie on his back, laid the rifle beside him, poured ketchup on his wounds and instructed him on how to stare away with his mouth open.

"Move a muscle and you're a dead man," he said in encouragement.

Clary and Simms arrived, and Clary commented on the amazing resemblance between the dead VC and the company's interrogator.

"Sir. I'm surprised at you," Wilfred said. "I mean I would expect a racial bigot to see similarities between Vietnamese that don't exist. But not you. You can see the differences, can't you? Surely. I mean they don't really look anything alike. Trinh is much taller—" Wilfred noticed a fly land on Trinh's cheek and begin marching toward his open mouth. "Get down!" he shouted and dove to the ground and fired six rounds into a nearby bush. Reckert and Henry also began firing, the captain and colonel hitting the turf a second later.

"Did you see that?" Wilfred asked Reckert.

"Those pith helmets in the bushes? I sure did."

"They's still in there, sir," Henry said.

Simms wasn't sure if it was a hoax or not, but Clary was shaken. It had been more than a decade since he'd seen combat.

"Captain Simms. You better get Colonel Clary out of here. We'll clear the area. There's no sense you risking your life along with ours. You're too important, sir."

Reckert and Henry opened up while Wilfred crawled forward almost as quickly as the two senior officers crawled backward.

Wilfred tossed two grenades for effect and when he was sure Clary was gone, said, "O.K. Get Trinh dressed. On the double!"

By the time Clary reached the interrogation area, Trinh was sitting, in full uniform, sweat dripping from his brow, talking to a prisoner, the faint taste of fly flesh bitter in his mouth.

"Oooh, that was close," Wilfred said to Reckert that night.

"I almost died when I saw that fly land."

"Clary might have died if he'd seen Trinh come to life."

"And we'd have been next."

"Yep. Well. Our score's improving," Wilfred said proudly. "That's four-zip now."

"That's not bad, but you're really gonna have to make a killing if you want to be best in the division."

"I know," Wilfred said, raising his canteen cup full of coffee to his lips. Then the cup was in the air, a finger-size stream of black gushing from each side. Wilfred hit the ground before the cup did, and this time the perimeter opened up.

"Thunks" of grenade launchers sounded followed by distant explosions, all amid the steady "chug-chug" of a machine gun and random splatters of rifle fire. By then, however, Colonel Dai was well along his escape route, crawling behind a dike, through bamboo and high grass, down a stream bank, and away.

"The rat," Reckert said.

"It was nearly four to one," Wilfred said.

The next few days were discouraging. "We don't have any weapons. How can we get any kills if we don't have any weapons?"

Their frustration peaked the day they found the three old fishermen who had drowned in the lake during a sudden storm and washed up bloated onto the shore.

"Three perfectly good bodies," Wilfred wailed. "And we can't even use them."

"Hey, man," Henry said. "You couldn't pass them off as no Charlies. They're all puffed up."

"Man, all you have to do is poke holes in 'em to let out the gas and cover 'em with blood. They'd be great!"

"Sheeit. They'd fall to pieces before you even got 'em where you wanted 'em."

"That's better yet. The worse they look, the less chance Clary'll look at 'em."

Wilfred began pressing his men to search the villages more carefully and promised a three-day trip to Vassar to any man who found a weapon. The new bonus system paid off at a fishing village on the South China Sea. The cluster of huts clung to a finger of sand three miles long with the sea on one side and a bay on the other. A Company marched toward the objective between dunes twelve feet high covered with waving grass.

He decided that the company was moving too secretively, so he paused for a bit of target practice at some Vietcong mirages, enlisting the aid of a large portion of his platoon. He would have been pleased had he seen the result: five enemy soldiers racing toward a sampan on the other side of the village, pushing off the sand into the surf, leaping over the side, sculling madly, and raising the sail.

When the company reached the village, the men quickly executed their nine to five cordon, and Wilfred's platoon went in for the search. They were unusually thorough—tapping, thumping, jabbing, sweeping away the sand, touching, looking.

While searching the hut of a young, tough-looking mother, Sergeant Matfield made a discovery—a glint of defiance in her eyes. He turned the two-room house upside down, personally tapping every square inch of floor, moving the furniture and a large crock full of rice. He thrust his bayonette into the walls in a hundred places, but found nothing. Still, he remembered the woman's eyes, and he looked around again. Then, from inside, he noticed that the rear wall, where it met the slope of the roof, was more than a foot higher than the front wall. He walked behind the house and saw what he had expected to see: outside, the front and back walls were the same height. Double wall, he concluded, feeling stupid to have nearly missed it. Back inside, he pulled two beds away from the high wall, drew his machete and chopped a hole in it. There it was: a cavity between the walls, a foot and a half deep. He called for his men and shined a flashlight inside.

In his peripheral vision, he noticed that the woman was edging toward the door. "Grab her," he said. "She goes first."

They brought her to the hole, struggling and shaking, and Matfield pointed at it and pushed her toward it. She resisted and began crying and talking rapidly in Vietnamese.

Wilfred came in first, smiling. "Good going, Sarge." He went to the hole, but Matfield blocked it with his arm.

"Hold on," he said. "I figger it's booby-trapped." Wilfred stopped short and stepped back. "The woman wouldn't go in. Get Trinh to tell us what she says."

Trinh came and Wilfred told him, "We want in. Ask her how to get in. Ask her where the booby traps are. Oh, and Trinh. If one of us dies, you die."

Trinh questioned the woman. She showed him a place where the side of the wall could be lifted out. She said it was booby-trapped, but she didn't know how because she didn't do it. "Ask her if there's anyone in there," Wilfred told Trinh. He did so and told Wilfred there were none. "O.K. Let's clear everybody out and frag the hell out of it."

They threw in eight grenades, one at a time. On the second try, they heard two explosions. The other grenades blew apart much of the thatch, but caused no secondary blasts.

Matfield and his squad went back in, removed the rest of the wall and found a stack of ammunition cases in the corner.

"Eureka!" Wilfred said. "We have found it."

Henry came in and disarmed another booby trap from one of the boxes, and they brought them out and looked inside. There were fifty-eight rifles, two machine guns, three pistols, ammunition, twenty-five sets of NVA uniforms, a mortar, radio, and several inches of documents. Wilfred had Matfield's troops hide the rifles, pistols and uniforms, then called for Charlie Charlie. Clary flew in and viewed the cache with mixed feelings. "No small arms," he said. "Strange."

When Simms began a sparkling rendition of how he, the captain, had led the operation, Wilfred cut him off.

"Let me tell it, sir," he said, and as Simms cringed and Clary waited in sadistic good humor for Wilfred to reduce the captain to the sniveling coward he was, Wilfred proceeded to describe how Simms had personally discovered the double wall and disconnected four other booby traps. "We'll write up the request for his Distinguished Service Cross tonight. There's no telling how many lives he's saved by his courageous action in capturing these munitions." He turned and whipped a salute on Simms. "Sir. I want you to know how proud I am to have had the privilege of serving in your command. Congratulations, sir."

"Thank you, Lieutenant," Simms said, returning the gesture with the total sobriety the occasion deserved.

Clary's eyes were popping. "C-congratulations, Captain Simms," he managed to utter. "Ou-outstanding!"

That night a band of thugs led by Henry, Matfield, and Rodriguez roamed the camp spreading the gospel, threatening potential snitches with horrible deaths, and getting every man's signature on the request for Simms's medal. Later that night Wilfred presented it to the ecstatic captain. "Just remember to keep your end of the deal. Don't forget your mother."

The next morning Matfield, who'd discovered the cache, left for Vassar—his reward for finding the weapons.

But Wilfred needed more than weapons.

CHAPTER 23

▼

HUNT, FIERDEN, AND MAUGHAM

Having relived his Vietnam experiences, Wilfred lay awake at LZ German making plans for the next day. He had all the weapons he needed, a bountiful harvest of bodies from fresh graves, and a plentiful supply of fresh blood, compliments of Reinholtz, the butcher. What's more, Frank Storp would be arriving in the field at 1000. Wilfred's plans made, he thought of sneaking off to see Can, but for once was just too tired. Dreaming of her, he fell asleep and awoke at 0500. At the shower tent was surprised to see a soldier he didn't know placing a drop of cologne beneath his nose.

He headed for the airfield and passed a new chapel on the way—beautiful, for ever, soaring skyward on Douglas Fir timbers from Oregon. From a hillock, he surveyed the entire base. A transformation was taking place. Permanent structures were rising everywhere, almost as he watched—wooden barracks, tin roofs, other chapels, clubs. We'll be here a long time. Thank you, most generous American taxpayer.

He hopped a ride to the field with the morning chow, and as he jumped to the ground in the roar of the rotor, his steel pot fell off. Bending over to pick it up, he discovered a new rip in the camouflage cover and a fresh dent in the steel. Laughing bitterly he lunged for the earth one more time. "God damn, it's good to be back!"

Fifty-five poncho litters carried the reeking human carrion to a new battlefield two kilometers away. The second ox followed the procession obediently, tethered and led by the company butcher. When they arrived, Wilfred set out his pieces in a new array. This time, for added realism, he dressed his platoon in NVA uniforms and had them join the enemy force.

Frank Storp and Lew Lance arrived promptly at 1000 hours, and Wilfred greeted them as they disembarked.

"Where did you ever dig up fifty-five bodies?"

"Back there two clicks."

"You actually dug them up?"

"Yep. Wait'll you see 'em. They're starting to rot."

"Great. That's what they like. But we need some dead grunts too."

"No problem," Wilfred said.

The two men collaborated on a storyline and the shooting commenced with Lance shooting both Storp and the firefight, and the A Company personnel shooting the breeze over each other's heads. Wilfred gave Lance some battle-hardened expressions as he crawled through the grass toward the enemy. Reckert offered him stark fear and unmanly tears. Rodriguez lay on his back with ox guts spilling from his belly. Henry caught a bullet in the chest as he angrily charged a machine-gun nest and nearly did a back flip for the camera.

When it was over, Lance walked through the enemy lines zooming in on torn limbs, bloody chests, visages frozen in terror, and a few decapitated heads. One event he neglected to record, however, was the amazing mass surrender—thirty NVA shouting "Chieu Hoi!" and "Hi, Mom" and laughing raucously as they came over to the American side and turned in their coats and pith helmets for jungle fatigues and steel pots.

The camera started rolling again when Clary arrived. "Some of these bodies are bloated."

"They're just a little fat, sir," Wilfred said.

"They're NVA, and the North Vietnamese don't feed their soldiers enough to get them fat."

"That's right, sir. They never have before. That's an excellent observation. You should include it in your report. The NVA soldiers appear to be better fed than in the past. The Pentagon will sure want to know about that."

"Now wait a minute. This one here is definitely bloated."

"Probably a gland problem, sir. They suffer gland problems too, you know."

"This one's got worms."

"From eating bad pork, no doubt. It's a common problem here. They don't burn their shit."

"But these are coming out of his cheek, not his ass."

"You're right, sir. That's the most advanced case of trichinosis I've ever seen. Amazing!"

"The worms are white. I—"

"God, yeah. They really look sick. But that's the way it is over here, sir. Even the diseases have diseases."

Clary was tired of talking. "Simms, what's the count today?"

"Fifty-five NVA KI—"

"Fifty-five! That's the same as yesterday."

"We were shocked by the coincidence too," Wilfred said.

"No friendly casualties, I suppose."

"Nope, but then casualties are never very friendly."

"How many weapons?"

"Three, sir," Simms said.

"Three? Three! You know, Simms. There's something funny going on out here." He stomped back to his Charlie Charlie as Wilfred turned off the mike and called to Lance who was hiding in a bush, "Did you get it?"

"Yeah, man, I got it. I got all of it."

"Great. I got a feelin' I'll need that tape soon."

Wilfred got word right after dinner when Simms called together the officers. The deck was getting shuffled. Clary had given Simms S-1 at battalion. Got him his medal and kill ratio too quick. I've still got 42 rifles!

"Who's taking over?" Reckert asked.

"Lieutenant Fierden," Simms said, hiding his glee. Oh, my, Wilfred thought, my very first choice. "There'll be a few other changes. Lieutenant Herbert Hunt will take Lieutenant Newcombe's platoon and Platoon Sergeant Maugham will go to yours, Carmenghetti. Last, but not least, Lieutenant Lorde, you—Lieutenant Lorde?" Lorde was in a fetal position, immersed in *Finnegans Wake*. "Lieutenant Lorde. Put down that book."

"Aw, let me finish it first, will you, sir? Please?"

Simms's mind stopped. "How close are you to the end?"

Lorde shook his head and said from far away, "There isn't any end. The end is the beginning."

Like war, Wilfred thought.

Simms gave up. "I quit. Fucking spaced-out hippie. Someone tell him, when he lands, that he's the new company Executive Officer. And Clary wants him to be the battalion poet and song-writer, too, to record our moment in history."

"XO," Wilfred said with the trace of a smile. "So if Fierden gets zapped, Lorde's the new company commander."

"Right," Simms said, and he laughed nervously.

"Who replaces Lorde in weapons?" Reckert asked.

"No one. The colonel said that if they've come this far without a lieutenant, they don't need one now."

"When does the change take place?" Wilfred asked.

"Tomorrow morning after chow."

After the briefing, Reckert spoke to Wilfred: "Fierden! He could really fuck things up. He's an idiot. Why do you suppose Clary picked him? He's not even a captain."

"Ah, but Fierden'll make a good snitch. I can just hear Clary: 'Listen, boys. There's something funny going on out at A Company, and I wanna know what. Find out and report back.'"

"What are you going to do, Will?"

"Prior planning prevents piss-poor performance."

Herbie Hunt was six foot eight, two hundred sixty pounds and strong, and wore a constant snarl on his face. Wilfred decided on sight not to call him Herbie. Herbie was said to have been first-string offensive tackle for N.J. State, and on a crucial play in the fourth quarter, told the coach to run it over him. But the coach ran it the other way, the ball carrier found no hole, and the game was lost. Afterwards Herbie punished the coach by breaking his jaw and kicking him in the groin. He was thrown off the squad as a result. But his devotion to winning was said to be highly regarded by Army recruiters. His training was abbreviated by nervous drill instructors, and he was rushed to the front to win the war.

"Big dude," Henry said to Wilfred as Herbie landed with a thud on the dry paddy grass.

"Maughamy" had beady black eyes and long, wide scars on both cheeks, the throat, and arms from a knife fight he had won in the Bronx as a boy. He was planning a second career as a mercenary when he reached his twenty-year retirement. Frequently he was observed sharpening his bayonet, bowie knife, and some say, his teeth, and was the quiet type, with no sense of humor.

Fierden was the same pimply old malefactor that Wilfred had known before, except that now he held the scepter of power. He greeted Wilfred with a vengeful smirk.

Colonel Clary was bursting with confidence as he followed the replacements to the company the next morning. The change of command ceremony was brief. It was against the rules to bunch everyone together in the field, since groups were too tempting targets, so only the officers were present. Clary had barely begun to speak when the merit of the dispersion precept was demonstrated by a bullet that whizzed past Wilfred's nose and split the air between the eyes of the colonel and Fierden.

"Sniper!" Wilfred shouted, and the officer elite scattered like bowling pins.

"Fierden gets Simms's job," Clary persisted, his cheek pressed to the ground, "Lorde gets Fierden's, Hunt gets Newcombe's, and Maugham gets O'Shaunnessey's. Let's get out of here, Simms. You too, Lorde." Thus ended the ceremony.

Wilfred put his arm on Simms's as he was getting up and whispered, "Remember, captain. Loose lips sink mothers."

"What are you going to do now?" Reckert asked. "Looks like a clear challenge to your authority. You seem to have most of the men behind you now, but they won't stick with you if you can't control those animals. And that won't be easy."

"Oh, Robbie. All I have to do is get their attention."

That night Rodriguez and Henry walked the perimeter, quietly circulating instructions from Wilfred. Then at midnight, Wilfred went into action. He led Rodriguez' squad to Hunt's hooch. The seven men fell on it and the struggling behemoth within, while Wilfred uncovered Hunt's gaping face and crammed a grenade into his mouth. "You look like a good listener," he said to Hunt.

Speaking slowly and quietly, Wilfred explained certain facts: That his finger was in the ring of the grenade pin. That Hunt should relax. That everyone had to work together in combat. That sometimes loners got fragged and sent home in body bags. That every man in the company was armed with at least one deadly weapon. That he, Wilfred Carmenghetti, was in command of the company. That killing anyone, friend or foe, was normally forbidden. That snitching to Clary would be extremely unwise.

"You see, Hunt. My family is Cosa Nostra. We have friends all around the world that I can call on to exact justice from those who would break our laws. I already know where your family lives in case you refuse to submit to my authority. I also have contacts in the Vietcong that I can turn you over to whenever I wish. So it would be clever of you to do exactly what I say." Lieutenant Hunt listened to the entire spiel with patience approaching reverence, uttering not a single word. They bound him, hand and foot, left the grenade in place, and repeated the performance for Maugham and Fierden. Wilfred, remembering his fraternity hazing, enjoyed it immensely. His only mistake was not knowing that Platoon Sergeant Maugham had no family at all.

When all three were thus instructed, Wilfred had them hop to the center of the FOB where a bonfire was blazing. He stood them beside it as Reckert shouted questions to the company.

"Who is our leader?"

"Carmenghetti," roared the ring of men from the dark.

"Who do we follow?"

"Carmenghetti."

"Who is our commanding officer?"

"Carmenghetti."

"Do we follow Fierden?"

"No."

"Do we follow Clary?"

"No."

"Who do we follow?"

"Carmenghetti."

"Who do we hate?"

"Traitors."

"Who do we despise?"

"Traitors."

"Who do we kill?"

"Traitors."

Henry removed the grenades from the mouths of the three and Reckert addressed them. "Do you pledge yourselves to A Company? If so, answer, 'I do.'"

"I do," they stuttered.

"Louder," Reckert said.

"I do."

"Louder."

"I do!" they bellowed.

"Do you promise to honor and obey Lieutenant Wilfred Carmenghetti and speak no evil against him?"

"I do."

"Will you dedicate your life to love?"

"I will."

Turning to the company, Reckert shouted, "Do we accept these soldiers into our company?"

"We do!" roared the crowd.

Wilfred had the three untied. He graciously shook each hand and welcomed them into A Company.

"Thank you, sir," PSG Maugham said.

"It will be a pleasure to serve you," Fierden said.

"Glad to be aboard, sir," Hunt said with a squint. It was a long way down to Wilfred's face.

The ceremony had been impressive. Everything had gone precisely as planned until the grenadier in Hunt's platoon lost control and snickered. His foxhole companion looked at him for a moment and giggled back. Twenty yards away another man heard the sound and tittered. Then across the field a chortle was heard and the distinct sound of a chuckle. Howls answered guffaws and shrieks begat cackles until soon the whole perimeter was reeling in gales of hysterical laughter.

The inductees, who had been led so carefully into the fold of docility, glowed now with humiliation and anger and mutely plotted their revenge.

Later that night, Wilfred's sources uncovered the snickerer in Hunt's platoon. Wilfred went for him. "Do you know what you did? You blew the whole god-damned thing!"

"I'm sorry, sir. It was just too funny," the grenadier said, and he snickered again until the lieutenant couldn't keep from joining him.

Still, Wilfred was more successful than he'd thought. The trio awoke with sore jaws, chipped teeth, the taste of blood and steel in their mouths, and the roar of the company in their ears. Though the memory of their embarrassment was strong, the unity of the hundred-plus heavily armed men and the lingering sound of Wilfred's ruthless voice was dominant. They would tread carefully and only confront their midget enemy obliquely.

Three days passed, and Wilfred used Trinh to get six more kills, shielding his actions not in the least from the newcomers and almost daring Clary to make an accusation. The results were expected. Several times he saw Fierden, Hunt and Maugham in a huddle, speaking in low tones and casting furtive glances at the company, with Maugham doing most of the talking. *The cancer survived my therapy*, Wilfred thought. *It's threatening to burgeon and send insidious cells throughout our system.*

Three times he confronted the new men, one by one, saying, "You're planning to turn me in, aren't you?" and three times before the rooster crowed each sang his denial, "Oh, no sir. I wouldn't do that. I'm for you, sir."

The tactic was ineffective. Twice after that he saw them talking to Clary. Once, the colonel's eyebrows lifted nearly off his face and then plunged into a most fearful scowl. Another time Fierden caught Wilfred peeking and smiled at him.

Wilfred responded to the menace with increasing carelessness, continuing to accrue KIA's, but on the final day not bothering to disguise Trinh at all.

"That's Trinh," Clary said.

"No, it isn't."

"He's even wearing his Kit Carson uniform."

"A clever disguise."

"He doesn't have any wounds."

"We scared him to death."

"He doesn't even smell like ketchup."

"Why should he smell like ketchup?"

"You know why."

"He's a hot dog?"

"The jig's up, Carmenghetti."

"I'm tired of your racial slurs, sir."

"You'll be tired of more than that, shortly."

"I've had it with your prejudice against short people. You've always held it against me—and the VC. Admit it, sir."

Wilfred knew he was in trouble when Clary walked away displaying not the least sign of anger.

Soon afterwards, Reckert cornered Wilfred. "What's going on? You're getting awfully reckless, aren't you?"

"Yeah. I'm sick of this shit."

"What are you going to do? Quit?"

"Fuck no. If Clary is gonna play these silly spy games with me, he leaves me no choice."

"But what?"

CHAPTER 24

▼

LIEUTENANT COLONEL CLARY

"It's time to take over the fucking battalion," Wilfred said, clenching his little fists.

"The battalion?" Reckert said.

"We've done all we can here. We've pacified A Company and given Simms and Clary an incredible kill ratio. We've put Simms where he can't harm anyone and satisfied his need for glory. We've given the American people one of the best episodes of the Vietnam War chronics ever to appear on nightly news and helped the networks with their ratings and their sponsors with their advertising. Big deal. It's a drop in the bucket."

"It's a significant accomplishment, Wilfred."

"It's not enough. And I'm thinking that maximizing KIA's, even if they're fake, might be the wrong way to bring peace."

"Why?"

"It's just another absurd contradiction. The more we kill, the less pacified our area will be presumed to be. Every enemy body we deliver is evidence of enemy strength."

"Victory implies defeat!"

"Exactly. The more we smash them, the more the American people will assume that we're losing, that we can't control them, that the enemy continues to resist in great numbers. Can you imagine what would happen if the NVA launched a massive, suicidal Tet offensive against the cities in this country, and we slaughtered thirty or forty thousand of them?"

"The press would say the military was lying about our strength and the enemy's weakness," Reckert said.

"Yepper. A victory like that would be a horrendous defeat for us. It would mean we weren't in control, and it would be interpreted as a defeat even though we stymied the attack and destroyed the enemy's ability to defeat us for years to come, until their toddlers become gun-toting teenagers."

"We can't win. But if we start losing, they'll still think we're losing!"

"I know. Both options are out. We're can't win or lose."

"And A Company's been winning!"

"And that means we're losing. But here's the problem: since America can't stand losing under any circumstances, if we win or lose over here, it'll prolong the war."

"We'll never get home."

"And the killing and destruction will continue."

"So how can you stop it?"

"I think we're not only going to have to stop the killing, we're going to have to stop pretending we're killing. We made a big mistake in that. The only way the American people will believe we've won is if the country is pacified. And the only proof of pacification is the elimination of the killing, real and pretend. A zip-zip kill ratio for an extended period."

"Great. And for starters, all you have to do is convince the colonel to go along."

"I'll convince him, all right."

He didn't have long to wait. The next morning after chow, Clary flew in and Platoon Sergeant Maugham informed Wilfred that the colonel wanted to see him.

"Good. I want to see him."

Instantly they were issuing simulcasts, nose-to-nose, hands on hips, the colonel bending over and the lieutenant on his toes.

"I want to talk to you," Clary said as Wilfred said, "I want to talk to you."

"You're in a heap of trouble," the colonel said as the lieutenant said, "You're in a heap of trouble."

"Stop talking while I'm talking," they said.

"Did you hear me, (respective rank)?" they replied.

"I'm warning you," they warned.

A rifle shot grazed Clary's steel pot. Dai had decided that having aimed at Wilfred and missed so often by so little, he now would intentionally miss him in order to hit him. Unfortunately, he missed. The two targets lunged to the ground—still eyeball-to-eyeball—fearlessly continuing their discussion. Wilfred was so close he could smell the dab of cologne under Clary's nose.

"You don't scare me," they hissed.

"I'll have your head," they threatened.

"I know you've been faking body counts," Clary said as Wilfred threatened, "You know I've been faking body counts."

"Don't try to deny it. I've got three witnesses," Clary said as Wilfred parried, "Don't try to deny it. I've got over a hundred witnesses."

"What?" Clary said.

"I said I have over a hundred witnesses."

"N-no. I have over a hundred witnesses."

"The hell you do. They're my witnesses, sir."

"Y-you don't deny you've been faking the body counts?"

"I'm warning you, sir. I have faked more than a hundred and thirty body counts."

"You admit it!"

"I'm not admitting anything, sir. I'm announcing it."

"Announcing? Warning? What are you talking about?"

"I'm letting you know what happened, sir, and if you don't do what I say, I'll tell the whole fucking world."

Wilfred waited for his reply, but Clary was speechless. The only sound was sputtering gunfire and the popping and thudding of grenades as the usual response to one of Colonel Dai's attacks took place on the perimeter.

"B-but they'll lock you up and th-throw away the key."

"Right, sir, and your career will come to an end."

"W-what do you mean?"

"I mean that the Army doesn't like scandals of this magnitude, and since I work for you, you'll be the goat. They'll hang you and drum you right out of the service."

"W-why?"

"You'd be breaking rule number one: don't make waves."

Fierden approached, but Clary whipped him away with, "Fierden, get that sniper." The company commander hastily about-faced and hurried away, and the rifle fire resumed.

"You're crazy," Clary said. "They'll back me to the hilt."

"Don't be a fool, Clary. You'd be giving the whole service a black eye. The whole war, for that matter. No sir. If the press gets hold of this, heads'll roll, and yours'll be first. You'll be crucified. Can't you see how stupid and incompetent you'd look? Why, the minute you leak it to a superior, you'll get gagged so fast you won't know what happened. But me? I don't care what happens to me. That's my ace in the hole. And brother, if you don't do what I say, I'll start singing like crazy."

"N-no one would b-believe it."

"As I said, sir, I have over a hundred witnesses. Not only that, but I have a TV tape of you accepting my inane excuses for fifty-five bloated bodies. The networks'll have a field day with that, now, won't they?"

"Y-you can't get away with—"

"You look so stupid that no one will believe that anyone could be that stupid. There will be no doubt in the public's mind that we were in cahoots, that you were fully aware of my actions and supported me."

"Y-you—"

"I also have plenty of witnesses to the fact that you and Simms covered up Simms's massacre at Quin Loc and exaggerated the enemy body count there." Clary's lower lip was trembling now. "What kind of discharge do you want, Clary, honorable or dishonorable? A kick in the pants or a proper pension?"

Clary was cracking. "W-what do you want?"

Wilfred let the question hang a moment, then said, "It's simple, sir. I want you to end the killing, them and us. No more KIA's, VC, NVA, civilian or friendly."

"Y-you want me to join your mutiny."

"Yes sir."

"But I'll get booted out just as quick that way."

"No sir. If you do what I say, the worst you can be accused of is bad judgment, and anyone can have that."

"What would I do?"

"First, sir, accept that I'm now the battalion commander. Second, send all the companies into unpopulated areas. Have them search deserted villages. Lose them in the mountains and swamps. Just keep them away from people. Your men are killers, sir."

"But how can I do that? Brigade, Division, they'll think we're not doing our job if we don't report some kills once in a while. I'll get busted for dereliction of duty. I-I—"

"Wrong, sir. You'll be hailed as a hero. You'll have the only fully pacified AO in Vietnam. They'll think you're in complete control, that the enemy is vanquished, that the VC don't dare set foot in your area. They'll make you a general."

Clary giggled. It was what he had always dreamed of. "You really think they'll make me a general?"

"Absolutely, sir." Wilfred was thoroughly enjoying lying on the ground this way, head to head, since it made him as tall as someone, in this case a colonel, and he seized the moment to gain an even greater advantage. He slithered forward a little in the grass, until he was actually looking down on Clary, and took on the gentle, superior, fatherly countenance of a big man. "Now that's not so bad, is it, colonel? Avoid all that vituperation and ugly publicity, keep your pension, and advance to general. That's not bad for a poor hero up from the ranks like you."

"I'll never make general. I didn't go to The Point."

"If you play ball with me, I guarantee you'll make general. You have my solemn promise. I have connections, you know."

"I know about your...connections."

"Don't turn up your nose at them. They're going to make you a general."

Clary looked deeply into Wilfred's eyes and couldn't help but believe, trust, and obey. He had seen the man in action. Carmenghetti had the courage to risk his life, the cautious self-composure to survive, the wit to deceive, the willfulness to win, and the ruthlessness to chip teeth, if necessary.

Wilfred closed the sale: "Do we have a deal, colonel?"

"Yes," he said with great relief.

"One other thing. I want you to ship out the animals, Hunt, Maugham, and Fierden. Put 'em on permanent R & R. Lose 'em in Hong Kong or Malaysia. Get 'em out of here today."

"O.K. But then Lorde'll be in command."

"He'll do just fine, colonel. We're not gonna kill anybody anyway. Besides, you know who's really in command."

Clary nodded, feeling worried and vulnerable. Then he was puzzled. "Wilfred, are you a communist?"

"Nope. Commies are pigs. I just can't stand the killing."

"Must be some sort of battle fatigue then."

"Yep. I'm tired of battle."

They rose and brushed themselves off. Clary was startled anew at how shrunken was his adversary.

"One more thing, colonel. We've been out an awful long time. We're ready for a stand-down."

"Is tomorrow soon enough?"

"Sure. Oh, and can you take back some rifles with you?"

"Rifles?"

"AKs and SKSs. We've got over forty of 'em and they're kind of hard to carry."

"Where'd you get them?"

"Like I said, sir. I have connections."

Three startled spies joined Clary on the Charlie Charlie.

"What happened?" Maugham asked.

Clary put on a fierce grin. "I've got him by the balls, gentlemen, thanks to you. And now, I have another mission for you, maybe the toughest you'll ever get, certainly the most important. Two men in the battalion went to Hong Kong on R & R and never came back. We suspect they crossed over into Red China and are dealing with the commies. I want you to find them and bring them back alive."

Hunt snorted and smiled savagely. Maugham bared his pointed teeth. Fierden, however, paled: "But, sir. I was supposed to run the company."

"You did, Lieutenant. So admirably, in fact, that I cannot allow you to continue to waste your abilities on such trifling duties. Yours is a greater calling. I'm sure you will not be found wanting."

CHAPTER 25

▼

CAN IN THE FIELD

They arrived at Sang Tran Bridge with gusto, only to find the town off-limits. Lieutenant General Panik, youngest general in the Army, had implemented his plan to get a piece of all the action in the AO for his boss, Major General Powers.

A sergeant in starched fatigues visited the company soon after it arrived and took orders for delivery that evening. The troops were disgruntled. Most of their favorite girls were not on the list, and prices had quadrupled.

"You're paying for service," Sergeant Williams explained curtly. "We have expenses, you know: administrative, sales, financial, inventory control, medical. We have to schedule, package, ship, fuck, pick up, and inspect them to make sure they're in proper working order for re-rental. You try and run a business some-time. You'll find out."

"Need any inspectors?" Rodriguez asked.

"You a doc?"

"I know what clap looks like. What it feels like too."

"Sorry, buddy. No vacancy."

"How come the town is off limits?"

"Security and disease control…"

"Cunt-roll, cunt-roll…" a soldier repeated, fascinated with his new word.

"…Too many G.I.'s passing secrets to broads. Too many broads passing the drip to G.I.'s."

When Henry heard, he flew into a rage. Quan was not on the list. She couldn't come and he couldn't go. "Filthy motherfuckers," he said to Wilfred. "I'm going anyway."

Can wasn't on the list either. "Well, we might as well get hung together." He put on an NVA uniform and sunglasses, and Henry took him to town under guard. Wilfred could have ordered special passes from his subordinate, Colonel Clary, but this was quicker and more fun. Their first stop was Paradise.

"Can not here," Mr. Tuong said, "but I get girl for you, half plice." Times were tough in Sang Tran.

Wilfred was stunned. I waited too long. She gave up on me. "Where is she?" he demanded, stepping closer to Tuong.

"She go Onkay."

"When?"

"Many day. Many day."

"Is she coming back?"

Tuong thought of Minh's fury when he heard that Can had left. "I think no."

"Why did she leave?"

"I don't know. Someone say you dead. She very sad."

Wilfred was overcome. All other concerns vanished. I've got to find her, he thought. He wanted to fly to Camp Vassar that instant, but was trapped by his uniform and his need to be guarded. "Let's go," he said to Henry. "I gotta get back fast."

"I gotta see Quan first," the black man demanded.

Wilfred was in the air by six the next morning and approaching Can's hooch by ten. "Ooooh!" she howled as she looked up from chopping vegetables with a huge cleaver. Her mouth fell open, her eyes exploded, and she began screaming at the ghost of her lover. Hearing her baby's cries, Má charged out of the hooch with a large bowl of rice and seeing the spirit, nearly swallowed her cheroot.

Wilfred, not wanting to deal with Má just then, raised his hands high above his head, put on a bloodthirsty smile, and lunged for the lady, shrieking, "Wooooooo…"

"Ooooooooo…" she wailed in return, dropping the bowl and running, hands high, along a dike and into the paddies.

Hmm, Wilfred thought. I guess ghosts in Nam go "Woo" too.

Can was up herself now, racing away from the specter, but Wilfred pursued with determination. They ran and ran with Wilfred hollering, and gradually gaining on her. When they reached the middle of the village, he overtook her with an open-field tackle, wrapping his arms around her legs. She landed with a squeal, twisted over, sat up, and began pummeling the back of his head, unwittingly driving it deep into her crotch. Not until she felt him trying to bite through the cloth did she realize that this was no spirit. "Wilfed!" she cried. She ceased her attack and hugged his head between her lap and breast.

Relieved, he mumbled a muffled "Can" into her lap, but with that one word went all his breath. He tried to gasp, but no air came. Her softness had formed a perfect seal, and though he struggled desperately, so great was her love that she could not let go. He panicked. Am I soon to be a ghost of a ghost? As he gurgled and grew faint, a circle of curious children who had crept in to see the spectacle delivered him from death.

"Oh!" Can said, and she relaxed her grip on him and chased the budding voyeurs with a flurry of words.

Gasping for air, Wilfred plunged forward, driving Can prone and blanketing her tender body with his own. "I love you," he swore, as she pushed him off.

"No here, Wilfed. Baby!"

Hand in hand they walked back to the hooch and made glorious daytime love. Then they talked.

"Who say I dead?" Wilfred asked, and he listened as she told him of Fierden and Minh.

"Fierden," he said, angry with himself for assigning the sadist beyond his reach. He cooled off, however, when he realized that with Fierden absent, he couldn't kill him.

He told Can of the atrocity and all the other deaths and how he had vowed never to kill again. At this Can grew even warmer and stroked his hairy chest.

Wilfred had never felt closer to her nor more at peace. Life with Can; how would it be? Tumultuous, for sure. But oh, the highs. He wondered what other people would think, but disregarded the subject harshly. Then he asked himself, will I still love her when she's old and fat? Probably, he decided. That's when gratitude and respect take over, lavished by memories, borne by familiarity, two lives and minds, one. He felt a twinge of fear and a sense of incipient loss. I can't let her go again. I can't leave her again. I must have her with me, to be with her, to protect her.

Can heard his frowning silence. "Why you no talk?"

"I'm thinking about Can and Wilfred."

"I think too."

Can's mother appeared in the doorway, saw them lying naked, and left without a word. What kind of a mother-in-law would you be, old hag? he thought. Then he realized she'd left them alone. If this was a pattern, she might be all right. From far away, he heard Madge preaching: "If you want to know what a girl will be like when she's fifty, just look at her mother." But maybe not.

"Wilfed," Can said breathlessly. "I love you." Her voice sounded urgent.

That was it. He looked into her eyes and vowed to himself, I'm going to have you, girl, and you're going to have me. He plunged. "Can, will you marry me?" Sometimes when he spoke, it was if someone else were talking, but not now.

"Oh, Wilfed, yes!" she said, and her whole body turned liquid and flowed over him like sweet oil. He held her close and nearly cried as she kissed and kissed him. Then he grew hard and they made love once more.

They dressed and emerged, hand in hand. Can's mother and siblings were sitting quietly, within easy earshot of the proceedings, but since Can showed no embarrassment, neither did he. She spoke to her mother who listened in silence, and Wilfred noticed with surprise that the old woman's eyes grew misty. She replied with but a few gentle words, and Can turned to Wilfred. "We go now," she said proudly, and they did.

He wondered what on earth Can had said to her mother since her return from Sang Tran. Whatever it was, it had tamed the wild beast. Perhaps she cried or said she loved me, he thought, and he felt the warmth of acceptance, the glow of victory. It wasn't until he and Can were walking away that he swallowed hard. My god, what have I done now?

Wilfred thought that having a girl in the field was a great improvement in the art of warfare—humping and snuggling all night in the great out-of-doors. But Can did not take well to the life of combat. She'd somehow expected a G.I. officer to have better accommodations than a shallow hole in the ground covered with rubberized cloth. Wilfred noticed her displeasure when they crawled over the threshold the first night. "Num ten," she mumbled.

Neither did Can enjoy the nomadic life of the soldier—aimless wandering, trailing a herd of ghosts through paddy and forest, rain and mud, heat and dust. Her pack was heavy, and she would have preferred a pole across her shoulders. Her steel pot made her neck tired and didn't protect her from sun and rain as well as a proper straw hat. Stupid, stupid, stupid.

She also was unnerved by that Vietcong soldier always shooting at her betrothed. "Kill him!" she screamed at the soldiers on the perimeter. But they never could.

The food was foreign—insipid and barbaric. She finally resorted to gathering rice and vegetables as they marched and preparing her own meals when they stopped. The thing that bothered her most, however, was the growing discontent of the other soldiers. If she'd known the words, she would have said they were horny and jealous.

"Where does he get off bringin' a broad out here," they grumbled. "It ain't fair."

Welbourne didn't appreciate being displaced by Can, though he was too polite to say anything. He had to sleep by himself now and had many a discussion with Deep Sky Six about Wilfred and Can's lack of matrimonial ties.

Wilfred noticed the pervading disgruntlement, but he couldn't bring out a hundred and forty girls—the company would be short on food. Maybe he could get some whores. But would they accept the lifestyle? Judging from Can, no.

Some weeks later, the men's dissatisfaction mysteriously began to wane. They started greeting him with smiles. Laughing and joking resumed. Wilfred became curious, until the night, a week or so later, when he came back early from his radio watch at the company CP and found two boots, toes down, protruding from his hooch. Moans and groans came from within and Wilfred saw a couple of soldiers who had been standing nearby, vanish into the darkness. "Shit!" he screamed. "Get out before I murder you!" and he fired his pistol into the air. The tent flew apart and away ran the soldier, stutter-stepping and stumbling as he pulled up his pants.

The row began: "You slut!"

"I do for you. Men no happy."

"You just can't get enough fucking. You're just a stinking whore!"

"I no take money."

"That's worse. You're a stupid nympho."

"You no love me."

"You got that right, baby. Not any more."

"Hooch num ten. Bed num ten. Hat num ten. Chow chow num ten. War num ten. You num ten!"

"So are you, baby."

"I go Onkay."

"Go, and good riddance."

In the morning they awoke in tight-lipped silence.

"I'm taking you back tomorrow," he said stonily.

"Good!" Can spat.

"Fucking women," he said to Reckert the next morning.

"Come on, man. You didn't really think it would work out, did you? Taking her home to momma and all? Jesus."

The primary beneficiary of this turn of events was Welbourne, who no longer had to sleep alone in half a hooch. One poncho overhead had provided poor protection from the rain when the wind blew the wrong way. And he was swollen with pride that Sky Six had deigned to act on his request that Wilfred and Can be separated.

Clary came in that morning. He seemed agitated as he approached Wilfred. "It's not working," he said. "The other colonels are catching on. "They're starting to play the pacification game too—turning in deflated kill reports, sending their troops into deserted areas, you know."

Wilfred was elated. His program was spreading of its own accord. "Great. What's wrong with that?"

"What's wrong? You said I'd be the envy of the division, that I'd have the only pacified AO in Nam. Now they're all doing it. I'll never make general this way."

"Oh, yes, you will. I told you you would, didn't I?"

"Yes."

"Well, take it easy, then. I'll deliver."

"When?"

"Tell you what. I have to go to Vassar on some other business tomorrow. I'll see Powers and get the ball rolling."

Wilfred found Reckert after Clary left. "I guess you're in charge again tomorrow, Robbie."

"Are you taking Can back?"

"Yeah. I think it's best for all concerned. And I've gotta see General Powers too."

"Powers? What about?"

CHAPTER 26

▼

PANIK AND POWERS

"I'm taking over the division."

Reckert laughed nervously, then droned, "Today the division, tomorrow the world. But why the division? I thought things were going pretty well."

"The problem is that most of the battalion commanders have caught on to Clary."

"That's hairy. Has Powers?"

"I don't think so. Not yet, anyway. Clary is Powers' pet since he pacified the battalion AO."

"Oh, I bet the other colonels like that."

"Clary says they were pretty pissed until they found out how he was doing it. Now they've cooled off."

"What? They didn't blow the whistle?"

"Hell, no. They're company men. They don't want to give the division a black eye. And they sure don't want to get the reputation of being tattletales—of showing disloyalty.

"So they can't squeal. But they can't let Clary get ahead of them either. So what've they done?"

"Most of them have started mimicking Clary by adopting our new game rules: no killing and no reporting of killing."

"But that means you've already taken over the division."

"A few colonels haven't gotten with the program yet."

"Taking over divisions. Wilfred, do you ever feel like you're losing touch with reality?"

"Maybe. But who cares about reality anyway? Illusion's the thing. If you want to change reality, you've got to change the illusion of reality. That's what counts."

He took Can to Vassar the next day, and when they reached the gate, she surprised him by coming near, and kissing him passionately on the mouth. What was more shocking was that he didn't resist and felt the same old fire within.

"Love Wilfed," she ventured sadly.

He pulled her to him. "Damn it. I love you too."

He didn't want to leave her, but he was still tortured with ambivalence. He didn't know what to do. He held her while their reflection traveled to the moon and back. "I gotta go," he said and watched tears flood her eyes.

"Wilfed come back?"

He broke away. "I don't know. I don't know."

He turned and went slowly down the road, and where it took a bend, he turned back to look. There she stood, her face obscure in the distance, watching him walk away. Fuck, he thought, as confused as ever, but he kept on walking.

"I want to see the general," he said to the corporal behind the desk.

"Which one?"

"General Powers."

"And who should I say is calling?"

"Wilfred Carmenghetti."

"Well…first I have to ask the sergeant, if he's in. And he has to ask the lieutenant. And he has to ask the platoon sergeant. And he has to ask the captain. And he has to ask the first sergeant. And he has to ask the warrant officer. And he has to ask the major. And he has to ask the colonel. And he has to ask the sergeant major. And he has to ask General Panik. We have a chain of command to follow, you know."

"Sounds more like a chain link fence. Who's this General Panik guy?"

"He's gives permission to General Powers to talk to people, and General Powers only gets it when he's good."

"Well, fuck this shit. Kindly tell General Powers I'm on my way." He marched through the door at the rear of the room.

"You can't do that," the corporal said as Wilfred slammed the door.

He slammed twenty or thirty other doors as he stomped through the maze of rooms past dozens of angry and astonished eyes. Speed and surprise were in his favor as were the rabid snarls and growls he flung into the faces of the inhabitants. It worked in the tunnel, he thought. It'll work here.

In the office next to the corporal, the sergeant E-5 raised a finger and barked, "Stop!" The lieutenant in the adjacent room rose from his desk and said, "May I help—" The platoon sergeant in the next office roared, "Ten-hut!" The captain next door looked up from a girlie magazine and said, "Halt, who...went there?" The first sergeant on the other side of the door rose so violently that he overturned his three hundred pound wood desk. "Stop that man!" he yelled to the major next door who stepped back, trembling. The colonel beyond, who was reclining on a cleaning lady, looked up aghast as Wilfred told him, "Carry on, sir. Carry on." The sergeant major in the next office attempted to tackle him, but came up empty. And Lieutenant General Panik in the next to the last office climbed under his desk, reached up for the phone, and calmly dialed the M.P.'s.

Major General Powers was seated with his feet on the desk reading the *Wall Street Journal* when Wilfred burst in.

"Sir!" Wilfred said as Powers looked in terror over the top of the paper, "I want to talk to you."

Powers dropped the paper, slapped his shirt pockets, and jerked out a little green bottle, holding his breath. Deftly, the fat fingers unscrewed the cap, shoved the nozzle up his snorting nostrils, and squeezed. Wilfred read the label: Cologne No. 10 Nasal Spray. Powers smiled. "Good to see you, boy. It's always good to see one of our fighting men from the field."

"Thank you, sir. It's good to see you."

"You're Lieutenant Carmenghetti, aren't you?"

"Yes sir."

"I've heard some fine reports about you and Captain Simms and Colonel Clary. Fine job you did on those rocks, boy."

"Thank you, sir."

"Yessiree. First you get the highest kill ratio in Nam and now you've got the most pacified AO. You whupped the VC so bad they're afraid to come near you. Outstanding."

"Thank you, sir."

"Of course, some of the other battalions are starting to look real good too..."

"Yes sir."

"You, uh, planning to go in business with your father when you get back?"

"I thought I might. I gotta admit that Nam has been fine training for that line of work."

"You know, Lieutenant, you should think about going Regular Army and staying in. The Army needs men like you."

Oh, you'd like that, Wilfred thought. Then you could control my whole life. "Don't get me wrong, sir. I like the Army. But I'd be crazy to turn down a job with Dad. And he needs me too. His business is kind of risky, and if he has to spend some time in the can, someone has to help him run it—you know, visit him, take orders, and make sure they're carried out. It's really a family thing."

"I understand. But there are some terrific opportunities in the Army, son, if you have the right friends."

"Yeah. I noticed. Wasn't General Panik a captain just a few months ago?"

"Sure was, but promotions come fast in time of war, and he needed the rank to do the job, and I must say, he's done an outstanding job for me here."

"I can see that, sir. But do you really think it was wise to have him promoted to a higher rank than your own?"

"I must admit I may have made a mistake there. He's acted a little uppity at times. On the other hand, business couldn't be better. He's got a real knack for it. And with him running the businesses, it frees me up to run the war."

"Ah, the businesses—boom boom girls, Sin City, and drugs."

"Don't forget the PX and commissary."

Wilfred noticed that the door to Panik's office had opened a crack. He's listening in. I better get him in here. If I want to take the division, I better take him too.

"Tell me, Lieutenant. What's your secret? How have you managed to be so successful out there in the field?"

Wilfred sprang to the door and jerked it open, exposing a crouching General Panik. "Come in, sir. You'll be much more comfortable listening in here." He grabbed Panik by the back of the collar and one withered bicep, led him in, and sat him down. Panik perched like an errant schoolboy in the principal's office. "Oh, my daddy could use a man like you."

Powers observed walleyed the inner violence of the Mafia lieutenant seeping to the surface like sewage from a cesspool and quickly grabbed his inhaler and sucked some more cologne.

"Now!" Wilfred said, eying his prey—Panik, then Powers. "You wanted to know the secret of our success. General Panik, could you please close the door?" Panik jumped up, shut it firmly, and sat back down. "Thank you. Our success in battle and our incredible kill ratio were due solely to one technique, the falsification of body counts. We counted the same bodies over and over, and when we ran out of dead bodies, we counted live bodies."

"What?" Powers gasped.

"Huh, huh, huh, huh…" Panik laughed.

"But—" Powers said.

"Wait, sir, there's more. Our total domination of enemy forces in our area was due to an entirely new set of tactics. Take notes on this, will you, Panik? It's important stuff. We developed revolutionary new types of operations. First was the 'Half Cordon And Search': we'd half encircle a hamlet before searching it, thus permitting the VC to escape. Then we had the 'Warn And Escape' mission: we'd warn the enemy of our entry into an area and then turn around and go the other way. This technique is highly effective against enemy ambushes. The third was the 'Hide And Stay Clear' type mission where we'd penetrate areas no mortal had ever before seen and simply hide out for a few days. The success of these techniques with regard to pacification is undeniable."

"B-but what you're describing to me is a total corruption of the war effort."

"That's right, sir."

"Do Simms and Clary know about this?"

"Know about it? They sanctioned it, implemented it, and concealed it. Not only that, but many of your other battalion commanders are employing the very same tactics. Why do you think their areas are becoming pacified too?"

"But—"

"I know what you're thinking, sir, that these events show every sign of ballooning into a scandal of major proportions, and you're absolutely right. Hundreds of men are in on it already, from privates to colonels, and now, to generals. That's why it must be handled delicately."

"Scandal…shame…oblivion…early retirement…"

"But, sir. Look what fame and glory we've brought you, and the opportunities you have to increase it further."

"Fame? Glory?" Powers' face flickered with hope.

"Yes, and wealth." The generals seemed to perk up at the mention of money. "That's what total pacification can bring you. But it must be total. You must rein in every renegade commander who refuses to pacify his AO. Put them back in school, instruct them, indoctrinate them, brainwash them, if necessary, into the new strategy and tactics. Then control, manipulate, and coerce them into cooperating. Eliminate enemy sitings by not looking. End enemy attacks by refusing to go in. Issue blank ammunition to all the troops. And most important, establish Free-Of-Fire Zones all over the division AO for the artillery, off-shore guns, and the Air Force."

"B-but we have to keep expending ammunition. We've got to keep dropping more bombs than we did in W W II, or my General Munitions stock will drop," Powers whined.

"Don't worry. Right now at every firebase you've got, the artillery pumps out hundreds of rounds a week in H & I fires aimed at probable enemy positions and avenues of approach. All you have to do is to change the aiming points to improbable enemy positions. You're already aiming at where Charlie could possibly be instead of where he is. Blast away at where he probably isn't. That'll really blow his mind."

"What about the bombs?" Powers asked.

"Easier yet. Call in missions on uninhabitable swamps and jungle areas. Build a bridge in the jungle, five feet long and three feet wide. Tell 'em it's strategically necessary to blow it, and let them take ten years trying to hit it. Use your imaginations, gentlemen. You have the power to expend as much ammo as you want to. Wilfred could feel the tug on the line and see the dip of the float.

The three doors of the room burst open at once, and white helmets were everywhere. A huge M.P. leaped on little Wilfred, twisted his arm into a hammerlock, and began choking him with a crushing forearm across the esophagus.

"Attention. Attention!" Powers shouted.

"You all right, sirs?" a burly captain asked the generals as Wilfred began turning blue.

"Of course we're all right," Panik said.

"Let go of him," Powers said. "He's O.K. If you haven't killed him, I'll probably promote him to Brigadier General!"

"And bust you to private," Panik told the captain.

"But you're the one who called us."

"I did not," Panik replied. "It must have been a prank by some perverted impersonator. And I want him found. You have two hours, captain, if you don't want to be a private again."

"Yes sir," the captain said. "All right, you idiots. You heard the general. Let's go." They double-timed out to the captain's "Lef, Ri, Lef, Ri…" and left Wilfred stroking his bruised throat with his good arm.

"Sorry about that," Powers said. "You all right?"

"Yeah."

"Now, where were we?"

"We were talking about pacification, sir, and glory, laud and honor."

"And wealth," Panik said.

"Yeah. Where does that wealth fit in?" Powers asked.

"Right now only ninety or ninety-five percent of your troops are in the rear on firebases. You still have at least five or ten percent in the field. These men, as you know, are beyond the reach of your businesses. They pick up girls where they find them, are too scared of getting zapped to get high on drugs, and since they're away from the bases, they can't blow their money on PX and commissary fare. They are, you might say, an untapped market."

"We know," Panik said. "We've been wondering what to do. We can't get our girls to volunteer to go out there, and boonie rats can't carry stereos and Hong Kong business suits on their backs. They have too much junk to carry already. And they're too skittish to buy dope. It's a problem."

"With an easy solution. Put all the troops in the rear. It's the ultimate step in pacification. No more contact, no more KIA's. Total pacification. You increase your rear-area security and the size of your market by five or ten percent."

"I wanted to do that, Powers, but you said it wouldn't work," Panik grumbled.

"I'm still not sure it will," Powers replied. "We have operations reports to file with MACV, you know."

"You can fake those, sir," Wilfred said. "We've been doing it for months. Just get the best creative writers in the Division to crank 'em out for you."

"I guess it wouldn't be too hard."

"Shit, no."

"But what about those TV reporters? They're always bugging me for action stories."

"Tell you what, sir. You leave me and my company out in the field. Just us. We'll take care of those TV guys."

"Would you do that for me, Wilfred?" Powers asked.

"I'd be happy to."

A specter came over Powers, darkening his jolly face. "Wait a minute. If we totally pacify the AO and the idea spreads throughout the country, those fools in Washington will decide that we've won and ship us all home."

"There go the businesses."

"And my kingdom," Powers said.

"The enclosed shopping mall."

"The walled city."

"The sports complex."

"The mile-wide moat."

"The Bob Hope Auditorium."

"Parks and playgrounds."

"The high-rise condos."

"The expressways and subway."

"The art museum and symphony hall!"

"Gentlemen, gentlemen," Wilfred said, hushing them with tiny raised hands. "Listen. We beat the Japanese and Germans twenty-two years ago. But have we brought home the boys yet? No. We still have hundreds of thousands of troops in Europe and Japan. We beat the Chinese in Korea thirteen years ago, but our army's still there. Don't worry. If we win in Nam, we'll be here forever, too, keeping warring tribes from fighting. Keeping things stable for business. It will be part of our empire, and empires must be maintained."

"Forever," the generals said with tears in their eyes.

"Pacification is really our only hope for staying here. You know, those people back home are getting tired of having their sons delivered to them in plastic bags. It hurts their morale. What they need are reports of peace. Victory. Letters telling them what a nice country this is. How their kids sleep under tin roofs, shower twice a day, play and frolic in the pools and clubs all night, eat three hots a day, instead of only two. We need to cut the tours-of-duty from one year to six months and send each man on six R & R's instead of three. Make the war palatable. Acceptable, hell—desirable! Their sons will be dying to come here. Then we won't need a draft. We can do away with it and have an all-volunteer army, and the end-the-draft demonstrations will stop."

"Very clever," Panik said. "But what if someone does rat on us to the press?"

"Oh, sir," Wilfred said. "Who could possibly believe it?"

"Very astute," Panik said.

"Carmenghetti, you're a genius," Powers said.

"Thank you, sirs. I trust, then, that we have a new program in the works?"

"Count on it, Lieutenant," Panik said. "We'll start pulling back the troops tomorrow. Right, Grant?"

"We'll start tonight," Powers said.

"Great," Wilfred said, rising to his feet. The generals leaped up in response, smiling warmly, and shook his hand.

"You deserve a promotion for this," said Powers. "How would you like to be a general?"

"No, thanks, sirs. My men wouldn't know how to act."

EPILOGUE

▼

Company A waited on the runway at Camp Vassar to board the planes that would take them on the first leg of the long flight home. Huddled with the masses of soldiers were dozens of Vietnamese—Quan and Can and most members of their families, as well as a number of other G.I. friends. All looked nervous and expectant, eager to be free of the conflict, and ready to begin their new life in the states.

When Wilfred had returned to the field, Reckert warned him, "The men won't put up with being the only ones in the field. You're likely to have a mutiny on your hands."

"I know," Wilfred said, "but it's only till Powers and Panik reach the point of no return."

That had been less than two weeks later. All the troops were withdrawn and operations officers throughout the division had rebuilt their staffs with creative writers. The new school was established at Camp Vassar, housed temporarily in the Division Chapel until the limestone halls of Pacification University could be constructed and the ivy planted. Manuals were hastily written in official Armese, instructors trained by the numbers, and dozens of dour-looking officers brought in cuffed for re-education. On Wilfred's recommendation, Colonel Clary was generalized and brought in as commandant because of his wide knowledge of pacification techniques.

"This place would be a lot more popular if it were coed," Wilfred told Reckert. "But I don't know where we can find enough girls. There aren't that many nurses and donut dollies."

"Admit Vietnamese girls. They'll attract men."

"Yeah, but do you think they'll be interested in nine to five cordons and free-of-fire zones?"

"No, but you could teach things like religion and philosophy and poly sci."

"No, we can't do that. If we teach courses like that, the students'll start squabbling and then go start wars to try to make other people think the way they do."

When Wilfred was satisfied that the program was well on its way, he called Frank Storp, who came out to see Wilfred the very next day.

"You don't really like this place, do you Frank?"

"Fuck, no. But what can I do? In my game, you make your name in the field, man. And I wanna make it big."

"I'll help you. But it's time to fade this scene."

Wilfred had little difficulty convincing Storp that the war should be moved to Hollywood, and all the shooting done with cameras. "Listen, Frank. They've got palm trees and swamps and the ocean and mountains. And the network's expenses would be so much less, and their profits so much more. All you'd need would be battle-hardened troops who can act. That's us. We're a proven commodity. You put A Company asses in the California grasses and who the hell will know the difference?"

"How would that save money—paying all those men?"

"Well, hell. The Army'll pay for us. Shit. On top of combat pay, we'll get temporary duty pay. We'll be flush."

"But we need guns, bombs, choppers..."

"Jeez, man. Splice in old footage. You must have hundreds of miles of it. It's all the same, anyway."

"O.K. But what about gooks?"

"You want gooks. I'll get you gooks. No sweat."

With Powers' aid, the idea sailed. He was happy to have at least one of the networks off his back, and when Wilfred convinced him the other networks were sure to follow suit as soon as they heard what Storp was doing, he backed it all the way. The network was delighted. They would leave a skeleton crew in Vietnam to cover unforeseen events, but run-of-the-mill daily reports could be covered cheaper and better on movie sets. They would bring some reporters home and fire others. Storp, of course, would escape the purge. He knew too much.

The need for Vietnamese actors fitted well into Wilfred's indecisive love life, relieving him of the necessity for making a final decision—setting the date. "I can't live with her and I can't live without her," Wilfred told Reckert.

"I understand. You're an incarnate cliché. Are you going to marry her?"

"Maybe. I know if I don't take her with me now, it may be impossible later on."

"You mean when the shit hits the fan."

"Yeah."

"You know, Wilfred, if you save her life, you're responsible for it for the rest of your life."

"Don't give me that shit. She doesn't have to come."

"They all think the U.S. is heaven, and everyone is rich. You going to take care of her or let her go on welfare?"

"I'll take care of her. What do you think I am?"

"And you're going to keep on screwing her?"

"That's none of your goddam business."

"Then you really ought to marry her, Wilfred."

"I'm only a kid!"

"I know, but kids have to grow up some time.

Wilfred had forgiven Can her breach of etiquette in screwing his comrades-in-arms, although his generosity had gone unrewarded by any remorse or gratitude from her—she felt she had done nothing wrong. We're all animals, anyway, Wilfred had reasoned. Why try to pretend we're something different? And besides, all she did was try to help me solve the morale problem. And she succeeded too, dammit.

Despite his ambivalence, Can was more than willing to fly away with him, especially since her family was going too. She hoped the stories she'd heard about America were at least partly true. She had no desire to take up the nomadic way of life she'd lived in the field, following herds and sleeping in little tents. But she couldn't really believe that all Americans were rich and that even the poor lived in houses and drove cars and had refrigerators, TV's, and plenty of food. That if Americans couldn't find work, their government gave them money and food every month. That most people worked only eight hours a day, and children, never. The children, she'd heard, all went to school and paid nothing! Some of these things must be true, though. She'd heard them from so many soldiers. But if any of them were true, it had to be better than living on the edge of starvation in a country always at war.

Her mother agreed. She wasn't beyond hoping for a better life for her family. At least they were going together and could help each other. And this way her sons wouldn't die as her husband had or end up killing each other.

Can's attachment to Wilfred was like the sea for the land: it came and it went, but it always came back. Most of the time, she drank of his waters and he fed on her bounty. But sometimes she lashed him with angry waves, and other times, his rivers went dry. She'd also grown stoical about Wilfred. She wanted to be with him, and she wanted to be available in case they could ever work things out. He was a little bit dinky dau, but if the storms reigned and the droughts persisted, she would let the currents take her to other shores.

Wilfred was readying A Company for the long ride to Hollywood, giving the men acting classes and instructions on how to tell their family, friends, and anyone else who was interested that their work was classified and that if anyone found out about it, the inquirer and inquiree could all be incarcerated and shot for treasonous spying.

His efforts were proceeding well when a Vietcong sniper shot a short soldier who happened to be talking to Welbourne at the time. The bullet struck four inches from the trooper's heart, creasing him between the arm and ribs.

The angry clamor "Get him!" sounded throughout the camp, and machine guns, claymores, rifles, grenades, and mortars opened up on the fleeing man with the long fingernails. Somehow the rule of love and the ban on killing had evaporated like a sliver of dry ice. Now, the company was boiling, unified by a desire for vengeance and a thirst for the blood of that sniper who had eluded them so often in the past. All three rifle platoons raced away in pursuit, but the escape of the assailant was guaranteed, as usual, by his careful planning and expeditious retreat, and by clinging plants.

"Shit," Rodriguez said. "These briars suck, man."

"They hold you till the tigers eat you," Henry said. He had gone on the expedition to ensure that no one was killed.

"Are there tigers around here?" asked Rodriguez.

"Believe it, man."

"Or till the snakes get you," said Wilfred. "Did you guys know that seven of the deadliest snakes in the world live in Nam?" Wilfred was tagging along to make sure they didn't shoot each other in the thicket. "Like that one back there—a bamboo viper, one of the most venomous in the world. You probably thought it was just a stick of bamboo."

The men soon lost their appetite for hunting snipers and vipers in the bush.

"It's all well and good that you got the generals to buy into your schemes," Reckert told Wilfred back at camp, "but how are you going to pacify the Vietcong? Seems like they haven't gotten the word yet, at least not all of them."

"You're right, Robbie. I've got to do something about their hearts and minds. The problem is, they've already bought into capitalism. They're always buying and selling stuff. They'll never buy our religion. And if we try to foist democracy on them, they'll just vote to send us home. They want to kick us out like they did the Mongols and Chinese and Cambodians and French and Japanese. But wait a minute. Maybe I can do something to stop the killing. Maybe if I start with that one-armed guy."

Back he flew to Onkay to see Can, but as soon as he arrived he received an urgent message. A General Dodge from MACV in Saigon wanted to meet alone with him right away at Division HQ. This time Wilfred was ushered through the doors like the general he wasn't.

"Come in, Lieutenant. General Dodge from MACV—Military Assistance Command, Vietnam." Three stars gleamed from his shoulders as he reached down for Wilfred's hand. "You know that MACV controls all the U.S. Forces in Vietnam, right?"

"To assist the Vietnamese people, right?"

"Right. Well, our commander, General Morelessthan, asked me to touch base with you while I'm here and pick your brain about this war. We know what you've been up to."

"Yes sir. Trying to bring about pacification, sir."

"Oh, yes. We'd all like that. But the President and Congress sent us here to do a job, and we've got to do it. Ever since the North Vietnamese attacked the USS Maddox in the Gulf of Tonkin."

"I heard about that. Sounded kind of fake to me."

"I won't comment on that, son. But what Morelessthan would like me to do with you today is to get your ideas on pacification and find out what you think we should do here."

"Well, sir. To pacify this country, sir, we need to send the troops home and claim victory. You know it's not necessary to change reality to accomplish our mission as long as we change the illusion of reality."

"What?"

"What I'm trying to say, sir, is this: we need to complete Operation Fake-In, Fake-Out. The Fake-In part, that was the Gulf of Tonkin. Now we have to do the Fake-Out part."

"Hmm."

"First we need to do something about the press. We've got to control the news and start telling those reporters what's happening instead of them blabbing everything to those folks back home."

"Right on, Lieutenant. What do you recommend?"

"Unbed the reporters from the military and inbed them with girls in Bangkok. Then have your writers do the battle reports and emphasize the increasingly peaceful nature of the country."

"Ah."

"And if the munitions manufacturers complain about losing business, start dropping their bombs in the jungle over in Cambodia and Laos."

"Good. What else?"

"Send the boys home."

"But we can't leave until we're victorious."

"Or until we have a successful negotiation, right?"

"Well, yes."

"So hire some Vietnamese actors to sit around and look official, and negotiate with them. Just don't put them around a table. They'll argue forever about what shape it should be. Put them all in chairs with wheels so they can move around and sit where they want to sit."

"But what would a successful outcome be?"

"Easy. We pull out, the commies take over, and they agree to do business with us, fair and square, and to sell us rubber and oil and give us cheap labor."

"Oh, Wilfed," Can said, delighted that he had returned to see her so soon.

"Hi, Can. Say, what was the name of that one-armed Vietcong guy who raped you at Sang Tran?"

"Oh," she said, knowing now that he had something cooking besides her. "He Mr. Minh. He a pig."

"Can, I need to talk to him. I have to convince him and the VC to stop trying to kill American troops. One of their snipers just shot one of my men. I think the sniper thought he was shooting at me."

"Ooh. You must stop that man with gun. But what you say to Mr. Minh? I wish you good luck. How you find him?"

"That's the other thing. I need you to help me find him."

"Can no sleep in hole in ground."

"I promise you the best accommodations in Sang Tran."

She agreed out of love, and soon they were walking into Paradise where Wilfred told the grinning Mr. Tuong, "I want to see Mr. Minh."

"Wait in room there, behind curtain. I find him." Tuong hated Wilfred for killing Trang and saw this as a twin opportunity to exact revenge and curry favor with Minh whom he knew wanted to send Wilfred to see his ancestors.

Wilfred unsnapped his holster as he and Can went in. Soon the one-armed man entered, boldly approached Wilfred, and shook his hand so the lieutenant could feel the strength in his arm, and then took a step backward as Can edged closer to Wilfred.

"Ah, the little whore and her lieutenant," said Minh in Vietnamese. "What do you want?"

"He want know what you want," she told Wilfred.

"Tell him I want all killing to stop." Can translated.

Minh snickered in deep, menacing tones. "Tell him to take all the American troops home. Then the killing will stop."

"But for us to go home, Nam's gotta be pacified—no killing by anyone. Then our people will be able to say we won."

"But why should we trust Americans to leave? And where do you get the power to make such decisions?"

He thought about mentioning his Mafia connections, but decided they would not impress the Vietcong. "You know I have special powers, Mr. Minh. You know how many of your troops I have killed and that I have ended killing in this entire area."

"Yes. I know you called on spirits in the tunnel and murdered nearly a hundred of us before you stopped killing."

"Well, take heed. The spirits are with me, and if you do not stop the killing, you yourself are in grave danger."

Minh stiffened. His eyes scorched Wilfred's. Then he stepped aside, and Wilfred watched a pistol, gripped by a slender hand with long fingernails, appear through a crack in the curtain.

The explosion was deafening, especially for Mr. Minh who lay on the floor with two bullet holes, one in the back of his head and one through his eye.

"Missed again," said Wilfred. Na na na na na na.

"Oh," shouted Can, pointing at the curtain. "Kill him, Wilfed. Kill him." Wilfred unholstered his pistol, ran out, and asked Mr. Tuong which way the gunman went. Tuong pointed to the street. Knowing he was being misdirected, Wilfred raced away in hot pursuit just to please Can who was trailing him a respectful six paces, her little legs flying like electric shears. Wilfred had no interest in killing the gunman, and was even less concerned about Dai now that he had seen how the long nail on the index finger of his firing hand struck the trigger guard when he fired, nudging the barrel off-target.

Not wanting to park Can in dangerous Sang Tran, he flew her back to Má in Onkay, and then returned to Sang Tran to make last-minute preparations for the trip home.

"You know what?" he said to Reckert. "That sleeper was still in the barracks last night. I couldn't stand it any more. I woke him up, sat him up, and shook him till his eyeballs flipped open like a baby doll's and asked him, 'What are you doing here, and why are you always sleeping?'"

"What'd he say?"

"He said, 'What are you doing out there? The world's in here. You're on the wrong side of your lids.' They flipped shut, and he started snoring again."

The day before the company flew to Vassar, Wilfred saw the company commander, Lieutenant Lorde, sitting in a cross-legged yoga position, notebook and pen in hand.

"Writing a poem?" Wilfred asked.

"A song, man. A song of love, for Clary."

"I bet you're glad we're leaving Nam, huh?"

"I'm not leaving."

"What? Why not?"

"You should know, man. Like I've never been here, so how can I leave?"

And now they waited to board. Can was squatting close beside Wilfred on the edge of the runway, looking as young and lovely as ever, her face shaded by her broad straw hat. She gazed steadily at Wilfred's face, watched his lips move as he talked to Reckert, and listened to the song of his voice, loving the sound, but understanding little.

The planes roared in, and as Wilfred walked aboard with Can, hand in hand, dragging his duffle bag on the ground, he felt guilty, somehow, leaving it all behind. The pacification might fail to spread, the war might flare again, all his efforts be negated. Fuck it, he thought. There's always Felicity's peace movement.

He looked back, and in the gaggle of soldiers from his company, and assorted Vietnamese actors, he spotted Henry and Quan, starting a new life together.

He and Can settled onto the webbed seats in the dim, roaring, rattling hole with an uneasy calm. Wilfred was grateful he hadn't been in country long enough to be short—he had a better chance of taking off without the plane exploding than if it were his 365th day. And now they were flying off to a country where they could love and argue in peace.

As the engines revved and the time machine rolled, accelerated, and left the ground, he turned to look out a window at this strange, beautiful land, one last time. Outside he saw an old farmer, squatting on a dike, doing his duty. Then he saw him wave good-bye with a rifle and fire a parting shot, which completely missed the plane.

And off they flew to the world.

THE END

CPSIA information can be obtained at www.ICGtesting.com
Printed in the USA
BVOW03s0032070514

352716BV00002B/9/P